Blood Wolf

Book One of The Blood Wolf Trilogy

K. R. Simler

For my parents, who always encouraged me to pursue my dreams, and my siblings for putting up with my requests to read the same chapters a million times.

Chapter 1

Jade

It was warm for fall, warmer than usual for a town located near the base of the mountains. Although summer still possessed most of the landscape, some of the trees had a few leaves giving up their lively green for richer reds and yellows that hinted at the new season. Sucking in a breath, Jade wrinkled her nose as it stung with the scents of too many people gathered in one place. Scents such as rotting food and sweat had a way of trickling through no matter how she tried to block them out. It all made her wish she were home or anywhere else if she honestly thought about it. It had been a long time since she had willingly been to a city so large or anything large enough to count as a real town for that matter. Like most rogue werewolves, Jade preferred to stay clear of places where packs had made their homes, and the Northwind Pack's home was definitely one that Jade would have been happy never seeing in person.

"Jade," James grumbled, dragging his feet as he followed her down the sidewalk. "When are we going to meet up with the others? I'm tired of walking around."

"Stop your whining; we just have a few more blocks to go before we can head back. If you hurry up then we'll get done a lot faster," Jade answered, rolling her eyes at her friend's complaints as she continued walking, forcing him to quicken his step to keep up with her. At fourteen, James was the youngest of their group and usually one of Jade's favorites. His quiet and shy nature made him easy to be around when he wasn't fussing like a pup.

"I don't know why we have to scout out this stupid town anyway," he continued, a little breathlessly as he jogged up beside her. "We're not going to be here long enough for it to matter. Besides, it's too big. I'm never going to remember where everything is!"

"We need to know the area while we're here. Don't forget, we are in enemy territory; we need to be ready for anything, and part of that means knowing the town's layout. We need to know the quickest ways through it, any alleyways, shortcuts, backroads. Anything that could help us get out of here quickly if things don't go well with Alpha Power," Jade explained, ignoring the dirty look from the couple who walked past them. The male pulled his mate closer to his side as if he expected either of the rogues to pose some sort of threat to them.

It seemed that everywhere they went, stares followed their every move. Mothers hurried their children along, and some uneasy individuals would walk across the street so that they wouldn't have to pass them. They were even met with the odd challenging growl every so often. It had taken a few years, but Jade found that every time a fellow werewolf looked at her with contempt, disgust, and even fear, the burning shame she had felt at the beginning of her life as an outcast had gradually melted away. Now she was just happy when she could get through a strange territory without a fight.

"I don't get why we have to be here anyway," James grumbled, "Why can't we just go back home? Alpha Power won't know the difference."

Jade ignored his last comment, but she couldn't stop her brows from falling into a concentrated frown. James wasn't entirely wrong.

About a month earlier, the rogue wolves had received a request from the Alpha Council, a council consisting of eight Alphas from the strongest packs. They requested that all rogues willing to continue coexisting peacefully with the packs report to the nearest official pack for further information.

All the rogues, including Jade, had scoffed at the arrogance of the Alphas. To approach the rogue wolves as if they had any authority to command them was bold. As rogues, they were not under the council's rule and were under no obligation to obey any orders created by the council. As long as they didn't trespass or cause trouble for the packs, the rogues could live as they wished. But Jade wasn't an idiot; it wasn't a request.

It was a threat.

A threat to any rogues that didn't show their support for whatever the packwolves were planning. A message for those who resisted; there would be no room for coexisting anymore.

So, there she was in the middle of the Northwind Pack's territory, trying to remember why she wanted to coexist with wolves who would be happy if she didn't exist at all.

"You know what?" Jade said, pausing on the street corner. "Why don't you just go find the others right now? Desert and Chris should be just a couple blocks that way by now," she said, pointing to her left towards the park that was in sight, the designated meeting spot. "I want to walk this block one more time anyway. I'll meet you guys back at the warehouse." James perked up, obviously liking that idea more than trailing along with her.

"Are you sure? Do you think you'll be alright by yourself?" he asked.

"I'll be fine. It's you I'm worried about," Jade laughed, standing up to her full height, which was a good four inches taller than James' skinny form to prove her point.

"Why don't we both just go over right now? You know Desert isn't going to be happy if we split up."

"Don't worry about Desert. I'll deal with him when I get back. Now hurry up and go," she said, giving him a push in the right direction. That was all the encouragement he needed before taking off in an energetic run, evidently hitting his second wind. Chuckling, Jade waited until she watched him disappear into the green grassed park before turning the other direction to finish her exploration. Walking down the sidewalk by herself, Jade felt herself beginning to relax. As much as she loved her friends, she also grew tired of always having them around. Sometimes she missed the peace and quiet that she had when she was alone. But there was a reason that lone wolves didn't last long; it was the same reason why Jade and her friends had finally come together. There was always safety in numbers.

Loud laughter shattered the quiet, turning Jade's attention to a group of wolves, all male, and none of them showed any intentions of moving out of her path. There were four of them, all around her age of seventeen or eighteen, maybe a little older. It only took a second for them to turn their eyes towards her and zero in, listening to her worn sneakers land on the cement. Their eyes lit up as they picked up her scent as the breeze blew their way, a foreign scent. Being a werewolf came with certain perks, such as heightened senses. All werewolves, those who had gained the title of shifters, and those trapped in their human form, were blessed with heightened smell, hearing, and physical

strength. Gifts that Jade used every day to stay alive, but now it seemed as if they were being turned against her.

Before any of the wolves could make a move towards her, Jade ducked into a small convenience store on the corner of the street. It wasn't even noon yet, far too early in the day to have any trouble. Ignoring the suspicious look from the lady at the front counter, Jade ducked through the rows of processed food towards the back of the store, away from prying eyes. But the short distance wasn't enough to protect her from hearing the harsh words from hushed voices that followed her down the aisles. Words such as rogue, mutt, and dangerous shadowed her every step; they floated around her as a constant reminder that she didn't belong here.

Jade looked back and breathed out a curse as the four wolves from outside entered the store as well, their bodies tense and their eyes hostile. She waited for them to go searching for her so she could double back and escape through the only entrance and non-emergency exit in the store, but they didn't move. They were waiting for her to try to leave. That left her with two options, hideout until they hopefully left or face them.

Her decision was an easy one. Snagging a bottle of lemonade from the drink section, Jade made her way to the front of the store, keeping her head high and staring straight ahead. She had as much right to be here as any of these people did. There was nothing to be ashamed of. Ignoring the obvious growls from the four wolves, Jade walked up to the cash register. Placing the lemonade on the counter, she met the cashier's glare. She was an unpleasant-looking woman; her cold, dirt-colored eyes might have looked pretty if it hadn't been for the bright blue eyeshadow and very poorly applied false lashes placed on her lids. Her lips were painted an awful shade of orange, and her

cheeks were far too red. Jade resisted the urge to shudder as the woman pursed her lips, revealing her yellowed, broken teeth.

"Just this, please," Jade said, pulling out a single ration chip from her pocket. The woman looked Jade up and down with disdain, her eyes resting on the three scars on Jade's forearm, the ones that marked her as an outcast. Jade resisted the urge to tug the sleeve of her jacket down to cover the scars; it was too late anyway. The horrid woman had seen them already.

"We don't sell to people like you. Get out," the cashier ordered, pointing her thin, wrinkled finger towards the door.

"Ma'am, I just want to buy a drink. I'm in town to do business with your Alpha, as the council requested. I don't want any trouble," Jade said. If only she could make these people believe that she wished she could leave their pathetic town more than they wanted her to.

"I don't care why you're here. I said we don't do business with people like you. Now get out." The four males by the door snickered, obviously enjoying the show in front of them. Jade felt the hair on her arms raise as her skin grew too warm.

"Fine, sorry to bother you," Jade said, biting down on her tongue before she said what she was actually thinking. Quickly, she turned away from the smug cashier. They weren't worth it; she wouldn't let their hatred, or their words get to her. That was what she repeated to herself as she marched out of the store. She repeated it determinedly as one of the men slammed his shoulder into hers on her way out, causing her to stumble, sending the others into an uproar of laughter. She repeated it out loud as she walked down the cracked sidewalk, letting each step pound the words a little deeper into her mind. By the time she made it to the abandoned warehouse on the edge of town, the sun was beating down on her back, her words a half-hearted mutter. It

didn't matter how much she repeated the same words over and over again; it didn't make them any more truthful.

As much as she wished she could forget their disdain, the disgust in their eyes, and how they acted superior, she couldn't just let it go. Every minute she spent in the Northwind Pack's territory, the more she felt their hatred piling on her shoulders. It weighed her down and filled her with unsatisfied anger. And her inability to let it go only infuriated her more. If she had stayed home and ignored the summon, then she wouldn't be dealing with any of the drama that came with a pack. There was a good chance she could pull it off. It was unlikely that the packs could track down every rogue out there. If she were on her own it would be simple for her to avoid the packs altogether and quietly slip through the cracks as if she didn't even exist.

But she wasn't alone.

"She's back!" James yelled as he jumped up, calling through the open door in the side of the abandoned warehouse that was temporarily home. Jade winced at the sound of his voice, calling unwanted attention to her. She held back a sigh as their friend Desert stepped out into the sunlight. His signature glare was, as usual, directed at her.

"Where were you? You've been gone forever. We were just about to go out and look for you," he said, ushering her into the building. He didn't even try to mask his frustration as she glared back and pushed past him. Desert meant well, but Jade was already in a foul mood, and his over-protectiveness rubbed her the wrong way.

From the outside, the warehouse looked shabby and old, but it looked even worse from the inside. The metal walls were covered in rust and dirt; when they first moved in there had been mice and rats infesting the whole place. It had taken a couple of

days to chase them out. A few windows were still intact; those that weren't were covered in trash bags or old tarps, anything to keep most of the wind and autumn rain from getting in. It may not have been much, but it was a roof over their heads, and there was more than enough room.

"Jade, where in the world were you? You had us worried," Lola, a small she-wolf said, tucking a piece of her fiery hair behind her ear. Her large, blue eyes were sincere with her concern and relief. That was one of the things Jade loved about Lola; she was an open book, always easy to read her true feelings.

"Aw, back off babe; Jade's a big girl. She can take care of herself," Chris said, giving Jade a clap on her shoulder as she walked past him. Chris was Lola's mate and the exact opposite of her in every way. Where Lola was petite and soft-spoken, Chris was a giant, loud, and had absolutely no filter. They were the perfect match. Although the couple had known each other for a few years, they had just held a bonding ceremony a year ago. Unfortunately, for the rest of the group, they were still in that love-sick honeymoon phase that new couples had.

"Maybe back home that's true, but we are in enemy territory right now and need to stick together. That's why we agreed to do the scouting in pairs. It's too dangerous to wander off alone," Desert snapped, still targeting Jade with his death glare.

"Hey now, that's no way to talk. We can't go into this place thinking of them as our enemies. Nothing good can come from that," Lola said, her voice taking on a motherly sternness. "But Desert is right, Jade. It isn't safe for us here, not yet anyway."

"Alright! I'm sorry, is that what you wanted to hear? Should I start calling you Alpha from now on too?" Jade asked, tossing herself onto the old mattress that she called her own, trying to

ignore the hurt that she knew was flashing through Desert's eyes at her remark. She knew he was right. They had all decided that it would be safer to stay as a group while they were in town. Jade had already witnessed the packwolves' feelings concerning rogues being in their territory; it was dangerous for them. But there was no way she would admit that out loud.

"Don't even start. You're a walking magnet for trouble, and don't even try to deny it. Stop trying to make us seem crazy for being concerned for you," Desert said, his glare melting away a little. Desert may have been quick to lecture, but his anger never lasted long. That was something Jade could always count on. "So, how was the rest of your walk?" he asked, finally giving up his frustration. Jade shrugged and laid back, closing her eyes.

"Uneventful."

Chapter 2

Darren

The Packhouse was unusually empty as Darren strode down the long hallway. With training just days away, most of the wolves were out enjoying the last bit of summer break. Parents took pups to the playground or swimming before they were sent back to training. Teens found the closest party or any other way to blow off the summer steam. Normally, Darren would have been out with his friends, but not today. His hands clenched into fists, wrinkling the paper in his grip.

When he reached his destination, a solid, dark oak door stood in his path. He ignored every lecture his mother had ever given him on manners as he stormed in without knocking.

"What is this?" he asked, raising the piece of paper, struggling to keep from yelling. You had to be careful when speaking to an Alpha wolf, even if he was your father.

Alpha Luke Power didn't even glance up from the paperwork on his desk as his son stood in the middle of his office questioning his sanity. He didn't even look surprised.

"What did I do to earn me a visit from my one and only son?" Luke asked, ignoring Darren's rudeness for the moment.

"When were you planning on telling me?" Darren asked, throwing the crumpled piece of paper onto Luke's desk, but he didn't give him time to answer. "Why didn't you tell me you're allowing, no, not just allowing, ordering the rogues to train side by side with us?" he asked, but he already knew the answer. "Did you really think that it wasn't important for me to know? I

thought I was supposed to be training to take over as Alpha. How can our pack trust me if I don't know about these decisions? I had to hear it from Spencer!" Darren said, trying to control his emotions, but he knew his frustration was not masked well enough from the slight frown on his father's face. Luke leaned back in his chair, finally giving Darren his full attention, his dark eyes betraying none of the inner workings of his mind.

"I was planning on telling you tonight before the pack meeting. Why? Is there something wrong with it?" Luke asked as if he genuinely was confused. He was playing games; Darren hated games. He knew Darren's concerns; they were the concerns every other wolf in the pack would have once they heard the order tonight. He probably had answers for ones no one would ever think to ask; that's just the kind of leader Luke Power was. But that wasn't enough for him. No, what he wanted was for Darren to voice those concerns, to doubt his leadership, then he would find some way to make Darren feel like an idiot for even thinking of them.

"There's no way to even begin preparing for this. We have no idea how many of them there are, let alone how many will be willing to function here long enough for you to get whatever it is you are looking for. And now we have to explain to the pack that not only will rogues be in the territory, but they will be inside the Training Center with their pups. Even if the rogues comply with the order, it will be nearly impossible to keep our wolves from wanting a fight," Darren answered. He could practically hear the outcries that his packmates would make. "None of the other packs that are calling for the rogues are training alongside them, so why? Why try to make an already dangerous situation more complicated?" he asked, wondering what could have driven his father to this level of insanity.

Luke didn't say a word the whole time Darren ranted, and he didn't say anything as his son stood there, waiting. The confidence Darren thought he'd had began shrinking rapidly as Luke slowly stood up and turned away to face the large window directly behind him. Silence filled the room. It stretched out and latched onto Darren's mind. He shifted his weight uneasily from one foot to the other; had he taken it too far this time? When Luke did finally speak, his words caught Darren off guard.

"You're right. This whole operation is risky; it's one of the most dangerous things I have ever willingly put this pack through. But for good reason," Luke said, staring out at the mountains that loomed above them. "Rogues are the greatest existing threat to the packs and our very way of life, and over the years, their numbers seem to have increased dramatically.

"To properly defeat or defend yourself from an enemy, you first need to know them. By bringing them to us, we will be putting them at a disadvantage. They're now in unfamiliar territory and outnumbered, giving us the perfect opportunity to gather first-hand information on them and learn how to better deal with them."

"Yes, I understand why they are here," Darren interrupted. "So why do it? Placing them with our newest wolves not only puts our own packmates in danger, but it's just asking for trouble! You know how some of the wolves can get. I know none of my friends will want to play nice with rogues. How could that possibly be good for us?"

"I can handle my own wolves; don't you worry about that. And as to how it could benefit us, just use your head, Darren. Many of the younger rogues were born into that kind of life. They may never have experienced what it's like to have the support of a pack. After living a life on the run, never knowing

where your next meal or shelter will be, do you really think that they'll want to go back to that once they see what their life could be like with us?" Luke asked, turning back to face Darren, his eyes flashing with an excitement Darren hadn't seen in his father for years.

"No, probably not."

"Exactly! Not only will we find out crucial information, but this could be the safest way to decrease the number of rogues while strengthening our pack. Darren, imagine the possibilities."

Darren had to admit, the idea of building the pack's numbers was appealing. The Northwind Pack was strong, one of the strongest packs in North America, but they wouldn't always be on good terms with the other packs as they were at that time, and having more wolves who could help defend them could be helpful. But there were still so many risks with this plan.

"They are still rogues, though," Darren said, mostly talking to himself. "Weren't they kicked out of their packs for a reason? Besides, we have plenty of strength already; we don't need them to defend ourselves."

"Never miss a chance to grow your strength. That is the mindset of the weak Alpha. As for the rogues, that's why we are going to focus our attention on the younger wolves. They're the ones who we will be able to teach and influence. If any of them can be saved from themselves, it will be the ones that haven't been caught up in the violence and hate of the rogues' lifestyle yet," Luke answered. It was clear that he had put a lot of thought into this plan, and grudgingly Darren was beginning to see the brilliance behind it all.

"Okay," Darren said, finally giving in. "What can I do to help?"

"Your job is crucial. You're going to ensure that the wolves at the Training Center stay in line. Try to convince your peers to befriend rogues they think have potential and keep things as peaceful as possible. Have them be our eyes and ears, and report back on which wolves would be good candidates to recruit. Can you do that?"

Darren's heart pounded in his chest. It was a huge responsibility his father had placed on him; maybe he believed Darren was closer to being a real Alpha

"Yes, of course, I can," he said, nodding confidently. This was his chance to be part of something that had never been done before, to be directly involved in what could mean the difference between the pack thriving or floundering. He had his chance. There was no way he would do anything to let his father down.

Chapter 3

Jade

Blood.

It looked like red cough syrup, thick and sticky as it spread across the hardwood floor, staining everything it touched. She stood in a puddle of red, watching as it spread out away from her feet; it seemed as if it came out of her, seeping out from the soles of her shoes. But that was just wishful thinking; of course, it wasn't hers, it never was.

Her eyes moved downwards to stare at her hands, hands that didn't look like her own anymore. They didn't shake like the last time. They were warm and still; they shouldn't be this still, not after what they had just done. They weren't nearly as still as the body that lay in front of her in the ever-growing puddle of red. If she looked to the right, she would see his face; he'd be staring up at her with big blank eyes-

"Jade, wake up!"

Jade jerked awake from her nightmare to see Chelsea standing over her and her makeshift bed. The pools of blood rapidly faded away, leaving a cold sweat causing her shirt to cling to her skin. "What are you doing, sleepyhead? You're going to be late."

"What do you mean?" Jade asked, bringing her hands up to rub her eyes, trying to ignore the memory of them covered in the red liquid. "Late for what?"

"For pack training, duh!" Chelsea laughed, tugging Jade's blanket away as she tried to pull it closer.

Training.

Jade cringed at the word, the one word she had completely forgotten about. Jumping up, she scrambled to find a clean shirt from her ragged duffel bag.

"Crap, crap, crap!" Jade shouted, changing into what she hoped was a clean pair of jeans. "Where is everyone else? Aren't they coming too?"

"They left a while ago. They're probably at the Training Center by now," Chelsea replied, uselessly watching Jade scramble around the warehouse in search of her other shoe.

"They left me? Why didn't they wake me up?"

"Lola was going to, but Desert convinced her not to. I think he's getting back at you for the other day," Kyler said as he walked through the door. "Sorry, I was going to wake you up earlier, but you looked like you could use the rest. It seems like you haven't been sleeping well lately."

"I can sleep later; what I need right now is to get to the Training Center on time, so I don't get in trouble on the first day," Jade said, finally finding her other shoe, nearly falling over as she tried to slip it on while standing on one leg.

"Who cares what those jerks think anyway? Besides, we won't be here long enough for them to even remember us. I thought you didn't want to go anyway," Chelsea said.

"Easy for you to say; you don't have to spend all day with them. And I don't want to go, but I don't want to be the only one on Alpha Power's bad side," Jade snapped, throwing her messy hair into an equally messy braid. Running to the door, she ran past Chelsea snagging her tattered backpack from her hand on the way out.

"Good luck, and whatever you do, don't get detention," Chelsea called cheerfully after her. Jade didn't have time to

respond as she sprinted down the street. She just hoped that being late was the worst thing she would have to worry about that day.

Chapter 4

Darren

"Long time no see!" Darren turned on the steps of the Training Center just in time for his friend, Spencer, to run up beside him.

"Took you long enough," Darren said, but he smiled as his friend caught up.

"Hey, look who's back!" a familiar voice called from behind them. Turning, they watched Michael, another one of Darren's friends bound up the steps to where they stood.

"Glad you made it. I hope tromping all over the countryside was worth it; you missed out on an eventful summer," Darren said, pulling Michael into a hug.

"Speaking of eventful, where is the lucky girl? It's not every day that you find your mate," Spencer asked, making a show of looking around.

"She's on her way. But if I'm being honest, I'm pretty sure that I'm the lucky one," Michael chuckled, rubbing the back of his neck in a bashful gesture.

"And don't you forget it," a sweet-looking girl said as she stepped up beside him, placing her hand in his without hesitation. "Hi, I'm Stephanie," she said, giving them a friendly wave. The boys introduced themselves, playfully teasing the couple as they slowly made their way up the remaining stone steps.

Watching his friends laugh, it was easy for Darren to forget about the trouble ahead of them. It was all so easy to place in the

back of his mind, to think of nothing but what was in front of him in that moment.

Until he saw them.

It was obvious who they were as they approached the four guards placed at the foot of the stairs. Their disheveled clothing and bags were the first clue, making them stand apart from the put-together Northwind Pack members.

Rogues.

Even if Darren hadn't been able to pick up their foreign, wild scent from where he stood, it was still apparent that they didn't belong. They stuck together in a small group, watching the packwolves warily, never stepping closer to anyone than they had to. There was a wildness about them that was apparent in the smallest behaviors. It was in the quick twitch of their hands and the way their eyes flickered around their surroundings, taking everything in. It was in the stiffness of their spines as they carried themselves forward. All of it screamed that they didn't belong.

There were four of them, three males and one small female, the sight of her surprised Darren. Female wolves were rarely kicked out of their packs, even for extreme crimes, although he had heard rumors of more and more female rogue spotted within the last couple of years. To force a she-wolf from her pack was an automatic death sentence since they were unable to shift into a wolf, a werewolf's strongest form. As rare as it was to kick a she-wolf out of a pack, it was even rarer to find one actually living as a rogue. A rogue's life was one of constant danger and uncertainty. Darren couldn't imagine how she had managed to survive unless she was with a mate.

"Are those some of the...you know...?" Stephanie asked, her voice trailing off as she stared with wide eyes at the rogues as the guards stopped them.

"The strays? Mutts? Troublemakers? Yeah, that's them," Spencer answered, glaring coolly down at the strange group. Darren's father had announced to the rest of the pack just a few nights ago what his plan was with the rogues and the reason for them coming to town. As Darren had expected, the pack was not thrilled about it. Many of the wolves had talked of pulling their children from training or chasing the rogues off themselves before they had a chance to infiltrate the pack. But just as he always did, Luke talked them down. No one was happy about it, but everyone had agreed to aid Luke in keeping the peace to help strengthen the pack, whatever that meant.

Darren watched closely as the first rogue, a young male probably close to Darren's age with dark brown hair stepped forward, holding out his left arm to reveal his old pack mark to the guards. He was too far away for Darren to distinguish which pack his mark belonged to, but even from a distance, he could see the three red scars that ran through it, marring the mark forever, proof that the rogue had been exiled from his pack. Once the guards had noted his status as a rogue, they motioned for him to another guard who handed him his open backpack and pushed him towards the sign-in table. The fourth guard watched the other rogues closely, giving them an intimidating growl when any of them looked his way.

One of the rogues, in particular, a mountain of a man, towered at least a head over the tallest guard. He was well-muscled, larger than any of the guards Darren had seen in their own pack. He was clearly an experienced warrior; the scars

scattered across his dark arms were proof of that. In fact, most of the rogues had scars in one place or another.

The last male was barely out of boyhood, his scrawny limbs still too big for him, his face still holding its baby roundness that would evaporate within the next few years as he matured. Darren quickly dismissed him as a potential threat, most likely just a rebellious teen who had run away from his pack as a way to prove his independence. It would be rogues like him that would be easiest to enlist into their pack.

Even with his quick evaluations, Darren knew that he shouldn't underestimate any of the rogues; each wolf was dangerous in its own way if they chose to be. But when he looked at this group, they didn't look dangerous. They looked nervous, just like his own packmates.

"Come on, let's get going; we don't want to be late," Darren said. The others nodded in agreement; the light, joking atmosphere was now heavy and quiet with his friends' fears. Stephanie's smile had been replaced by a blank look, her eyes holding traces of worry. Michael had his arm wrapped protectively around her shoulders; his eyes darted around the room as if he were searching for potential threats to his mate.

Rumbling from within Darren's mind, his wolf was on high alert as well. He didn't like seeing his packmates scared for their safety. It was their job to keep them safe, and here they were helping bring one of their biggest threats into their homes. With so many wolves feeling skittish, there was bound to be some violence. Darren just hoped he would be able to stop it before anyone got hurt.

Chapter 5

Jade

Breathlessly, Jade stumbled up to the Training Center; her side pinched from sprinting several blocks from the warehouse to the center. Just ahead, walking up the steps into the building were the people who had failed to wake her up yet still dared to call themselves her friends.

"Hey, wait up!" she called out, running toward them. If her reflexes weren't as well trained as they were, she would have run straight into the man who stepped out in front of her, abruptly blocking her path. He stared her down with what Jade assumed was supposed to be an intimidating glare.

"Not yet, mutt, show me your pack mark and hand over the bag," he ordered. Giving him a quick once over, Jade determined the man was probably just a few years older than her own seventeen years. Most likely a guard wolf judging by his stance and muscular build, he was even large enough to be a warrior. A glance around revealed three more guard wolves at the foot of the stairs, all tall and well built. Jade wondered if Alpha Power just had a higher standard for his guards than most packs or if he had pulled in some of his actual warriors to protect the underage age wolves from the big, bad rogues. If the second one was true, she wasn't sure whether to feel flattered that the Northwind Pack thought so highly of their skills, or to feel offended that they already thought they needed to protect themselves.

Slowly, she rolled up her jacket sleeve on her left arm, exposing the now pale fang-shaped mark on her forearm. Once,

it had been a symbol of pride, a sign that she belonged with a powerful pack, a family, but now with the three long scars that went through it, all it was only a reminder of what she had lost.

"The Darkfang Pack? Their territory is nowhere near ours; how did you make it out here?" the first guard asked. Jade merely shrugged in response. She didn't blame him for being curious; she would have questioned the sanity of the wolf who traveled a thousand miles away from their home also. It was odd for any rogue to travel that far from their birth home, even less likely for a defenseless female rogue to do so. Narrowing his eyes in suspicion, he grabbed a clipboard from one of the other guards and scribbled something on it.

"From what I hear, they're one of the more ruthless packs this side of the plains. You must have done something pretty bad to have them kick you out," he said, glancing up from the clipboard to gauge her reaction to the accusation. She stared back at him, keeping her expression blank, pushing the anger down before it had a chance to bubble up. He didn't know her or what she'd done. Or why she'd done it.

He wasn't wrong, though. The Darkfang Pack was made up of warriors who valued strength and power above all else, but even according to their laws, what she had done was unforgivable. The three red scars running through her pack mark where her old Alpha had run his claws through it, successfully severing her link to the pack, was proof of that.

"Alright, the bag now," the guard snapped as he deepened his glare, annoyed at her lack of response to his obvious jabs. Sliding the straps from her shoulders, she kept a steady glare on the guard as she did so, feeling a little more satisfied than she should have when he looked away first. Ignoring the way he snatched the bag from her hands, she tried not to flinch as

another guard stepped up behind her and pushed her arms out to the side as he began to pat her down roughly. She could feel her face growing red as the guard with her backpack dumped its few contents onto the ground, handing the empty bag to her. Staring straight ahead, she tried to overlook the stares from the local trainees as they watched their packmates manhandle her and her belongings. She struggled to push her pride aside; it didn't matter what they thought; she was just as good as any of them. That's what she told herself, but the words couldn't keep the blood from creeping up her neck and face.

"Your pack mark must be visible at all times, for identification purposes and your protection. Should you be caught hiding your status of a rogue, there will be consequences," the second guard said once he was done patting her down. His voice was monotone and bored, making it sound as if it had come from a script he had been forced to memorize, which wouldn't have surprised her at all.

Looking down at the exposed scar on her arm, Jade felt almost naked with her shame displayed for all to see, marking her as something dangerous. Someone to be feared.

"And what happens if I do cover it?" she asked, tearing her eyes away from her arm to turn her gaze to the guards.

"Once your business with our pack is done, you will be sent on your way, and you can do as you choose with it."

"I get that," Jade snapped. "What about while I'm here?"

Jade tried not to flinch as the first guard stepped forward, close enough that she could smell the sour scent of his hostility rolling off of him and grabbed her arm. She tried to keep her expression bored as the guard gripped her jacket's sleeve and ripped it off, letting the stray fabric fall to the ground, leaving her mark for all to see.

"As he said, there will be consequences," he said, his dark eyes promising more pain than his words did.

"Wait, so not only did you people make me leave my home, drag me all the way out to your smelly territory, now you are also forcing me to deal with your Alpha's poor fashion choices?" Jade asked, her voice dripping with mockery to cover up the fury that would leak out otherwise.

"You should just be grateful that you're even allowed on our land at all, pup. Now move along and let us get back to our jobs," the guard replied, crossing his arms in front of his chest, making his arms look even larger in an attempt to intimidate her. She'd taken on bigger in the past, and it would take more than a couple of wolves who thought themselves formidable enough to make her back down. She took a step forward, ready to let the spoiled packwolves know just how lucky she had been when she was kicked out of her pack. How lucky she had been when none of the other packs would take her in, simply because of a mark. She was about to tell them where they could shove their ideas of lucky, but before she could get the words out, her eyes flickered over the guard's shoulder to the steps of the Training Center where her friends stood. They watched the exchange with tense shoulders, Chris and Desert's bags already on the ground, waiting to come to her aid if she needed it. If she had been on her own, she would have torn into these arrogant packwolves without hesitation, but she wasn't alone anymore and if she acted rashly the consequences wouldn't be solely hers to bear, and her friends didn't deserve that.

"Whatever," she said, bending down to pick up the stray notebook and pens and other odd items that had fallen to the ground. Her anger intensified when the first guard kicked her water bottle before she could pick it up, sending it spinning away

from her. She wanted to look up, to yell or hurt them, to do anything besides sit there and take their abuse. But there was already too much attention on her and she needed to calm down before she did something rash. Taking a deep breath, she finished scooping up the last of the stray items and tossed them into her backpack, and stood, striding over to where her friends were. She hoped that the red was fading from her face; no one needed to know just how upset the guards had made her.

"Just ignore them, Jade. They're all idiots anyway," James said once she had reached them. He moved his hand to give her a comforting pat on her shoulder, but she shrugged him away.

"Come on, guys, we don't want to be late," she said, her voice snapping more than she intended. She couldn't help it. Her friends looked at her as if she was a kicked puppy, their eyes wide with sympathy. Jade hated it. Sympathy led to pity, and she didn't need anyone's pity. Walking up the steps, she watched the lingering students scurry away, throwing worried glances over their shoulders at the rogues. Their eyes darting away whenever they made eye contact with any of them. The day had barely begun, and Jade already wished that she were back in bed, even if it meant dealing with more of the nightmares.

"Oh yeah, and thanks for waking me up this morning," Jade said to the group, but she directed her glare at Desert to let him know that she knew he was the one to blame.

"Maybe if you didn't spend so much time wandering around all alone you wouldn't be so exhausted and would wake up with the rest of us," he replied, shrugging his shoulders, looking very unconcerned about being the target of her frustration.

"Oh, ignore him, Jade!" Lola exclaimed, linking her arm through Jade's in a familiar gesture. "We're sorry we didn't wake you up, but we knew that Kyler and Chelsea would get you

up in time to get here. Please don't be mad," she said. Her green eyes were so serious and pleading, Jade would have had to be completely heartless to stay angry.

"Fine, I guess I can forgive you guys this time, just don't let it happen again," she said, allowing her shoulders to let go of the tension they had been holding. It was a new day. Her friends were there, ready to face whatever came next with her; it was going to be okay.

The inside of the Training Center was larger than Jade had expected it to be. Bland white walls were so spotless they seemed to reflect the light off of them, as did the too shiny tile floors. The wide hallway was crowded with Northwind teens. Some leaned against the walls casually; others rushed past their peers in a flurry of paper, books, and excitement. A few sat or stood on the outskirts, headphones over their ears or a book in their hands. There were so many bodies, so many pairs of eyes, so much variety all in one place. But even with all their differences, there was one thing that they all had in common. Everywhere Jade looked, she could see the three dark lines curving upwards that made the Northwind Pack's mark. These people may have all had their own unique traits, but they all knew that they had someplace they belonged, something bigger than themselves that they were a part of. Jade wished she could remember what that felt like.

"Anyone else ready to kick some spoiled pups' butts?" Chris whispered, staring down a group of guys who had been glaring openly at their group until they realized they had caught Chris's attention. Casting their eyes downward, they avoided looking at any of the rogues as they walked by them. These wolves were all bark and no bite. Not that Jade blamed them. Most people were too scared to look Chris in the eyes, and that

was before they realized he was a rogue. Even without the visible scars that were scattered along his arms, proof of the numerous battles he had survived, he was still one of the most intimidating wolves Jade had ever met.

"Chris, keep the butt-kicking to a minimum, please. If I can control myself with those jerks outside, then you can too," Jade said, earning herself a shrug and one of Chris' customary grins.

"Will do. But, fair warning, I'm not going to take any crap from these guys," he replied.

With her friends at her side, she made her way through the crowd towards the large glass wall with the word "office" painted above it in big, red letters. Behind the glass was an older woman with very round glasses that Jade guessed was just a little too large for her since she kept having to push them up her nose. Her white hair still had hints of brown in it from her younger years. It naturally stood out from her head, making her appear taller than she was. The wrinkles by her eyes and mouth were barely noticeable, but they seemed to give her a softer look. Jade couldn't have imagined someone who looked more of the part of a secretary if she had wanted to. A middle-aged woman was a little further in the room, a few grey strands just starting to show in her dark hair. When she made eye contact with Jade, her eyes narrowed into an unpleasant squint, apparently not happy with what she saw.

"Hello dear, what can I help you with today?" the older woman asked as she slid away from the layer of glass between them, beaming up at the rogues as they approached her desk.

"Uh...hi," Jade said, somewhat taken aback by the woman's friendliness. Maybe she hadn't noticed their rough looks or their damaged pack marks. "We're just wondering if this is where we find out which training group we're supposed to be part of?"

"It sure is," she replied, tapping on the keyboard in front of her a couple of times to bring something up on her computer. "If I can just have your first and last name, I'll pull those up for you right now."

"Sure, my name is Jade Lenoir," she answered, giving her the name she had used for the last few years. They all waited as the secretary's fingers flew over the keyboard, the mouse clicked a couple of times, her eyebrows drawn together in a slight frown.

"That's odd," she said before turning back to face the rogues. "I'm not finding your records here. What pack role are you training for?"

"Ehem!" Chris cleared his throat loudly, holding up his arm so she could see the three-peaked marks that stood for the Stonehill Pack, the faint mark looked more like a scar on his dark skin now, but it didn't hold the banishment scars like Jade's own. The older woman's eyes grew wide once she saw the mark, but her smile didn't falter.

"Oh dear, silly me! You must be some of the rogues we have visiting. I'm sorry I didn't recognize the marks before; I feel like I'm blind as a bat these days," she said, jumping up to scurry across the room. "Give me just a second; I'm sure that I put that folder down over here somewhere," she muttered, searching through a stack of folders on the table in the back of the room as her younger coworker continued to direct her withering glares at the rogues. Jade could hear the older woman humming a light-hearted tune from where she stood, one Jade didn't recognize. Out of the corner of her eye, Jade could see James and Lola exchanging confused looks with one another. Glares and rude remarks were something they were all used to, but being treated as an ordinary pack citizen was...unsettling.

"Ah, here it is!" she exclaimed, scurrying back to the front desk, a manila folder in her tiny hands. "Alright, if I could just have each of you sign your names here," she said, handing them a clipboard full of blank spaces. Evidently, they were the first rogues to show up for training. Jade wondered how many more would come.

Scribbling her name on the paper, Jade passed the clipboard to her left to Desert before turning back to the older woman who was pulling out documents from the folder. "I combined all of the classes from the different pack positions into a system and randomly generated schedules for the next few weeks for each of you, just to give you a chance to experience each of the roles. If you end up finding one that you'd like to focus on for the remainder of your stay, then please let us know. I'd be happy to make up another schedule that is centered on that role. And if for some reason your business keeps you here longer than planned, we can always adjust the schedules as needed," she said, handing Jade a piece of paper with a list of names and times that Jade didn't bother to look at. With any luck, she wouldn't be here long enough for any of them to matter anyway.

"Well, if it means we get to see more of your lovely face, then let's hope Alpha Power takes his time with this business," Desert said, throwing in a quick wink that would have made any woman blush. The older woman rolled her eyes and waved a hand dismissively, but the grin on her face indicated that she wasn't entirely immune to Desert's charms. Jade resisted the urge to roll her own eyes.

"Oh," the older woman said as an afterthought, her cheerful smile still as sincere as it was when they first walked up. "And my name is Thelma, and that's Kathy over there," she gestured towards the sour-faced lady. "You can pick up your ration chips

here each week. Alpha Power had a supply sent down for each of the wolves that are participating in the program. If you have questions or need any help at all, please feel free to drop by; one of us is usually around."

Each of the rogues murmured a thank you before turning away to walk around the corner to a larger room, each examining their class schedules. Looking around, Jade watched many of the other packwolves doing the same, most were already hurrying off to their first classes. How could these people let such a flimsy piece of paper control such a big part of their lives?

"Guess I'll see you all later if I make it through Pack History without falling asleep," Jade half-heartedly joked, pulling her backpack up her shoulder.

"Alright, see you at lunch," James replied, his shoulders hunching in a sulk as he looked over his schedule, not happy with what he saw. Jade didn't blame him; it had been years since any of them had been forced to sit through any of the training young werewolves were required to go through. If they were anything like the ones she'd had as a pup, then the next few weeks were going to be torture.

Jade turned away from her friends to start down the hallway in what she hoped was the right direction for her first class. She was only a few paces away when she was frozen in her tracks by a high pitch scream. Whirling around, Jade was caught by surprise when a set of arms immediately wrapped around her waist—stumbling back a few steps from the force of the other person running into her. Her heart was pounding in her ears as she raised her hands to ward off the sudden attack, her instincts kicking in.

Except they didn't continue the attack, they just held on with what Jade now recognized as very thin arms.

Whoever had pounced on her was almost an entire head shorter than Jade and had a head full of vaguely familiar frizzy, dark hair that blocked Jade's view of the rest of the room. She also realized with some shock that the small person was a girl, probably around James' age, barely old enough to be in the older training classes. She was even more surprised when she realized that not only was the screaming still going strong but was coming from the tiny person who had her locked in her tiny death grip. But the scream started to sound more like an excited schoolgirl squeal.

"Jade! I knew it was you. I just knew it. At first, I thought it was crazy because I knew that there was no way you would be down here since you live so far away in the mountains, but then I got closer, and I could just tell it was you. I'm so glad you're here! Wait, why are you here?" the girl rambled, her words muffled since her face was still buried against Jade's shoulder.

"Valery?" Jade asked, trying to pry herself out of the girl's steely grip. "It's good to see you too." Valery loosened her hug just enough to look up at Jade, flashing her a big toothy smile.

"I still can't believe you're actually here. What are you doing here? I thought that you lived too far away to come down the mountains?" she asked, completely oblivious to the stares they were receiving from everyone, including Jade's friends, who were watching the interaction with interest.

"My friends and I are just in the territory for a few weeks because of the order from the council. We'll be going back to our home once Alpha Power gets whatever he needs from us," Jade answered, motioning behind Valery to where her friends stood. Following the gesture, Valery glanced over her shoulder to look at the other rogues, sending a shy but bright smile their way before turning back to Jade.

"You're here to see Alpha Power? That's great! I've told my family all about you at least a hundred times, and now that you're here, they can finally meet you. Of course, you and your friends can come over to our place too. You'll have to come over to dinner and-"

"Whoa there, Valery!" Jade interrupted the girl's ramblings, placing her hands on both of her small shoulders. How could such a small person talk for so long without taking a breath? "Slow down for a second will, ya?"

"Oh yeah, sorry. My brother always says I talk too much, but it's not my fault-"

"Hey!" a boy from just a few feet away yelled, cutting Valery off mid-sentence. "Get your hands off of my sister, you filthy mutt!" he yelled before charging forward and tearing Jade away from Valery and shoving her against the wall with such force that Jade knew it would leave a bruise.

"Spencer, get off of her!" Valery yelled, another boy coming up to grab her arm to hold her back. But evidently, the wolf named Spencer didn't hear her or didn't want to.

"Valery and I were just talking. She's an old friend of mine," Jade said, keeping her hands raised in what she hoped looked like a harmless position. She didn't have to see Desert and Chris to know that they were already moving forward, pushing their way through the crowd that had formed around her and the Northwind wolf. Using one of her hands, she held up a finger, a small motion, barely visible to anyone else, but Desert and Chris would know its meaning. She had it under control. She could handle one kid.

"Stupid rogues," Spencer spat. His hands were hard against her shoulders, pressing them into the wall. "You think you can just walk in here and start pushing people around? Well, you

don't get to do that here! Not in our territory and not to my packmates, to my family!" he shouted, spittle flying onto Jade's cheek.

"I'm not looking to cause any trouble here, and I've done nothing wrong. As I said, Valery and I were just talking. Now get your hands off me," Jade said, keeping her voice as even as she could, though she could feel her own temper rising as the group that surrounded them grew tighter. It didn't matter what she said, this Spencer kid didn't want to listen. Packwolves never did.

"You mutts are always looking for trouble; you all screwed up your own lives, and you just can't let the rest of us be happy," he sneered. The disgust in his eyes could have burnt a hole through her head, probably even through the wall behind her.

"I said get off of me," Jade shouted, shoving Spencer away from her, breaking the grip he had on her shoulders and forcing him to stumble back. Spencer's eyes were bright with more than just anger; they weren't his eyes at all. His once brown eyes now glowed an unnatural yellow. They were eyes that didn't belong to a human. They were the eyes of a wolf, and Spencer's wolf was dangerously close to the surface.

"See, what did I tell you?" Spencer asked, turning his glowing eyes on Jade. "Pushing others around is what these mutts do best. Even their females are brutes," he said, his voice growing deeper, a feral growl embedded in every word. If Jade didn't tread carefully, things could get dangerous, not just for her but for everyone in the hallway. But then again, Jade always had a knack for getting into dangerous situations.

"Better to be a brute than a pampered brat whose whole life revolves around whatever some old man tells you. I bet you do everything you're told to just like a good little boy too," Jade

taunted. She couldn't help it, these packwolves had been harassing her since she stepped foot in their stupid territory, and she was tired of taking it silently.

"You'll regret talking about Alpha Power with such disrespect," Spencer snarled, taking a threatening step forward, but that one step was the closest he would get to her. Something was stirring deep inside Jade, something she had buried within her for years, something she couldn't allow out.

Spencer made another move towards her. Before Jade had time to react, Chris was in front of her, tossing Spencer halfway down the hallway, a growl of his own tearing through his bared teeth. His eyes were a similar shade to Spencer's yellow ones. His wolf was dangerously close to taking control. Desert was by her side in an instant, his hand on her arm in a gentle but firm grip, his body angled in front of her in what Jade was sure looked as if he were protecting her, but she couldn't help but wonder if it was actually an attempt to protect them from her. She looked over Desert's shoulder in time to see James ushering Lola up the staircase to the second floor. Good, at least two of her friends could avoid the drama she had caused.

"The rogues are ganging up on Spencer!" Someone from the crowd yelled, spurring other shouts of anger or surprise. Jade felt a pit form in her stomach as she looked around them. Throughout hers and Spencer's exchange, a circle had slowly begun forming around them, but what was once a crowd of spectators was thinner than before. Most of the girls who had been watching had either left the hallway entirely while others had moved to the very back corners of the hallway, their eyes wide with anticipation or fear. All that was left of the crowd was twenty glowing orbs, just waiting for a chance to strike.

And they had surrounded the three rogues.

Chapter 6

Darren

The red bricks that made up the outside of the Training Center felt warm against Darren's skin as he leaned on them. Normally, he would have taken a moment to relish the autumn sun and cool morning air on his face, but he would have to enjoy it another time; at the moment the young wolf in front of him held his full attention.

"I don't know what I'm going to do," Henry sniffed, his eyes growing teary as he looked down at the ground to avoid looking at Darren. "All of my friends can shift already. I'm the only one who can't! And now they put me in the warriors training; my dad was so proud when he heard. But how can I be a warrior if I can't connect to my wolf? I'll be the only boy in the pack that can't shift. They'll have to put me in the nursery like my mom and sister or one of the lame jobs," the boy practically wailed.

"Hey now," Darren said, bending down so he was eye level with the younger boy, placing his hands on Henry's shoulders. "Your wolf will show himself when it's time. Lots of wolves don't learn how to shift when they first start training," he said. Making a show of looking around to make sure they were alone. Darren leaned in closer. "Don't tell anyone, but I didn't learn how to shift until I was almost two years older than you are now," he lowered his voice as he confided in the younger boy. He couldn't help but smile as he watched Henry's eyes grow wide with surprise.

"Really?"

"Yep, really. Don't worry. I know that it may feel like it will never happen, but it will. Just give your wolf some time; he'll come around, I promise," Darren said. He couldn't help the pride that swelled in his chest as Henry looked up at him, a hopeful grin on his face.

"I guess you're right. Thanks, Darren."

"Hey, I'm here if you ever need to talk, okay?" Darren said, smiling once Henry's head bobbed up and down in an energetic nod. "Alright, now let's go in before classes start."

The two made their way through one of the side doors into the empty hallway on the first floor of the Training Center.

That's weird, Darren thought. Usually, the hall would have been buzzing with trainee wolves rushing to get to class that would begin in just a few moments. Where was everyone?

Darren said goodbye to Henry and made his way to his own class when a sudden shout drew Darren's attention further down the hallway. There were still people in the commons area, a lot of people. All of them had their backs to him; most were gathered or focused on something going on by the hallway as shouts rose from the crowd.

Pushing his way through the crowd, he was more than a little surprised when those he passed looked up at him with a bit of panic in their eyes once they recognized him. A few even turned away, hurrying towards the stairs or down the other hall as if they'd been caught red-handed.

When he finally pushed his way to the front, Darren couldn't believe what he saw. Spencer, Michael, and four other Northwind male wolves were very close to losing control of their wolves. Darren could smell their wolfs' scents already, their eyes no longer their own but the eyes of the creatures that lived

within them. His packmates were in the middle of the circle, along with three rogues. All of them fighting.

His mind kicked into overdrive, taking in the scene before him in what could have only been seconds, but Darren watched it all as if it were taking place in slow motion before him.

The giant rogue he had seen earlier was fighting three Northwind wolves. His fangs already lengthening, making him look more animal than human as he picked up and threw one of Darren's packmates against the wall. Michael and another Northwind wolf were up against the other male rogue. He was less brutish than the giant but still just as vicious in his attacks, lashing out quickly, often before Michael or the other wolf could even try to get their own hits in. Darren expected to see the baby-faced rogue fighting, but the third male rogue was nowhere in sight or the small female he had seen earlier. Instead, a different female rogue was battling Spencer; her face was blank and cold as she swung out at the other wolf. She didn't even seem to mind that it wasn't his human eyes that glared at her but the eyes of the animal in him. Like her friends, she lashed out aggressively and with enough force to make Spencer stumble backward. She was strong for a female, but she didn't stop when he fell away from her. She swung at him, again and again, making it impossible for him to do anything except raise his arms in defense and try to hold his ground.

Blood.

Darren could smell it in the air, his own wolf coming forward in his conscious, triggered by the scent that usually accompanied danger. The scent came from multiple wolves, the shorter male rogue with a cut on his cheek, Spencer had a bloody nose, and Michael was bleeding from a cut on his arm. Darren's wolf wasn't the only one who had been aggravated by the scent

of his packmates' blood. If he didn't stop them someone was going to shift.

"Stop!" he roared, allowing his wolf to come forward enough to try to push his own power into the command. Some of the bystanders fell silent, staring at him with wide eyes, but his order went unheard by most. The wolves in the center of the circle continued to fight. Darren watched in horror as two more Northwind wolves jumped into the fight as the giant rogue tossed one of their packmates into the crowd, knocking over three of the bystanders as he landed on top of them. Spencer and the female rogue each had ahold of each other, but there was no way she could compete with him, not while he was able to draw on his wolf's strength as well as his own. Darren had to make them stop now before anyone got seriously hurt.

Lunging forward, Darren grabbed the wolf that was the closest to him, the female rogue. Pulling Spencer and her apart, he pushed her away as he shoved Spencer against the wall. He placed directly in front of his friend, forcing Spencer to focus on him.

"I said, that's enough!" Darren shouted, causing everyone to go silent. Both male rogues turned their eyes towards Darren. They both let snarls slip from them, but they weren't looking at Darren anymore. Turning around, Darren felt his own heart falter at the sight before him. The female rogue was on the ground, struggling to pull herself into a sitting position. Her face turned, so she looked at the floor, blood running down the right side of her face from a gash on her forehead. She must have hit her head when he pushed her. He hadn't meant to hurt her; he'd only wanted to get her out of the way. Another growl tore through the male rogue, drawing Darren's attention away from the injured female.

"Chris, don't you dare!" the female shouted, but it was already too late. One second the giant rogue, Chris, was running down the hall towards Darren. The next second, a massive grey wolf was in his place. Screams erupted from the crowd; some ran in terror, friends and mates gripped at each other, while others ran forward, ready to fight.

"Get down!" Darren yelled, he and Spencer diving out of the way as the wolf lunged, but he didn't come for them. Instead, he landed beside the female, standing directly over her, protecting her.

She must be his mate, Darren thought, as he stood up slowly, keeping his eyes on the wolf directly in front of him. You had to be cautious with werewolves. Their minds may have been half-human, but once the wolf came out, the human rarely had any control over the actions of his other part. Especially when their mate was involved.

Even once Darren was standing up to his full height, the dark grey wolf stood nearly eye to eye. He was massive. But he didn't charge or lash out. He stood his ground, continuing to growl threateningly; his ears pressed back against his head. Still, he made no move to attack anyone yet.

"Let's all just take a minute to calm down," Darren said, holding his hands up in a non-threatening gesture. "Everyone, leave now. Except for you guys," he ordered, making eye contact with Spencer, Michael, and the other packwolves that had been involved in the fight. He didn't bother ordering the rogues to stay put. The dark-haired one didn't look as if he would be going anywhere as he stood off the side, openly glaring at Spencer and the others. The female rogue was forced to stay put until the male who had shifted moved out of the way.

The crowd dispersed quickly, the hallway buzzing with the nervous chatter as they hurried away. If none of the adults were aware of what had happened yet, they would be in a few moments, then Alpha Luke Power would find out after that. It was Darren's first day in charge of the trainee wolves and already he had wolves fighting and shifting. His father would never trust him with anything ever again.

"I'm fine, Chris," the female rogue snapped, seemingly unafraid of the dangerous beast that was practically on top of her. "Get off of me," she said, pushing at the wolf with her hands. Hesitantly, the wolf moved away, his eyes shifting from Darren to each of the packwovles left in the hall. He was still anxious but hopefully calm enough so that he wouldn't do anything stupid. But then again, you could never know what to expect with rogues, at least that's what his father always said. "Oh, come on," the female said. "Quit your growling and shift back already. No one wants to fight anymore," she said, standing up now that he was out of her way, but Darren still couldn't get a good look at her since he wasn't willing to take his eyes off the wolf, at least not while the animal in him was still in control.

Much to Darren's surprise, Chris's human side was close enough to the surface to actually listen to what the female had said. In the blink of an eye, where the wolf had stood was the giant rogue, his face grim and his human eyes just as angry as his wolf's had been.

"Alright, who's going to tell me what happened here?" Darren asked, letting his eyes graze over each of his packmates. Most shifted their weight around nervously, their eyes on the ground, except Spencer, who kept his glare directed at the female rogue. Darren almost felt sorry for the girl, Spencer was Darren's best friend, but he knew how hard Spencer made life

for the wolves that he had a grudge against. And she was definitely on his list now.

"Your buddies were looking to pick a fight with our friend. That's what happened," the giant rogue rumbled, crossing his arms across his chest. The simple action made him look more threatening than before.

Friend, not mate, Darren noticed, a frown twisting his mouth. It didn't matter whether they were mated or not; they still had acted just like everyone had said they would. Already acting out violently on their first day. Although Darren had to admit they all seemed more in control than he had expected them to be.

"I didn't ask you," Darren said calmly, forcing himself to hold the rogue's glare for a moment before turning back to his packmates.

"Sorry, Darren," Michael said, speaking up when no one else said anything. "Spencer and I were on our way to training when we noticed Valery being harassed by that one," he said, pointing to the female rogue. "Then the big one threw Spencer, and I just lost it," he finished, looking down at the floor. Darren turned to the female, a growl rising in him at the thought of tiny Valery being terrified by the violent rogue. She didn't avert her gaze when his eyes met hers the way most wolves did to show their respect for his status; she obviously didn't know he was the Alpha's son or simply didn't care. Each wolf gave off an aura of their power that other wolves sense. Even females, with their limited wolf senses, could feel it. Usually, Alphas and Betas would use it to keep unruly wolves in check or in brief frights for dominance. It was the reason that not just any wolf could be an Alpha. No self-respecting wolf would follow someone that didn't have the power to protect them. Darren's own power

hadn't reached its full potential yet, but it was still enough that any wolf could tell that he came from a bloodline filled with power. Maybe being out in the wild so long had dulled the rogue's senses enough that she couldn't feel his wolf's influence or the urge to submit that came along with it anymore.

There wasn't anything extremely remarkable about her at first glance besides the blood drying to the side of her face. She wasn't all that tall, but she wasn't as petite as her redheaded friend; she probably was a few inches shorter than Darren was. Her dark hair was pulled back in a messy braid showing off her slim face and the barely noticeable scar across her jaw. Darren wondered how she had gotten the scar and if she had any more hidden under her jacket sleeves, like the ruined fang-shaped packmark on her arm.

It was her eyes that drew Darren in, making it hard for him to focus on anything else. Her eyes were an odd shade of light and dark grey swirling together, the kind that reminded him of a storm cloud just before it released its rain. They were simple but held a strange beauty, or maybe that was just the light reflecting off of them that made them look so enticing. He felt his wolf stirring restlessly within him, but he was too distracted to listen to whatever it was that his wolf wanted. He was probably still just anxious from the fight.

"Darren, aren't you going to do something? You can't just let these mutts come in and act like they own the place!" Spencer snapped, breaking whatever spell Darren had been slipping into.

"But she didn't do anything!" Everyone's heads turned at the shout from the other end of the hall where Valery stood, her tiny body stiff and her chin held high. When her eyes landed on the female rogue her eyes went round, her jaw going slack. "You

hurt her!" she exclaimed, her voice full of accusation, though Darren wasn't' sure who it was directed at.

"You don't need to worry about this, Valery," he said. "Go back to training. I'll take care of it," he assured her, turning back to rogues. How he was actually going to take care of the situation, he wasn't quite sure, but he would figure it out. His father was counting on him. If he couldn't sort out a few unruly teenagers, then how could he ever expect to one day lead an entire pack?

"No!" Valery said, running forward, shoving past Spencer, who moved to block her path and ran straight to the female rogue, throwing her arms around her. Darren's eyes widened as he watched his cousin wrap her arms tightly around the other girl's waist, pulling herself as close to the rogue as she could.

Stunned into silence, Darren and the other packwolves stared at their packmate in confusion and horror. Spencer was the worst, though; he looked as if he had punched right in the stomach. Darren was stunned as well; what could have come over his cousin to make her go towards the rogues who had just frightened her moments ago?

"What are you doing?" Spencer yelled. "Get away from them, Val!"

"Valery," Darren said slowly, trying to keep his voice calm. "Just come over here, and then we can talk about this, alright?" But Valery was already shaking her head.

"No, I'm not leaving Jade until you listen to me," she said, sticking out her bottom lip in a slight pout, her arms still wrapped tightly around the rogue.

Jade. The name suited the rogue, her face as hard and cold as the stone she was named for, but undeniably beautiful as well. The question was, how did Valery know her name?

"I promise that I'll listen to whatever it is that you need to tell us. But I need you to come over here and tell me about it," he tried to reason, holding out a hand, motioning for her to come closer. She looked as if she were about to argue with him some more, but Jade, keeping her hands away from Valery, bent down to whisper in something in the younger girl's ear. Valery looked up at her, a bit unsure, but Jade nodded. Slowly, almost cautiously, Valery turned back to Darren and her other packmates. The fire that was in her eyes had dimmed a bit. It was a look that Darren knew well. It was the face of someone whose resolve was about to cave.

"Fine," Valery conceded, allowing her arms to fall to her side and taking a small step away from the female rogue, but that was enough. Spencer sprung forward the moment Valery released her grip on the other girl, latching on to her arm and dragging her over to where the rest of the packwolves stood, to safety. "Hey! You don't need to be so rough," Valery grumbled, yanking her arm away, glaring at her brother, but he didn't seem to notice. His glare was still trained on the female rogue, her grey eyes filled with untempered anger of her own.

"Alright, Valery," Darren said, never taking his eyes off of the dark-haired girl in front of him. "Tell us what happened."

Chapter 7

Jade

Jade watched as the wolf who had first attacked her, Spencer, pulled Valery towards the rest of his group, an attempt to keep her safe from the monsters he saw in front of them. They all circled her protectively as if they expected the rogues to suddenly jump up and attack them. It was impossible to keep the anger from flaring up when she saw the look in their eyes when they watched her and her friends. The disgust and hatred, the way they looked at her like she was nothing more than an annoying piece of gum that they had the unfortunate experience of stepping on.

Worthless.

Jade could feel the familiar heat in the pit of her stomach start to rise as her anger sparked. It spread throughout her entire body, filling her with an odd feeling of power. A kind of power that she hadn't felt in a long time, one that she shouldn't be feeling at all. It was all-consuming, making it impossible to think about anything besides the flames that were coursing through her blood. Until she felt the firm pressure of Desert's hand on her shoulder, cooling the fire within her. Desert didn't need to say anything; she knew what he would say, and he was right; her anger wouldn't help any of them right now. She needed to get control, now.

"Alright, Valery, what is it that you need to tell us?" the newest male wolf asked, the one that Spencer had called Darren. Usually, she would have enjoyed the sight of lively blue eyes

and muscle-packed shoulders, but she found it hard to appreciate his good looks when her head was still pounding from where it had been hit when he pushed her. There was something about his voice, though. When he spoke, Jade could feel something settling in her chest with every word, gently tugging at her heart. It wasn't an unpleasant feeling, just an unfamiliar one.

"She doesn't need to explain anything," Spencer growled, turning his glare back to Jade. "These mutts cause nothing but trouble. We need to do something about it."

"No, Spencer, you don't understand. Jade is the one who saved me!" Valery yelled, fisting Spencer's shirt in her hands as if she were trying to hold him back, but it wasn't necessary. The second the words were out of her mouth, everyone froze. Jade could see their confusion as if it had been stamped on their foreheads.

"Saved you from what?" Darren asked, something in his tone softening. His eyes shone with something more than the judgment that the rest of his packmates held in their own, something softer. Could he be willing to actually hear the truth? Jade smothered the thought before it could take root. There was no use getting her hopes up, especially where packwolves were concerned.

"Remember when we went to go see the Crystal Mountain Pack three years ago?" Valery asked.

"Yeah, I remember," Michael said. "Didn't you wander off and get yourself lost?"

"No! That is not what happened," Valery said, her face flushing pink with embarrassment. "Some of the trainees were showing us the forest and took us off-trail. It's not my fault that you guys all left without me. I didn't even know that I had fallen behind until I realized that I couldn't hear or see anyone else.

We were in new woods, so I didn't know how to get back," she continued, shooting dirty looks at Michael and a couple of their other packmates as they rolled their eyes. "I was stuck in those woods all day without food or water, and it was getting dark, and no one had come back for me yet. I thought I was never going to find my way back! Until Jade found me," Valery said, shooting a grin at Jade. "I was so turned around that it took us three days to find the way back, but she helped me find the trail again and even stayed with me until we found the packhouse to make sure that I got home. I wanted her to come in and meet everyone, but she said that she had to go,"

It was true, all of it. What Valery didn't know was that Jade had stayed behind and watched to be sure that Valery was welcomed back by her packmates. She also stayed long enough to watch the hunting party head out to track down the rogue that was trespassing, according to the lost girl. Evidently, good deeds and intentions didn't mean much when you were a rogue.

"Is it true?" Darren asked, turning those impossibly bright eyes towards Jade. "Did you help bring her back to us?"

Jade could only nod in response. She met his gaze without hesitation, expecting to see the same wariness and disbelief in his packmates' eyes reflected there. Instead, there was only the innocent curiosity that she had caught a glimpse of earlier and an openness that made Jade feel vulnerable. As if she could see straight to his soul if she wanted.

"And you approached Jade this morning when you recognized her?" Darren asked Valery, though it sounded as if it were more of a statement than a question. She nodded earnestly in response, a satisfied smile lighting up her face.

"Then it sounds like we were wrong," Darren said, turning to face Jade directly. "I'm sorry for the trouble that we caused

today, and for the part I played in it. I hope you can forgive us," he said, meeting each of the rogues' shocked gazes. The sincerity in his eyes nearly knocked Jade to the floor. A packwolf willingly apologizing to rogues, within his own territory even!

Impossible.

Jade opened her mouth to say something, anything at all, but Spencer's harsh snarl stopped her.

"You can't be serious? Darren, we don't owe them anything."

"Spencer!" Darren snapped. "That's enough. Everyone head back to your classes." No one moved. Spencer and the other packwoves kept their steely glares on the rogues, and the rogues did the same, no one wanting to be the first to turn away, to be the first to back down.

"Come on, guys, you heard him. Let's go find our classes," Jade said, turning around to walk down the empty hallway before her. Jade wasn't one to hide from a fight, but she also knew that some battles weren't worth the outcome. In a heartbeat, Desert and Chris's footsteps followed close behind her own, but she could still feel eyes boring into her back as they walked away.

The light tugging that had started in her chest spread until it settled in her toes and fingertips, where it was replaced by a light but pleasant tingling. It was that tingling that seemed to stir awake something inside of her, something that she had shoved a dark forgotten corner of her mind. She pushed back at it, reinforcing the walls within her until she felt it settle again, going back into the deep slumber she had sent it into years ago. But the tingling remained, even after the darkness inside of her was once again asleep. It was troubling that a mere unfamiliar

feeling could break through the walls she had spent years building up. She would have to take extra care while she remained in Northwind territory to ensure it never happened again.

As she walked away, Jade heard some of the remaining packwolves turn away, but she could feel one pair of eyes that still followed her movements, eyes that sent shivers down her spine. Jade wondered if it was just the foreign territory, the stress of dealing with the packwolves, or maybe even exhaustion that gave those ice blue eyes their magic. Or perhaps that was something they possessed all on their own.

Chapter 8

Darren

Darren watched the rogues as they strode away from him and his packmates. He kept an eye on all three of them, but he found his eyes kept slipping to one as if they had a mind of their own. Some of his packmates slipped away quietly to their own classes. Still, he continued to watch the rogues until they were out of sight before turning to face Spencer, who stood just a few paces behind him. His friend's hands were still clenched into fists at his side, his eyes bright with his unspoken outrage.

"I know you were just protecting your sister," Darren said, trying to keep his own frustration at bay. "But I don't appreciate you questioning my decision in front of everyone the way you did. With my dad giving me more responsibility and all of these rogues around, I need to know that you have my back."

"I do have your back! But I can't stay quiet while you side with those strays over your own pack, over your own family," Spencer said, his voice rising with every word until he was nearly shouting. "You should have made them apologize to us! They're the ones who waltzed in here and started picking fights. Now they're going to think that they can walk all over us."

"Valery said that they weren't bothering her, and you threw the first punch Spence, not them," Darren said, but Spencer was already shaking his head.

"Valery is confused! She's always been naïve, and you know that. She wants to see good in everyone, even in those criminals. You can't trust her opinions of them."

"And I'm supposed to just trust yours?" Darren shouted back, his patience finally snapping. "You're not always the most level-headed or trustworthy source. You've always been more inclined to swing first and ask questions later."

"Well, at least I do something! Do you really think that you helped anyone today? Do you think that your dad will be proud that you defended a rogue instead of one of your own?" Spencer asked, but he didn't give Darren a chance to respond as he stormed past him, slamming his shoulder into Darren's forceful enough to make Darren stumble back a step before he righted himself.

It took all of the self-control he could muster just to hold himself in place so that he didn't go after Spencer, but what could he do if he did? Throttling him wouldn't help either of them at this point, and Darren didn't know what else he would say even if Spencer gave him the chance to speak. He was right; his father would disapprove of how Darren had handled the situation with the rogues. Luke would have unleashed his wolf's dominance on them. He would have forced everyone who had taken part in the fight to submit and would have made the rogues participate in extra training. Or worse, even throw them in the pack's dungeons for a night.

Werewolves may have been half-human, but the animal instincts were often stronger than their human mind, logic, or manners. The social games that were played when humans still ruled the Earth were nearly nonexistent now. Instead, their laws were determined by the laws of the wild, of nature itself. The law of the wolf. When there was danger, you fight, the safety and future of the pack come before all else, and above all, the Alphas' word is absolute. Of course, it could be harsh and bloody at times, but that was how they had thrived all these years

while humans had slowly died out, leaving a few left throughout the world. It was how the packs kept order and functioned while the rogues spent their days in bloodshed and hunger.

Is it really the only way?

Darren hushed the questioning voice within. Of course, that was the way it had to be; that was how it always had been for the wolves. It was how they lived. If the Alphas couldn't use their power to force submission, then there would be no order. They would be no better than the rogues.

Rogues. Violent, moody, lawless rogues.

Or at least that's what he had thought. These ones were definitely violent enough, and from their short encounter, they already seemed angry but lawless…Why would someone who had no moral code help a lost and defenseless she-wolf when they stood to gain nothing from it? None of it made sense.

Shouts and cheers floated down the hall from the slightly ajar door that led outside to the sparring field. The warriors in training grappled with each other, honing their brute strength into skills that would one day help them protect the pack. Normally, Darren's father or the pack Beta would observe the warriors' training regularly, but since Darren was in charge of the training wolves, it was probably one of the duties that he was expected to take charge of. Letting out a sigh, he started down the hall towards his ever-growing burden of responsibility. Red blood still stained the floor where the female rogue, Jade, had laid on the floor after he had thrown her. He still couldn't believe he had hurt her. Since he was a pup, it had been ingrained in him what a dishonor it was to harm someone unable to protect themselves. Since females hadn't been able to access their wolves for generations, they were some of the most defenseless members of the packs.

Yet there her blood was drying on the floor, taunting him and the guilt that tugged at him once again. Even her scent still lingered, fallen rain and freshly cut grass tickled his nose. Powered by the scent, Darren felt his wolf surge forward, breaking through the barrier that was around him when Darren was in control. There was only one thought in the animal's mind.

Mate

Mate!

Mate?

No, that wasn't possible. Something had to be wrong. Mates were supposed to recognize each other as soon as they saw each other. If that rogue was his mate, why hadn't his wolf sensed it before? His thoughts raced within, spiraling out of control with little to no sense coming from them.

Darren knew it wasn't himself that led his body down the halls, following the overpowering scent of rain through the building despite there not being a single cloud in the sky. Still, he followed it until he stood outside a single classroom, the closed door the one thing separating him from the girl on the other side. Blinds were closed over both of the windows to the room, but one small window in the door remained uncovered, allowing Darren to view the trainees within. Nearly twenty young wolves sprawled throughout the room, watching the pack history mentor pace slowly in the front of the room, probably trying to not bore the young wolves to death on their first day back.

In the very back of the room, almost completely hidden from his view, Jade sat in the darkest corner, as far away from the other wolves as she could get. Despite the distance, she was all that he could see.

He couldn't help but wonder if she purposefully kept her expression so bored or if it was genuine. Despite the initial appearance of disconnect on her face, her eyes were alert as she watched the mentor's excited gestures, her gaze flickering away for a brief second to scan the room. Taking in every detail of her surroundings.

The blood from earlier had dried on her forehead; most of it had fallen off, but a few specks still clung to her skin and hair. A dark bruise formed on her cheek as well. The mere sight of it triggered his wolf's instincts, fueling the beast forward. Knuckles white from clenched fists and ragged breaths were all that held him back from barging through the door and begging for her to forgive him.

No!

He was Darren Power, the future Alpha of one of the most powerful packs of their time. He was expected to protect and defend his packmates from people like her; he couldn't be mated to a rogue. What would his father say?

The hairs on his arm rose in alarm at the thought. The words sent a shock through him as if a bucket of ice-cold water had been dumped over him, waking him from the dream he'd been in since he saw those stormy eyes. Even awake, he was still in a nightmare. How could he explain to his parents that the she-wolf they had spent his whole life preparing him to meet was a rogue? His mother would be heartbroken to learn that her son had been destined to find his other half in someone so rash and violent. The complete opposite of what a Luna was supposed to be. And his father-

Darren didn't want to think about what his father would think.

She could be different, something inside him whispered. *Remember, she helped Valery.*

It was true, she had helped Valery, and she had proven that she was capable of stepping away from a fight.

One thing was certain, despite whatever intentions or plans the Goddesses had for him, and Jade would have to go unfulfilled for now.

As if sensing his presence, those grey eyes snapped to the door, and although Darren knew that he was out of her line of sight, he couldn't help but feel that she knew exactly who stood on the other side, watching her. That was all it took for Darren to retake control of his body, banishing his wolf back into the corner of his mind as he pulled himself away from the door.

Darren had been in plenty of skirmishes and even a few battles in his life. He had fought wolves twice his size and come out on top. He bore the scars that proved his bravery and willingness to face his enemies head-on like any other warrior in the pack, the way a true Alpha should. But turning away from the classroom door, Darren found himself doing something he had never done before.

He ran.

Chapter 9

Jade

Jade let out a loud yawn and stretched her arms above her head as she strode out of the training building; her last training session finished for the day. The movement allowed her to feel every ache in her bruised and battered body. If she were a male like Desert and Chris the aches and bruises would already have disappeared, healed by the wolf's superior healing and strength. As a female, she still healed faster than a human would have, but she would have to make do with Lola's herb concoctions and bandages for the next couple of days until the pain subsided completely.

She wasn't the only one that was a little tense from spending the whole day with the packwolves. Her friends already gathered at the foot of the stairs, each one stiff and weary from the long day of stares and whispers from the timid ones and outright insults, jabs, and harassment from the brave ones who felt like testing their luck. It pained her to see them all so serious when they were usually such an energetic bunch.

Bracing her shoulders and lifting her chin, she pushed through the dark thoughts. They were rogues; they had each survived being disowned by friends, family, and packmates and lived on their own until they had found each other. They could survive this too, with their heads held high.

"What's up with all the long faces?" She asked, bounding down the steps with an energy that she didn't know she

possessed. Evidently, Desert didn't believe that she had newfound positivity from the skeptical look on his face.

"Well, it's not as if life is all rainbows and sunshine at the moment," he replied, readjusting his ragged backpack on his shoulder.

"Let's be honest, though; when has it ever been?" Chris asked, holding his hand out towards Lola. Inside of his hand, hers looked even more fragile and delicate than usual, but somehow still the perfect fit. Jade wondered if the couple seemed so perfect together because they were made for each other, or if it was because they were both her friends, and the idea of the people close to her finding happiness gave her hope. She knew that last thought was a little morbid and sad, but she couldn't help but wonder how much truth it held.

"That's true," Jade said, ruffling James's hair causing a small smile to appear on his face. "I'm going to go for a walk by the river. Anyone want to join?" she asked. Immediately, the group perked up, everyone chiming in their agreement.

It didn't take long for them to make their way away from the rough sidewalks and packwolves' eyes on them to soft grass and nothing but chirping birds surrounding them. Tense shoulders began to loosen, smiles began to creep back onto her friends' lips. It was what they all had needed, to be removed from the watchful eyes and to pretend that just for a little while, that they were back home. Even with her own senses clearing with the fresh air, Jade couldn't seem to clear her mind of the events that happened earlier that day and the boy with blue eyes that had intervened.

She'd learned his name was Darren Power, future Alpha of the Northwind Pack and son to Alpha Luke Power. It explained why he had stepped in to break up the fight, but it didn't explain

his lack of anger or judgment when he spoke to them or his willingness to listen to Valery's story.

"What are you thinking so hard about?" Desert asked, falling back to walk beside her in the rear of the group.

"Just the mess that today was. I knew being here was going to be hard. I just didn't know it was going to happen like this," she replied, gesturing around them. "Thanks, by the way, for today. I'm not sure how that would have gone down if you and Chris hadn't stepped in," she said, but Desert was already shrugging.

"It was bound to happen sooner or later; at least it happened when we were all together. It could be worse next time," he said.

Next time.

There was always a next time to worry about. The next fight, next meal, next place to sleep. It wasn't an easy life, always living with that uncertainty, but in a way, Jade almost found it comforting. If she didn't know where her next meal or shelter would come from, it just meant that she could find them anywhere. She was free to travel as far as she could walk, stay however long she wanted, sleep under the stars, hunt for her own food, and befriend who she wished. That was the type of freedom that most packwovles would never know.

But she knew that not all of her friends felt the same way. Many of them were still new to her lifestyle, still longing for their old pack or at least missing the stability that they offered. As optimistic as they tried to be, Jade could see they were struggling.

A scream shattered the silence that had wrapped itself around Jade, shaking her from her thoughts.

Desert and Jade exchanged a brief, frightened glance for a single breath before they took off. Desert shifted mid-leap into

his wolf, the animal's legs carrying him ahead of Jade, trapped with her human ones. Trees blurred in her vision as she sprinted towards the continued, panicked screaming. How had they gotten so far ahead? She should have never let them out of her sight, not after the fight that morning, not with the packwolves so hostile towards them. Bursting through into a clearing, Jade found not only Desert but her other friends caught once again in a battle. Lola screamed once again as Chris, in his wolf form, was attacked by four other wolves. James's wolf rolled around with another one, teeth flashing and frightening snarls filling the air. Leaping into the fray, Desert joined his friends in their battle as Jade stood by, watching in horror. The strange wolves fought furiously, their auburn fur matted and coarse, and Jade could see their ribs starting to poke through, their summer coats not thick enough to hide their hunger. They weren't Northwind wolves.

Rogues.

Watching mutely on the sidelines, Jade felt as if she was seeing it all from underwater. Lola's screams muffled, the growls and yelps of pain coming from the fighting wolves just background noise to her own beating heart. But the blood wasn't dulled. Bright red blood speckled the grass as it dripped from tooth and claw from random wounds scattered across bodies. A familiar feeling clawed inside of her chest, fighting against her control, a primal, animalistic instinct to protect her own. But as a human, she was useless.

A low growl had Jade turning slowly to her left; a sixth strange wolf stood just a few feet away. His grey fur along his back stood at attention as he let out another menacing growl as he took a step forward. Bright yellow eyes watching Jade's every move.

Raising her hands, Jade took a slow step back, never taking her eyes off of the danger in front of her. One wrong move and the wolf would have his teeth around her throat.

"Let's not do anything rash; I'm sure we can talk this out," she said. The wolf took another step forward; he wasn't going to back down on his own. Slowly Jade bent down, even when that made the rogue let out a harsh snarl, but he didn't move forward. Picking up the only potential weapon within reach, Jade found a sharp rock. It wasn't the perfect choice, but it would do the job.

She didn't have time to think about how she would use it as the wolf let out one last snarl before leaping forward. Rolling to the side, she barely made it out of the way before he landed where she had been. Scrambling to her feet, she whirled around to face him, but he was coming again and quickly. He charged her again. This time she wasn't fast enough; one of his paws caught her in her shoulder, knocking her to the ground. Her shoulder stung; that was going to leave a mark. It was too late to roll away as her attacker stood over her, teeth snapping mere inches from her nose; his hot breath brought tears to her eyes. There weren't many options for defending herself pinned under a two-hundred-pound wolf. There was only one place she could reach. A yell was pulled from her as she jammed the point of the rock into the roof of his mouth, his teeth scraping her hand as she pulled away, his blood spraying her hand and face. Howling, he reared up, allowing Jade to scramble away from him. It also caused the rest of the wolves to turn their attention towards them.

"Now, let's try this again," she said, turning around to look each wolf in the eye. "It's time to talk."

It didn't take long for the wolf Jade injured to shift back into his human skin, cradling his mouth gingerly with one hand. He was clearly the oldest of the group, his dark hair showing signs of graying along the edges. One by one, the rest of the wolves slowly shifted back until finally, Jade's friends stood there in their human forms along with six strange rogues. None looking especially friendly.

"Anyone want to start?" Jade asked, glancing around the group. She was met with silent glares and crossed arms, even from Desert. "Fine, I'll go first. Hi, I'm Jade. I'm an Aries; I like bubble baths, hiking, and not acting like a freakin' idiot and starting fights everywhere I go. Especially while I'm in packwolf territory!" she yelled, her face sticky from the blood that still clung to her skin. James and a couple of the other rogues suddenly found the grass incredibly interesting; Chris let a snicker slip earning him a sharp elbow to the ribs from Lola.

"Well, we wouldn't have needed to fight if your friends hadn't barged into our camp. We thought we were under attack," the rogue that had fought Jade snapped, spitting a mouth full of blood into the grass. "Oh, and I'm Aiden," he grinned, his teeth stained a bloody red.

"I'm sorry we surprised you; we just got here a few days ago. We didn't know anyone was out here," she said, looking around the campsite.

Campsite was a loose term. As far as Jade could see there was one small, very cold fire pit and a bed of loose leaves and other plants large enough for a few wolves to curl up on if they didn't mind sleeping close together. It was the home of people

who had no real home. It was a sight Jade was familiar with, one that most rogues had seen at least once in their life.

"When did you guys get here?" she asked.

"Two days ago. We were actually closer to Twin Peak's territory, but Kacen here has had a few run-ins with their guards already, so we figured the extra day of travel wouldn't hurt if it meant we could avoid them," he said, pointing out one of his companions, a younger dark-haired wolf who merely shrugged unapologetically in response. "I'm guessing you runts came from their 'mandatory training'," he said, his tone left no question about his feelings. Jade kept her face blank, but inside she bristled at the apparent jab.

"Yeah, we figured we could play nice until we figure out what the packs want. I think the phrase is keeping your enemies closer," she said, flashing a smile that she hoped could only be described as sickly sweet. "Speaking of which, we better be getting back to our place, early morning training. I'm sure you understand."

"Where are you guys staying?" one of the other rogues asked, a scrawny wolf, probably close to James's age.

"We're just a little way outside of town, north of here," Jade answered as her friends slowly started to gather their scattered belongings back up.

"Do you guys have a good camp?" he asked, his eyes hesitant as if he wasn't sure if he should be talking to her.

"Oh yeah," James said, perking up. "We found this warehouse that we're staying in; it's huge."

"You found a building?" Aiden asked, his younger companion's eyes wide with wonder. There were three things most valued by rogues: freshwater, a food source, and a roof

over your head. The first two were hard enough to come by, but the third was nearly impossible.

"There's plenty of room if you guys are interested, as long as you and your friends can keep your teeth to yourselves," Jade said, ignoring the surprised and concerned looks from her friends. She wasn't sure where the invitation had come from either. It was as if someone or something else was running her mouth for her, but there was something about the cautious eyes of the young wolves that reminded her of when she was new to rogue life. How different would her life have turned out if someone had just given her a safe place to sleep, even for just one night? The younger wolf opened his mouth to respond, a smile starting to show before he was interrupted.

"We don't take charity," Aiden snapped, "we're doing just fine on our own."

"I prefer to call it taking advantage of opportunities and taking care of your friends, but to each their own, I guess," Jade shrugged; spinning on her heel, she walked away.

Two fights in one day, one with packwolves, the same wolves that had treated her like an outcast. Then with rogues, the ones who should be able to understand their life better than anyone else. Nowhere was safe, not for her, or for anyone who lived as a rogue, and she was tired of it. Maybe it would never be safe for them, perhaps the packs were right, maybe they were nothing more than lawless monsters who thrived off of the chaos. But that didn't mean they had to eat, sleep and live like it.

"Are you coming?" she called out over her shoulder, her friends close by her side. Jade didn't have to turn around to know the glances the other wolves would exchange among themselves or to feel the cautious footsteps that followed them home.

Chapter 10

Darren

Knuckles bleeding, Darren's legs and shoulders burned angrily. He had almost forgotten what his legs were supposed to feel like besides jello. He couldn't stop, though. When he stopped moving it meant his mind was free to think, and when it was left to its own devices, all it could conjure were images of *her*. Her face, bleeding and bruised, haunted his every waking moment. Forget sleeping. Darren didn't even want to think about what kind of dreams he would have once he did fall asleep.

He still could hardly believe it. He had hurt her.

Meeting your mate was supposed to be a magical moment, love at first sight. That's how his mother and friends had always described it. That's how it was supposed to be. But he hadn't recognized her for who she was, and he certainly didn't think that she had sensed who he was to her. Had he just been too concerned about breaking up the fight and ensuring that his packmates were safe to be able to really see her?

Did it even matter now why he hadn't realized who she was? He had blown it; if she hadn't hated his guts before then, she certainly had reason to now, and there would be no way for him to redeem himself.

Did he want her forgiveness? After all, she was a rogue.

His wolf crushed that thought immediately. Of course, they still wanted her forgiveness. It didn't matter who she was; she was made for him just as he was for her. It didn't matter if she

was a rogue, a witch, a human, or even a hunter; he would always want her.

It didn't matter what he wanted. His future Luna would have to be accepted by the pack. She would have to be someone they could trust even more than their Alpha. There was no way the Northwind Pack was ready to accept a rogue as their Luna. His father would never accept her into the pack.

For now, he would have to avoid her, at least until he figured out his next steps. Even if he couldn't talk to her, Darren knew that he wouldn't be forgetting the girl with stormy eyes anytime soon.

Chapter 11

Jade

Two weeks. It had been two agonizing weeks since Jade and the other rogues had come to the Northwind Pack's territory. As strange as it had been, the group had slowly found a rhythm, the teens and pups going to the pack's Training Center and the adults assigned odd jobs within the pack in exchange for ration chips. But finding the rhythm of their new life did little to ease Jade's concerns. Or the whispers, and there were plenty of whispers and rumors speculating the Alpha Council's reasons. Maybe they wanted to recruit the rogues as for-hire soldiers to help fight against the hunters. It wasn't an unheard-of idea. Packs had been known to hire rogue wolves as mercenary fighters before, usually in fights against other packs. The most concerning rumor and the one Jade feared had the most truth behind it was that the Alpha Council finally recognized the rogues' strength, and they were afraid of it. They wanted to know their numbers, know just how many rogues there were and if they posed any real threat to the lifestyle that the packs currently enjoyed. Why else would they be taking and keeping records on each of them?

With all the rumors going around, things were tense within the rogue community, but they managed to get by with little to no drama with the packwolves besides the fight on the first day. Jade couldn't say the same about the residents of the warehouse.

After Aiden and his group had joined them in their temporary home, it seemed their numbers had swelled within the

last week. Every day more rogue wolves made their way into Northwind Pack territory, and many of them found their way to the refuge that Jade's friends offered them.

Wolves were naturally pack animals; they enjoyed being around others of their own kind. But Jade found herself feeling wary and often tired of being surrounded by the crowds, first with the packwolves and then with the rogues. And others were starting to feel the same way. Although they were avoiding more fights with the packwolves, it seemed that every time Jade turned there was a new tussle to starting up between her new roommates. Especially between the younger wolves.

"Break it up!" Jade yelled, stepping in between two fighting wolves, Prince and Kacen. Both were younger males that seemed to be at each other's throats every time she turned around. Prince was newer, but Kacen had come with Aiden's group, and one of the most difficult to calm down. "Back off now; I'm not telling you again!" Jade shouted again, shoving Prince away when he tried to go for Kacen again, snarling and eyes glowing.

"I'll back off once you tell this mutt to stop stealing from me," Prince growled, still obviously furious, but his eyes lost their animalistic glow and were going back to their normal brown.

"I already told you, I didn't take that dumb necklace! What would I even want with it?" Kacen asked, flipping his long, dark hair out of his face. His unapologetic scowl didn't help the situation.

"I don't know, you tell me. Why were you lurking around my stuff earlier?" Prince accused, taking an advancing step forward, only backing off when he met Jade's cold stare.

"Slow down and catch me up. What is missing exactly?" Jade asked once both of them had taken a step away, forcing the males to turn their attention to her. Prince turned towards her, his face flushed a bright red; Jade wasn't sure if it was from the recent fight or his following words.

"It's not a necklace, well, not really. It's one of my fangs that I put on a chain. I'm giving it to my mate Lucy when I see her again," he said, pain alive in his eyes. Like many rogues, Prince was forced to leave his mate when he was banished from his pack, and the thought of getting back to her was sometimes the one thing that held him together.

"I understand; we'll help you find it, but that means I need you to stop jumping down everyone's throats anytime something happens. There are too many of us in here to be fighting. Got it?" she asked, watching Prince carefully until he gave a hesitant nod. "Thank you. Chelsea, did you hear that?" Jade asked, turning her attention to where Chelsea and Kyler stood nearby, watching the whole interaction closely.

"Everyone keep an eye out for a necklace made from a fang, got it. Kyler and I can spread the word," she smiled, springing out of her seat to drag Kyler along behind her. Just like that, the watchful eyes turned away back to what they were doing before the fight had started. Kacen and Prince exchanged glares one more time before going to their separate corners.

Closing her eyes, Jade let out a deep sigh. It was a good thing she was a rogue; she obviously wasn't cut out for pack life. How could Alphas do this all day, every day?

She wasn't quite sure how or why she had been the one that got stuck fixing the issues within the group. It seemed to have happened overnight as many rogues had started to seek her out to help resolve disputes, arrange sleeping spaces for newcomers,

and assign duties as needed. Desert said it was because she had "a powerful aura", but Jade suspected it had more to do with her being an ex-member of the Darkfang Pack and her years as a rogue. With so little to go on in their world, rogues had little need for power that the Alphas thrived on. Every pack knew they were as strong as their Alpha's control over them was, but power was only helpful when you needed to ensure power stayed in the right hands. Experience and common sense were what kept you fed, warm, and alive.

Even as she told herself she'd be glad once everyone went their separate ways, she couldn't completely ignore the comfort she felt walking through the crowded building. Stepping around the obstacle course of random bedding and bags of belongings, their owners smiled at her or called out a greeting as she passed by. Like Malcolm, the elderly wolf that always had a story or words of wisdom to share. Or Maryanne and her daughter, Kendra. The single mother had followed her mate into roguehood when he had been thrown out of their pack to lose him weeks later to illness.

Not everyone was friendly. There were plenty of wolves like Prince and Kacen who were only with them to have a roof over their head and someone to help them figure out where their next meal would come from, but they were by no means a danger to the group. Besides constantly testing Jade's patience.

Needing to find some of her sanity, Jade found herself making her way to the back corner of the warehouse, towards The Lost Children. The name was given to pups born into the rogue life or the ones abandoned or orphaned before they received their packmark. They were the children that had never belonged to anyone, a feeling Jade was a little envious of. The list of things she wouldn't give just to remove her own

disfigured packmark was small. To have the freedom of belonging to no one but herself.

Jade wasn't surprised when she found Lola sitting on the ground playing with some of the smaller children. Lola was a natural when it came to nurturing and being motherly. She would have fit into the role that most packs wanted their females to fulfill, a position that Jade had always felt a little awkward and out of place in.

She was surprised to see a familiar head of dark hair bobbing among the others, one that most certainly did not belong.

"Valery, what do you think you're doing here?" Jade sighed, approaching the younger she-wolf where she played with the young pups; Lola watched the whole scene with a smile from where she was seated. The girl grinned up at Jade, completely unapologetic or unaware of the danger she could have been in.

"Oh, hi, Jade! I just wanted to come by and say hello to everyone. I didn't know there were so many of you guys staying here," she said, glancing around the room, her gaze void of any of the judgment Jade expected to see. Of course, she should have known better. Valery didn't have a critical bone in her body.

"Does your family know where you are?" Jade asked, already suspecting the answer but the sheepish grin Valery displayed confirmed it for her.

"No... I didn't think it would be that big of a deal."

"Really? So, if I let your brother know where you are, you think he'll be fine with that?" Jade asked, unable to hold back a smile as Valery's dark eyes widened into saucers.

"Uh, you know it probably is time that I head back. I'll see you guys tomorrow!" she said, leaping to her feet, scurrying

towards the door, but not before she gave a parting hug to each of the pups. Jade watched as she nearly skipped out of the warehouse, shooting smiles and waves to any of the rogues that cast confused glances her way. She was completely oblivious to their bemusement.

"She doesn't mean any harm," Lola said, also watching the younger she-wolf, a small smile lighting up her face. Jade let out a sigh, plopping down on a wooden box, keeping her eye on Valery's bouncing hair until it disappeared out of the double doors completely.

"We've all done plenty of harm to others, even if that wasn't our intention," she said. "The last thing we need is for the pack to think we kidnapped her."

"I just don't want us pushing her away; it's nice having a friend outside of these walls. We need more wolves like her who are willing to bridge the gaps between us. Maybe she can help convince others that we aren't as dangerous as they think we are."

"Maybe," was the only reply Jade could muster. Lola was right; she should find it encouraging that even after all this time, Valery was still so willing to look past their rough exterior. But she couldn't help unwanted thoughts that Valery would get hurt just from her close proximity to them no matter their intentions. Like so many before her.

"You handled that well," Lola said, nodding her head in Prince's direction, successfully changing the subject. Jade rolled her eyes.

"Bunch of immature pups if you ask me; they can't get anything done without throwing fists and snapping their teeth," she said, watching as the other she-wolf bounced a drowsy toddler on her knee.

"That's males for you," Lola laughed. "They would always be fighting if we weren't around to bring some common sense."

"Yeah, I guess you're right," Jade sighed, bringing a hand up to rub her eyes. Between training with the packwolves, keeping peace within the rogues, and avoiding the boy with blue eyes who made her tingle, she was going to run herself ragged.

"You know you're doing an amazing job here, right?" Lola asked, genuine concern crossing her face. "I don't think we could have done this without you."

"What do you mean?" Jade asked. She wasn't doing anything that Desert or Chris couldn't have done themselves if they were inclined to do so. She just happened to be the one stepping up this time. "I mean, look at all of this," Lola said, gesturing around the warehouse and everyone inside it. "All of us living together like this; it wouldn't have worked for this long without someone leading us, without *you* leading us." Jade scoffed.

"Breaking up a few fights is hardly leading."

"Is that really all that you think you're doing? We're all fed because of your idea to pool together our ration chips. We have a roof over our heads and are safe because we listen to you. Even if you can't see it the rest of us can. You're a good Alpha," Lola assured her, placing the now sleeping toddler under a blanket, brushing a lock of hair behind his ear gently.

"Don't underestimate yourself, Jade. Things are going to get harder from here on; we need a strong leader to help us get through it," Lola said, patting Jade's shoulder as she walked away to comfort a crying child. Leaving Jade alone to process her words. She wasn't really an Alpha; she didn't know anything about leading people. She had barely kept herself alive all those

dark nights on her own; could she really be expected to be able to help others as well?

"Jade!" a tiny voice squealed. Jade looked up to see Kendra running over to her. "Look what I found, do you like it?" the girl asked, holding up a simple chain with a single wolf's fang hanging from it.

"That is beautiful. Where did you find it?" Jade asked, offering a relieved smile which made Kendra's grin larger.

"I found it outside in the grass. Do you want it?" Kendra asked, holding out the necklace to her in a simple but selfless gesture.

"You know what, I think I know someone else that will be happy to see this. Do you want to help me give it back to them?" Jade offered, taking Kendra's hand when she nodded enthusiastically.

Jade still wasn't sure if she believed Lola, but she did know one thing she was right about. Tensions between the rogues and packwolves were going to grow, and if the rogues didn't try to find peace together, it might mean the end of life as they knew it.

Chapter 12

Darren

Weeks crawled on by since the rogues had arrived, and Darren had lived in his own personal hell since then. Every day tensions grew in the pack, the whispers louder each time the rogues passed in the halls or were seen around town. It didn't help that the rogues were uneasy as well.

More and more fights were breaking out across their territory, and it was Darren's job to investigate all of them. He was rarely at his regular training, which was a blessing in its own way. Nearly every moment of his day was dedicated to furthering his growth as the future Alpha of the Northwind Pack. And it was exhausting, but there was one thing that kept him going.

Darren had never seen his father more proud of him than he was the last few weeks. There was no hint of disappointment in his eyes at the weekly pack council meeting where Darren had to share his report on each rogue he encountered. And after each meeting, his father would pat his shoulder, grinning from ear to ear as he thanked him for his hard work. It made him stand a little taller, knowing that maybe he could live up to his father's expectations.

But at the end of each day, Darren was beyond exhausted mentally and physically. Since his birth, he had been told he would be Alpha one day. He had been groomed and continuously built into the Alpha that his pack would need him to be. Somehow when he was younger, he had imagined it would

be more fulfilling work, but every night he fell into bed feeling drained, empty, and dreading the next day. This couldn't be what he was destined for. If it was, then he had a very long and tedious future to look forward to.

There were few moments in his day where he did find his peace of mind. Such as dropping by the basics Training Center where the pups went before moving on to the Training Center with the maturing wolves. Problems there were simple, and pups were straightforward with their issues. He wished he could have all of the packwovles and rogues spend just one day with those pups. Maybe he would have fewer disturbances to report if they could be a little like the young wolves.

Those moments with the pups were too brief, something always pulling him back into reality. If those moments were few and far between, then the moments that he saw *her* were even rarer.

Jade had mainly kept to herself for the first week, only interacting with her friends that she had come into the territory with. Slowly her group had grown as more rogues came into the territory. Darren had noticed more and more rogues following her around the Training Center, mostly unmated males, which made his wolf uneasy. Valery had also somehow worked her way into their group, chatting with different rogues in the hallway or taking her breaks with Jade.

Darren hadn't spoken or interacted with Jade since the fight that first day, and it was driving his wolf crazy. As far as he could tell, she either didn't know or didn't care whether he was there or not. When he was near, she never made a move to talk to him or even look his way. There hadn't been any more incidents involving her that he had to manage. In fact, most of the rogues that followed her around stayed out of trouble. Darren

often caught himself wishing she would cause some kind of trouble, anything to prove that it wasn't safe to have her in his life. Mostly, though, he hoped it would happen simply so he would have another chance to talk to her.

What would he even say if he did get the chance to talk to her face to face again? As if accidentally injuring her wasn't bad enough, so much time had passed since the incident that he didn't even know how to apologize for it. Every time he considered throwing away any caution he had and letting her know how he really felt, it all felt too little too late. No, it was better if he stayed clear of her for now, at least until he knew what he wanted.

Though it seemed that plan would be short-lived.

"Good, you're here," Luke said as Darren walked into his office.

"You are the one that asked to see me," Darren replied. "Looks like I'm not the only one who is part of this meeting," he said, glancing around the room at a couple of dozen other wolves already in the room. Most of them were various members of the pack council like Johnathan, his father's Beta. There were others whose presence surprised him like the dozen of their strongest warriors, who were usually left out of pack politics. And Spencer, who avoided Darren's eyes. They still weren't on good terms after Spencer accused Darren of taking the rogues' side in the fight, despite Darren's repeated attempts to repair their friendship.

"It's less of a meeting and more of an outing," Luke said, standing from his desk and striding out of the room without explanation, forcing everyone to follow him.

"Where are we going?" Darren asked, trying not to show the spark of excitement he felt at the odd turn of events. Maybe he would finally find out the interesting parts of being an Alpha.

"The rogues have been joining into small groups ever since they arrived, which we expected they would. Most of the groups haven't lasted long; they split up and join up with different ones like rogues tend to do. But there is one group that has remained together. In fact, they have just continued to grow enough that our own wolves that live near where they are camped have started to raise concerns."

The longer Luke explained their mission, the weaker Darren's excitement grew until it felt like a stone sitting in his stomach. He knew which group Luke was referring to. It was the group Jade was part of.

"Our job tonight is simple; we will be meeting with them to see how many of them there are and to see if there is any tension within the group. Any chance you have to let them see our strength, take it. Any questions?" Luke asked, finally turning to face the group he had assembled, completely blind to the turmoil and panic that was settling in Darren.

When he was met with only silent eagerness from the group, Luke turned and shifted into his sizeable dark grey wolf and started the run towards the other side of town, the other wolves close on his heels. Darren followed as well, but there was hesitancy in his step. Maybe he should have told his father about Jade and who she was to him, at least to give him a heads up. But Darren found himself holding his tongue. Jade didn't even know what they were; it wasn't fair for others to know before she did.

It didn't take long for the group to reach the outskirts of town, where a large warehouse stood right on the edge of the

forest, the temporary home of some of the rogues. Jade's temporary home. Dingy and rusted with broken windows, but those at least had been covered with either blankets or plastic, it was hardly what Darren would consider a decent shelter.

Even from where he stood in the trees, Darren could smell the individual scents from dozens of wolves. Evidently, a dingy warehouse was good enough when you had no home.

The Northwind wolves followed Luke's lead and shifted back into their human forms, still standing within the trees, no sign of the rogues besides their scent.

"We go in peacefully but ready for a fight if that's what they want. Understood?" Luke asked, but it was clearly a command.

"Yes, Alpha," Darren answered in unison with his packmates, their eyes alight with excitement that Darren had seen in wolves before going into battle. Swallowing his dread, he moved forward, following his father's footsteps, every step taking him one step closer to his mate.

Chapter 13

Jade

"Packwolves are coming here. There are packwolves right outside!" James yelled, running to the back of the warehouse where Jade was watching Chris and Kyler set up makeshift shelves.

"Do you know how many there are?" Chris asked, dropping the long slab of wood directly onto Kyler, earning him an annoyed huff from the other wolf.

"I'm not sure; I counted at least fifteen, but I think there were more," James answered breathlessly. Jade could hear his racing heart from where she stood, its pounding echoing the hammering of her own pulse.

"Nothing to worry about," Chris grinned. "We can take 'em."

"No one is fighting anyone," Jade snapped, making Chris's smile droop. "They're probably here to see how many of us are here, and just to scare us enough into behaving. If we fight them now, we'll just be asking for trouble."

"Maybe some trouble is exactly what we need. Come on, you agree with me, don't you, Desert?" Chris called out as Desert approached the group.

"Sorry, but I think I'm with Jade on this one, again," Desert answered, his words finally deflating Chris as his shoulders slouched forward in defeat.

"Fine, but if we aren't going to rough anyone up, what is our plan?"

"Let's find out what they want first, then I promise if any roughing up is needed, you will be the first to know," Jade said. Walking towards the large double doors with Desert and the other following behind her, she tried to steady her breaths.

Aiden and a few of the other rogues already stood by the doors, leaving their sleeping spots to watch whatever drama was about to unfold.

"Is it true the packwolves are out there?" Aiden asked, just as riled up as Chris had been.

"That's what we're checking now," Jade answered, not slowing her pace.

"They want to see our strength; let us show it to them," Aiden said, a few of the other wolves cheering in agreement. Jade raised her hand to silence them.

"We don't know why they are here. If anyone tries to start trouble before we know what's going on, they will have to deal with me later. Got it?" she asked, turning her back to the double doors to face the wolves that stood behind her. There were grumbles of acknowledgment from the audience. Most didn't try to hide their disappointment at the missed opportunity to let off some steam. Jade let her eyes wander over the crowd until it began to dwindle as wolves were driven to the edges of the room.

Turning back to the doors, Jade placed her hand on it and drew in a deep breath. "You ready?" she whispered, knowing only those that were close could hear her.

"I'm ready whenever you are," Desert said, placing his own hand on the other door.

"Let's do this," Jade said, as she and Desert both gave a shove and let the doors open.

Clouds glowed pink in the burning orange sky. Even though the sun had sunk below the tree line, it gave enough light for Jade to see the group of wolves that made their way out of the forest. They were in human form, which was a good sign. No one went into a planned fight in their weakest form; it meant they were here on business. Because they had their backs to the setting sun, Jade couldn't see their faces until they were a few feet away; but she could count their figures, and from what she could tell, there were at least twenty of them that were out in the open. There could have been more in the coverage of the trees that she couldn't sense yet. Once they were close enough to see their faces, Jade was surprised to see Alpha Power in the lead. She had never seen him in person before, but he had an aura of power around him, one that only an Alpha would have. And a powerful one at that. What was so important that Luke Power would feel the need to come out there himself? At least it explained the number of wolves. They were merely a precaution in case the big bad rogues were foolish enough to attack Northwind's most powerful Alpha.

Another wolf had caught Jade's eye. Just behind Alpha Power stood the boy with the bright blue eyes from the Training Center. Darren Power, Luke Power's son. Although she could hardly call him a boy, he wasn't built quite as large as a typical warrior, but he was no twig either, and the two scars running up his well-shaped bicep showed that he had some experience in battle. No, he wasn't a boy; by wolf standards, he was a full-fledged member of the pack. He was already watching her when she noticed him, his eyes intense as they bored into hers. She

was used to packwolves gazing at her with intensity, but usually, it was with emotions such as rage or disgust, but not his gaze. It was full of something for sure, something that Jade couldn't quite define. Whatever it was, it didn't seem hostile.

"Alpha Power," she said, nodding her head in what she hoped he viewed as a civil enough greeting. "It's a pleasure to meet you; what brings you out this way?" she asked.

"I make it a habit of meeting all of the wolves that make it into my territory, and I heard that a number of you had gathered here," Luke answered, but his eyes glanced her way for a moment before they shifted to Desert. His deep voice was soft, but even then, it was clear and easy to hear. Jade could imagine how powerful it must be when he was trying to be intimidating. She also couldn't help noticing that he didn't mimic the pleasure it was to meet them. "This is my Beta, Johnathan, and my son Darren. I'm sure you've had the opportunity to meet him already at the Training Center."

"Yes, I believe we have," Jade answered, even though the question hadn't been addressed to her. She allowed her eyes to meet the blue ones that still stared at her, trying not to get lost in their depth. She pushed away the awakening she felt building within her chest. She would need to worry about it later.

"Would it be alright if we came inside?" Luke asked, once again looking at Desert as he gestured towards the doors behind them.

"Of course," Desert said, stepping aside. "Come on in."

Jade and the others stepped to the side to allow the packwolves to pass. Chris crossed his arms and puffed out his chest as some of the warrior wolves walked by him, making them speed their steps up. Jade tried to avoid looking at the blue-eyed boy as he walked past her, even though she could still feel

his gaze on her. Goosebumps sprouted on her skin when his arm brushed hers, and for a split second, it felt as if a bolt of electricity coursed through her. As suddenly as it was there, it was gone, and Jade found herself following the last of the packwolves inside, stealing a look with Desert, and he allowed his unease to show. It had been difficult enough to keep the rogues off each other when they were all under one roof. Would they be able to keep this visit civilized and quiet? She could only hope.

Chapter 14

Darren

Jade was here. This was the closest Darren had been near her since the fight on the first day of training. His wolf was struggling to remain calm with her scent so close to him. Rain, cut grass, summertime. It was intoxicating. He reigned in his wolf's excitement; now was not the time or place, not when she didn't know she was his mate and certainly not in front of his father and packmates.

Brushing past the rogues, Darren made his way into the shabby warehouse. He was unsure if the hairs on the back of his neck stood at attention due to the close proximity of his mate or because of the sight that lay ahead of him. The large room was divided into smaller areas, mostly by wooden pallets or crates. Each area had blankets and mats laid out for rough sleeping areas. Darren found it difficult to hide his surprise at the number of wolves already in the building just from looking around the room. From quick calculations, there had to be over a hundred and fifty rogues there already, and they were still expecting more to come within the next few weeks. If they all came here, how large would this group get? He could see the same thoughts going through his father's mind as well. This was a bigger concern than they had initially suspected.

"It may not be much, but it's what we all call home for now," Jade said, catching the uneasy glances Darren and his packmates gave the room. "Us rogues know how to rough it,"

she grinned. He knew it wasn't a genuine smile from her, but even her sarcastic one made his heart thud like a jackhammer.

"It looks like you have made yourselves comfortable," Luke said, hiding the disdain well enough that an untrained eye could easily miss it. But Darren noticed. And he had a suspicion that Jade had seen it too by the way her eyes darkened from their blue-grey to a stormy grey. "I assume with this many wolves in one place, you have a designated Alpha?" Luke continued; his question sounded more like a statement.

"Actually, we tend to make most decisions as a group," Jade replied, crossing her arms as she faced Luke, that defiant spark in her eye that Darren had seen the first time he met her. She certainly was a talker, Darren thought, surprised that more of the group didn't speak up.

"But you're right, sometimes we do find it helpful to have one person in charge," the wolf Darren had learned was called Desert answered, "And I think I speak for the group when I say we are all in agreement with who we follow."

"Perfect," Luke nodded, "is there a place we can speak somewhat privately?" he asked, gesturing towards Desert. It was a decent choice. Desert seemed confident and capable in their current situation. Clearly, he was respected among the group from what Darren had observed at the Training Center.

"Oh, I'm not our Alpha," Desert answered, his eyes widening in surprise at Luke's suggestion. "I do help keep order here, but I'm not running the show."

"Fine, then who is 'running the show'?" Luke asked, his eyes flashing. Darren tried not to wince; his father was not known for his patience, even on his best days. It was true of most of the powerful Alphas, but it didn't mean that Darren had to like it.

"I am," Jade answered, flashing a wicked grin as many of Darren's packmates failed to suppress their surprised gasps.

Luke looked back and forth between Desert and Jade, not a single muscle moving on his face. Which wasn't a good sign.

"In case you hadn't noticed, I am an extremely busy man. I don't have time to waste on what you may find amusing," Luke said, a growl coming through at the end of his words.

"As difficult as it may be for you to believe I am the one our group has chosen to lead them while we are here. And no, I don't find it amusing at all," Jade said, not appearing the least bit intimidated by the Alpha in front of her. A murmur went through the packwolves. It had to be a joke. But if they were so inclined to humor themselves at the packwolves' expense, Darren didn't see any sign of mockery in the rogues' faces.

"That's impossible," Spencer snarled, voicing the outrage of his packmates. "Females can't shift; why would anyone choose a non-shifter to lead them? Especially a worthless stray like you!"

"Insult her again, and you'll find your arms disconnected from your body," the giant wolf, Chris, snarled back, flashing his fangs. Spencer made a move forward, his eyes glowing a dangerous yellow hue. "How dare you disrespect Alpha Power with these lies. Do you think any of us are stupid enough to believe them?" his voice steadily rising with every word.

"Spencer, that's enough!" Darren commanded, grabbing his friend's shoulder to keep him from advancing further. "I apologize for Spencer's behavior. He should know better than to act so rudely to our guests," Darren said, meeting each of the rogues' eyes before removing his hand from Spencer's still stiff shoulder.

"But I think you can understand our surprise and doubt at this information," Luke added, retaking control of the conversation. "It is rather...unusual to have a female as a dominant leader." Darren wondered if Luke purposefully didn't use the title of Alpha when he was talking to Jade. Somehow it seemed as if it was a snub all on its own. If Jade felt the insult in the words, she didn't let it show on her perfectly calm face.

"I completely understand your reservations, but just because it's strange doesn't change the fact that it is the truth. Now, if you are ready, would you like to get down to business?" she asked, dismissing their current conversation, a clear move for control. Luke narrowed his eyes but nodded and followed as she led them to the front corner of the room where random chairs and a couple of old couches had been placed in a small circle. After everyone had found a seat, Jade turned to Luke. "So, why exactly have we been called out here?" she asked, getting right to the point.

"We'll get to that soon enough," Luke said, waving a dismissive hand. "Over the past few years, the Alpha Council has noticed a significant increase in the number of pups that are part of.... the rogue community," Luke said, choosing his words carefully. "As I'm sure you understand, this is very concerning."

"I agree that it is a concern. But since we are the ones that end up in charge of their care, I don't see how it is a concern for the council," Jade said. Her voice was just as steady and fearless as she had been against Spencer in the hallway, as if she didn't care that she was speaking to an Alpha. Was the girl afraid of anything?

Darren's packmates all stiffened at Jade's defiance, but Darren found himself fighting back a grin at the pride his wolf felt; their mate could hold her own in a battle of fists and wits.

Luke also didn't appear to be phased by her confidence; he simply continued.

"I'm just as aware as you are of the difficulties our people have with one another. But even with our differences, I can't pretend to enjoy seeing children struggle through the hardships that come with your lifestyle. I'm sure even someone like yourself can sympathize with that."

"So, you called all of us out here because you are worried about our pups?" Jade asked incredulously. Luke offered a tight smile.

"No, of course not. We have other purposes to accomplish in having you here, but that is not what I am here to discuss. As a gesture of goodwill, the Northwind Pack is willing to offer housing, food, and medical care for all the rogue pups while in our territory. It would mean a warm bed, full bellies, and guaranteed safety while we deal with our business. After all that they've been through in their short lives, some stability would do them some good, and the Northwind Pack is more than happy to offer that."

Jade listened quietly while Luke explained his offer, her face betraying none of her thoughts or emotion. "What do you think?" he asked, shifting back in the chair to display a look of ease, but Darren knew that look. He could see the tension in his father's shoulders as he awaited Jade's reply.

Darren didn't blame him for waiting impatiently. It was a huge offer, one that could impact the whole relationship with the rogues, especially grateful parents who could be persuaded to join the pack ranks after seeing their children happy and healthy.

"You said all of the pups, not just the orphaned ones?" Jade clarified, her eyes never leaving Luke's face.

"Yes."

"You can't honestly expect us to just hand them over to you? Most of us here have been separated from our loved ones already. How can you expect any of them to trust their children into your care?" Desert spoke up, skepticism at the idea written plainly on his face.

"Because, unlike you, these pups have not sealed their fate by making themselves into criminals. Even criminals can want what is best for their children, and that's something that I can respect," Luke explained; his voice was calm, but his eyes had a hardness to them.

"I can't speak for everyone, so there is no way for me to give you an answer at this time. I can relay it to the parents here and let them make their own decision for their pups. When do you need an answer by?" Jade questioned as Luke's expression soured slightly.

"I had hoped for an answer tonight."

"I'm sorry if you feel like you wasted your time, but this will not be an easy choice for any of the wolves here. Choosing to allow their pups to be cared for by the same people that have rejected them may not be as appealing to everyone as it is to you," she answered, a fire in her stormy eyes. Somehow it gave her a fierceness, more so than she already had as a female sitting across from an Alpha. She met his challenges in a way that no other wolf would dream of, except another Alpha.

"Two days," Luke growled, rising from his chair. "It's time we were leaving."

"Two days it is," Jade said, rising from her seat as well. "We'll see you out."

The group made their way to the door in silence, Jade and Luke walking at the front of the group while the rest followed. The rogues that were not part of the meeting watched warily as

the packwolves walked past them, but they all left the group alone just as they had done when they had first entered the warehouse.

As the packwovles stepped back out into the cool evening air, Darren sucked in a shuddering breath. The sun had sunk completely, allowing the sky to fill with stars and for the chilled breeze from the mountains to be felt, without the warmth of the sun chasing it away. It all looked so peaceful, as if nothing could disturb it.

If only that had been true.

Darren turned back to see if he could catch one more glimpse of Jade; what he wasn't expecting was to see her standing in the doorway still watching the packwolves. No, watching *him*. Her stare was unapologetically and intent, as if she was trying to see inside his mind. There was part of him that wanted her to see. To be able to look past everything that he seemed to be to the rest of the world, the Alpha's son, a packwolf, even the man standing in front of her. If she could look past it all and see his wolf, the most genuine part of himself, and see what he felt for her, then she would know how sorry he was. So, Darren stared back and hoped that everything he felt could somehow travel straight from his soul to hers. And she stared back, taking in everything he gave her.

Even with several feet between them, it was the most intimate moment Darren had ever had with someone, as his wolf reached out to her, his mate, and he saw something light up in her eyes.

But the moment shattered around him when she shook her head at him and mouthed two words,

Not now.

Pushing the double doors to the warehouse closed, she severed the connection, leaving him standing alone, breathless and shaken.

She knew.

For the second time that night, Darren found himself striding down the dimly lit hall towards his father's office. He had to tell him about Jade; he didn't know what else to do. This secret was eating away at him from the inside. Spencer wouldn't want to hear anything about it. He hated all rogues, especially Jade, and most of Darren's other friends were in a similar mindset. But Luke constantly reminded Darren of the importance of finding his mate and establishing that connection before he became Alpha. Luke would have to understand what Darren was going through. Now that he was sure that Jade knew they were mates, he had to find a way to win her over, a way to redeem himself in her eyes. And it wouldn't be easy, even if she did forgive him. Darren wasn't sure if she would want to accept him as her mate, especially since that meant joining him in the Northwind Pack.

After a swift knock on the office door, Darren slipped inside and found the once calm and composed Alpha Power was long gone. Pacing back and forth in front of his desk, Luke was tense and appeared less and less like the powerful Alpha he was.

"What took you so long?" Luke snapped, the pivoting in his pacing becoming more aggressive with each turn.

"Sorry, I came here as fast as I could," Darren answered, but Luke waved off his apology.

"It doesn't matter now. What was your impression of this evening? Did anything stand out to you?"

Darren needed to answer carefully, knowing with his father there would be a right answer and many wrong ones to choose from.

"The fact that the meeting was civil is comforting, but I was a little disturbed to see that many rogues under one roof," he answered slowly, wracking his brain for everything he had noticed that hadn't been his mate and the way her scent seemed to cling to him still.

It was not the right answer.

"A little disturbing? It's appalling!" Luke bellowed, pausing in his pacing to face Darren, blotches of red appearing on his cheeks and neck. "For the last five years, the council has seen more rogues gathering, but I've never heard of that many living together at once. Can you imagine how detrimental it could be to us if they remain together? If they continue to grow?" Luke sank into his large armchair, looking older than Darren had ever seen him. "Darren, if this continues, we could have an all-out war on our hands. The rogues already are the greatest threat to us. If they discover the depths of their strength when they are together, then there is nothing to stop them from claiming pack territories as their own," he said, his face resting in one hand. His eyes closed as he considered the weight of his concerns. Darren felt a pang of guilt slice through him at the sight before him; he knew that being an Alpha was often a thankless position, but he had never seen his father so defeated. And here he was completely infatuated with the source of his father's distress.

"Maybe they won't choose to stay together even for the remainder of their time here. It can't be easy controlling that many wolves in one setting, especially when they aren't used to being together," he said, his attempt at comfort falling flat even

to his own ears. Letting out a sigh, his father looked up at him, letting his hand fall to the armrest.

"Them remaining together isn't my *sole* concern tonight," Luke said, his words causing a confused frown to pull at Darren's brows.

"Your visit wasn't just about seeing how well they would cooperate, was it?" he asked as Luke shook his head in confirmation.

"Within the last week, the hospital has reported a handful of females have been admitted. The doctors are unable to determine what is causing it, and none of them have recovered so far."

"What's happening to them?" Darren asked, his heart speeding up at the look of defeat on his father's face at the question.

"It seems to just start as a headache, but slowly it increases to fever, vomiting, and finally they seem to go into a comatose state that the doctors are unable to wake them from. All of their vitals are strong for now, but that's not even the most concerning part."

"What's more concerning than comatose she-wolves?" Darren asked.

"None of the sick wolves have been rogues, and tonight, did you see any sign of illness among them?" Luke asked, continuing before Darren had a chance to answer. "No, not a single one appeared to be ill, so why our people?" Darren stood in silence, mulling over the news. If his father was right and the rogues did have something to do with the sick wolves, did that mean they knew something about it or were they in the dark as well?

"And now to add to the list, I don't know how they have survived this long with such a young *female* leading them?

There's no way she's able to keep them in line on her own. Females can only access an Alpha's power if she's mated to one, and she clearly hasn't been claimed by anyone. Why would any of them choose to follow her? Any of those males could easily claim the position," Luke continued, speaking more to himself than Darren.

"I don't know Father; the rogues have always worked differently than we have. That's why they aren't part of the packs anymore. But either way, I don't think they will be here long enough to cause those kinds of problems," Darren tried to reassure, but Luke wasn't listening.

"I have to report this to the council. We need a plan for what to do if they continue to grow, and more importantly, I need you to keep an eye on that girl. We need to learn all that we can about her. As long as they allow her to lead them, she is going to be the key to finding out their secrets."

"I really don't think this is necessar-"

"Taking your pack's safety seriously is always necessary!" Luke yelled, springing up from his seat to stand in front of his son, still towering a few inches above him, making it easy for Darren to avoid eye contact. No reason to test his temper even further. "This is not a joke or a game Darren; this is about survival. It is about us or them. I thought you would understand this based on your objections to having those mutts here in the first place."

He was right. Darren had been the one arguing for the safety of the pack just weeks ago, but he had been so wrong about what the rogues would be like. Besides the first fight, they hadn't shown the violence or brutishness that he thought would be there. They were by no means model citizens, but just in the short time he had observed them, he had seen close, complex

relationships. And wolves who were willing to protect and stand by their loved ones, who wanted to live their lives in peace; just like packwolves.

But Luke wasn't looking for comparisons or someone to defend the rogues. He was looking for Darren Power, the future Alpha of the Northwind Pack. And that's who Darren needed to be.

"I'm sorry. You're right. I'll make sure we keep a closer eye on them. I won't let anything happen to our pack," Darren answered, giving Luke exactly what he wanted to hear. Even if the words felt too practiced on his tongue.

"Good. Keep this up, and you'll be a fine Alpha someday," Luke said. His words should have been encouraging, but his voice was void of any real pride for his son. Its absence stung.

"Thank you, Father," Darren said before backing out of the room, closing the door behind him.

He should be excited. Jade knew that they were mates; that was a good start to begin growing closer to her, and now his father had just ordered him to keep close to her. It was all working out in his favor.

Then why was there a pit in his stomach telling him to run?

Chapter 15

Jade

"You should have seen the look on their faces!" Chris howled with laughter as he retold the story of the meeting with Alpha Power for the third time that evening. "Even that Alpha Power didn't know what to say. Jade was brilliant. You all saw the way they stormed out of here."

"Maybe they'll think twice before messing with us again!" Prince said, causing a few of the others to cheer in agreement, but Jade found it difficult to smile. Today had been a win for the rogues; there was no doubt of that, but Jade had learned that there was little that Alphas held more dear than their pride. An Alpha that had no pride in himself would be unable to earn the pride of his pack, and if that pride was injured there would always be retaliation.

Painful retaliation.

But the fear of Alpha Power's anger wasn't the only thing fueling the worry that ate its way through Jade's mind, specifically the boy who smelled of fresh pine and mountain air. The boy with eyes as blue as the summer sky. The boy who was her mate.

Darren Power.

The future Alpha of the Northwind Pack was her soulmate, given to her by the Goddesses to make both of them complete. The whole thing was ludicrous. Jade had never believed in soulmates. Even with Chris and Lola, who were so perfect for

each other it was sickening to just be around them; there was always a part of her that doubted the idea.

She had known something was different about him the moment she had laid eyes on him, but it had taken her nearly a week before it had clicked. After that, all she could do was wait to see how it all played out. He hadn't spoken to her, and she didn't speak to him. She had begun to think that he either hadn't felt the beginnings of their mate bond or was even better at ignoring it than she was. After the night she'd had, she guessed it was the second one.

He felt the pull as well. She had seen the pain of fighting it in his eyes as he turned back to her, just before she had closed the doors in his face.

She couldn't sit still anymore, she needed to move, needed to feel free. Shooting out of her chair, she strode towards the doors, ignoring the alarmed looks of her friends as she walked by without a word.

"Jade, wait up!" Desert called, jogging to catch up with her, but she didn't turn around. As supportive of a friend that he was, Desert was not who she wanted right now. "Where are you going?"

"Out," she answered, not offering further explanation. She should have known that he wouldn't have been satisfied with that.

"It's completely dark; you shouldn't be out by yourself. Especially not after tonight," he said, casting a wary glance out the doors, to the forest that lay just within sight. Jade couldn't help but roll her eyes.

"I'm not afraid of the dark or whatever is in it. And I was alone before you all came along. I think I'll be okay," she said, but he was already shaking his head.

"That was when you avoided pack territories like the plague and before you pissed off not only an Alpha but his entire pack. I get it; we're all going stir crazy in here. Just let me come with you."

She wanted to refuse; she needed time alone, but she knew he would probably just follow her anyway if she didn't agree. Plus, she had been telling the rest of the group to stick together, and why would anyone listen to her if she couldn't take her own advice?

"Fine, but give me some space. I don't need you on my tail the entire time," she snapped, continuing her path outside, Desert stepping out with her, closing the doors behind him.

Crisp air filled her lungs the moment she stepped into the darkness; the cool bite of fall was in the air. Soon enough the snow would be back, but for now, Jade would enjoy the warm days and cool nights.

Moving away from the dirt trail, Jade trudged to the tree line, the pines towering above her. These trees had been here for years, growing and learning from their surroundings. With all of the secrets that they must have held within, could they handle another one tonight?

"You know, it's okay if you want to," Desert said, standing beside her, staring up at the trees. "I'll keep watch; you don't have to worry about anyone finding us out here. We can cover our scents also, just to make sure no one follows us," he said, this time glancing over to gauge her reaction. She didn't say a word or look away from the forest. She didn't know what to say.

She wanted to take him up on his offer so badly; part of her wanted it more than anything else.

But she couldn't, not now.

Not ever.

"Not tonight," she said, finally looking over to where he stood, still watching and waiting. She could see the war that waged in his eyes as he debated arguing to convince her to take what she needed. Shrugging, he finally turned away.

"Fine, bet I can still beat you," he said, raising his eyebrows mischievously.

"Want to bet?" Jade asked before taking off running into the trees.

And they ran, bounding over fallen branches, winding in and out of the trees. Lungs and legs burning, Jade pushed herself, sprinting as fast as her human legs would carry her, Desert running at her side.

This was what she needed, to run, to feel the wind in her hair, the cold on her skin. The way she could focus on her breath, on matching Desert's stride and ignore the blue eyes that were branded into her memory.

Covering her yawn, Jade leaned against the table, elbow propping her head up as she watched Matthew Doyle pace across the floor. The mentor talked with his hands making slow movements in front of his round belly as he retold one of the most over-told histories of the werewolf packs. It was a story she'd heard a hundred times, even as a pup in her old pack. The first werewolves were all in one pack, then divided into two, then four, and so on and so forth until there were the dozens, if not hundreds of packs that there were now. Frankly, she had more important things to worry about, such as Alpha Power's request. Most of the wolves had opted to keep their pups close to them, not trusting the pack to care for them properly. The few that had

chosen to hand their pups over, for the time being, were dropping them off at the pack hospital later that day. If Jade was being honest with herself, it made her more than a little nervous about sending any of their wolves into the pack's hands, but she knew how enticing of an offer it was for many, and she couldn't blame them for wanting the best for their pups. Against her advice, the group had voted on sending the youngest orphaned pups into the pack's care as well. Why should they continue to struggle to feed them when the pack had offered to? The pups that were old enough to decide for themselves had been offered a choice, and all had chosen to stay with the group, much to Jade's surprise. She was busy contemplating the dangers of handing Alpha Power more bargaining chips when Mr. Doyle's voice rose in excitement, drawing her back to his lesson.

"Now all packs have a mixture of different wolves, but when these packs first split, it was usually to wolves who came from a similar background," Doyle said. "For example, we have the Mountain Wolves, mostly various shades of gray. The Forest Wolves, usually consisting of dark browns and reds in their furs," he stopped talking when a hand went up. It was a twig of a girl named Katy. By her appearance, Jade would guess that she was the kind of girl who would rather be in the library than going out on pack runs. "Yes, Katy?"

"We know all of the wolves that we have here in our pack, but why is it that we no longer see wolves that are fully black or white coats?" she asked. Doyle nodded his head, a sober look coming over his thin face.

"Ah, you mean the Blood and Phantom Wolves?" he asked, and Katy replied with an enthusiastic nod. Jade felt her own interest perking; it wasn't often that they heard this part of the story.

"There actually isn't much that is known about them besides a few stories that have been handed down. Keep in mind we have no way to discern fact from fiction from these. No one has seen a Blood Wolf or Phantom Wolf in centuries."

"But where did they go?" Katy asked, impatience in her tone. Jade wanted to roll her eyes, but she was more curious about what Doyle would have to say. And she wasn't the only one. The rest of the class had perked up as well, many sitting up and eagerly watching Doyle and awaiting his response. Hesitant, Doyle glanced across the room, one hand stroking his greying beard absentmindedly, but seeing the same eagerness that Jade had observed, he gave in with a sigh.

"As I said, when separate packs did start to form, wolves would join packs that were similar to themselves. Two of these packs were known for their mental power and physical strength; few could challenge them. Humans have believed in the existence of werewolves for centuries, in nearly every culture, but the Nordic culture was the closest to our true origins. They believed that our father, Fenrir, was meant to bring about the end of the world, but he was the beginning of ours.

"Blood Wolves were said to be the first wolves, direct descendants of Fenrir and the Goddesses. Every other wolf in existence can be traced directly back to a Blood Wolf somehow. Known for their ferocity in battle, they were said to be demons on earth with coats of midnight and eyes red as the blood of their enemies, which they were sure to spill. No wolves were their rival. They ruled with an iron fist and sparked fear in even the most impressive warriors. Everyone except the Phantom Wolves.

"Phantom Wolves were a secluded pack; some thought they were just a rumor. Known for their spirituality, it's said the

Goddesses spoke directly to them and gifted them with unique abilities. Hence, why they were blessed with pure white coats

"For years, the packs lived relatively in peace, until the Alpha of the Blood Wolves realized the full power of his pack and decided to expand his territory. Determined to unite all of the packs together once again, he started a harrowing war. And it could have happened. Any of the packs that tried to take a stand against them paid for it in their own blood and the blood of their families. We would still be one pack today if the Phantom Wolves hadn't stepped in." Doyle said, pausing for dramatic effect, casting his gaze around the room. Jade felt a slight shiver shudder down her spine. This was not a version she had heard before, but something about it felt eerily familiar.

"The final battle fought between Blood and Phantom wolves was bloody and horrific," Doyle continued, his voice steady, but there was a guarded look in his eyes. "It is said that it lasted for days with no rest for any; some would fall down dead from exhaustion. Males, females, even pups all fought and were killed; no one from either pack was spared from the fight. After five days of endless fighting, finally, the last wolf fell, leaving no known survivors from either pack." A hush fell over the whole room as Doyle finished his story; the only sound that could be heard was the soft breathing and fast heartbeats of everyone. No one dared break the almost sacred silence until Katy raised her hand again.

"Yes, Katy?"

"So, there's just no Phantom or Blood Wolves at all anymore? I find it hard to believe that there were no survivors from two whole packs," she asked, folding her arms and leaning back in her seat, raising a skeptical eyebrow.

"That's why they say known survivors," Doyle said, a small smile appearing on his face. "It's very likely that some wolves may have lived through the battle, but if they did, then no one has seen or heard from them since."

"So, what you're saying is that there still could be Blood or Phantom Wolves out there?"

Jade jumped at the sound of a familiar voice. Flipping around in her chair, she tried to keep her face expressionless as she found the source of the voice. Darren sat just a few seats away, his eyes on Doyle as he awaited a response to his question. Jade hadn't even heard him come into the room. Frowning, she turned back to face Doyle. She'd worry about him later when they didn't have an audience.

"I always like to think that there's a chance. There were times when humans thought we were just the stuff of myth and legends, and now any surviving human knows of our existence. I think it makes sense that just like their legends, there may be some truth in ours," Doyle answered, finishing just as the clock in the corner of the room chimed, signaling the end of class.

Jumping up with the rest of the class, Jade snatched up her backpack, weaving her way in between people to get to the door, trying as best she could to avoid looking back at the blue eyes that she knew would be watching her

"Jade, wait up!" Her feet froze instantly at the sound of *his* voice calling out to her. She didn't dare turn around even though she knew he was standing directly behind her.

"What do you want, Darren?" she asked. The invisible line that connected them sprung to life with their close proximity, sending shivers down her spine and stirring something inside of her. Something she was trying desperately to push deep, deep down.

"I was wondering if we could talk. Alone," he said; he sounded calm enough, except for the faintest waiver at the word *alone*. Could it be that he was nervous? It wasn't likely, as an Alpha's son's confidence in all situations was a must.

"Fine," Jade said, spinning on her heel to turn around, coming face to face with her mate's startled expression. "Where did you have in mind?"

"Really? Um...follow me," he said, seeming surprised by her answer. Not that she could blame him, she hadn't known what she was going to say until the words had come out of her own mouth.

Stepping around her, Darren led the way through the crowded hall, packwovles throwing them questioning glances as Jade matched him step for step. It didn't matter what they were thinking. Whatever fantasies their bored minds came up with couldn't be anywhere close to the truth of the complex situation she was facing at that moment.

Weaving through the crowds, they strode down the halls until they reached the back of the Training Center, where only a few stray students lingered, but that was still too many eyes and ears on them. Heading towards a door in the back of the building, Darren pushed it open, leaving one arm on it to hold it open as Jade followed him out. There was no way to know for sure, but she could have sworn that she felt him shiver as his arm brushed against hers as she squeezed past him. Was he that horrified by even the slightest touch from her?

The door had brought them outside of the Training Center; a cool breeze and the warm sun was the perfect combination to clear her head. Sucking in a deep breath, she kept her back to Darren as the door swung shut behind him, clicking shut and sealing them off from the other wolves.

Alone.

This was the first time they were together without watchful eyes on them. It was the first time they were really, truly alone. The thought by itself was enough to make her heart pick up its pace a notch or two. The whole thing was ridiculous. Jade had fought every day of her life just to survive. And from that fight had gained not only friends but the loyalty of dozens of rogues when everyone believed it was impossible. She had seen things that packwolves couldn't dream up in their worst nightmares. Most wolves considered it a miracle that she had lived this long. Yet, even with all of that strength and fight in her, she still couldn't bring herself to look her mate in the eye.

"Jade…" Darren finally spoke, his voice quiet but not timid, as if he was speaking to a frightened animal. "I am so sorry for everything. I never meant to hurt you, and then I found out you and I were-I mean, we are..." he paused, swallowing what his next words would have been. She didn't blame him. She didn't know if she would have been able to say the word out loud either.

Mates

"I don't expect you to forgive me, but I would like to try to get to know you and to try to redeem myself," he said, the certainty in his voice surprised Jade enough that she turned around to face him. His eyes held the same quiet surety, nothing wavering in their blue depths as he asked her for a chance.

He didn't hate her for who she was. He wasn't disgusted by her. Instead, she saw a boy, waiting anxiously to see if she would reject his apology, if she would reject him.

She should reject him, just get it done and over with now before either of them really got hurt. He was a future Alpha, and she was a rogue through and through. Neither of them had a

place in the other one's world. But his words echoed through her, drowning out the logical thoughts in her mind and filling her stomach with fluttering butterflies.

"I'm not going to lie to you," she started slowly, struggling to find the words that would help him understand the tangled mess that her thoughts were. "I'm not very good at trusting people, especially after they have already hurt me once. But…" a flicker of hope flashed in Darren's eyes as she continued. "But I think it would be a good idea to get to know each other. It looks like we will be in your territory for a while, and I'm sure it would be helpful if you and I got along at least. You know, set a good example for everyone," she hurried to finish, ignoring the part of her that wanted to jump out of her skin from excitement or anxiety, Jade wasn't sure which one, but it didn't matter because when she looked up at Darren his face was stretched into a huge grin, his eyes nearly sparkling.

"What are you grinning about?" she asked, frowning slightly when his smile grew as he shook his head and chuckled.

"Nothing. You're right. It would be a good example for both of our packs, show them that all of us can get along," he said, but his smile said it wasn't nothing, and the way he looked at her sent her blood rushing to her cheeks.

"Good. Well, I'll see you around then," she said, hoping he hadn't noticed her blush. Judging from the mischievousness that had made its way into his grin, she suspected he had seen it already. She needed to get away from him before she embarrassed herself even more. Silently cursing herself, she turned away and hurried to the corner of the Training Center, hoping to make it to safety before she could embarrass herself further.

"Hey, Jade," Darren called out, just before she rounded the corner to safety.

"Yes?" she asked.

"You look really pretty when you blush like that," he said. Her blush deepened even more as she threw him a scowl before marching around the corner out of his sight. But that didn't block out the laughter that followed her.

Chapter 16

Darren

Young wolves spilled out of the doors of the Training Center, another day of training leaving them free to blow off steam. Normally, Darren would have joined them. He and his friends would have found some corner of the woods to call their own for the day, letting their wolves stretch their legs and maybe enjoy a hunt, but today he had different plans. Leaning against a tree directly across from the doors, Darren watched patiently for his target, unable to keep a smile from his face. He had been that way since his conversation with Jade earlier that day; his spirit lifted as well as his wolf's.

Finally, he had found a way to tell her the thoughts that had plagued his mind for days, and she hadn't turned him away. She felt their bond just as he did, and now that he knew that Darren prepared to do everything in his power to earn her trust. He would just have to deal with his father and packmates and their concerns later.

His patience was rewarded when she stepped through the doors into the afternoon sun. Shading her eyes, she looked up at the sky, a weight seeming to lift from her shoulders at the sight; Darren understood that. Something about being out in the fresh air made him feel so free, he wondered if it was the same for her.

Bounding down the stairs, she seemed clueless to his presence, but he had a suspicion that she knew exactly who was watching her and where he was. Walking up to her friends, her grin grew wider; from where Darren was standing, it looked

genuine enough, but he wouldn't help but wonder if she had to fake any of her smiles the way he faked his for the sake of others. He almost felt guilty interrupting what was probably the first moment of freedom she had that day. His guilt was short-lived, though, as he strode up to the group and her eyes met his. Her dark hair was pulled back in its signature braid; the black t-shirt she wore made her skin look lighter than it was from years in the sun. Scars littered the bare skin on her arms, symbols of the struggles and battles she had survived. As a warrior in Darren carried a few of his own proudly, but the sight of hers made his chest tighten. She shouldn't have had to carry all of them; she was supposed to be protected by her pack, her Alpha, but instead, there she was, damaged pack mark and all.

"Hey, guys," Darren said, but it was unnecessary; all of their attention was already on him. As expected, the two males she was closest with went on high alert immediately, the taller one moving ever so slightly in front of the small red-headed female. The shorter one moved closer to Jade, but she leaned slightly away, her way of letting him know it was safe. When he had first seen the group in action, Darren had thought for sure one of the males was her mate. Packs were meant to protect their own, but even within the pack, each member had their priorities, mostly involving their mate, pups, and other close family members, but outside of that, it was rare to find such binding loyalty, the kind Darren had seen in action with Jade's friends.

"Is there something we can help you with, Darren?" Jade asked.

"There sure is," Darren said, ignoring Jade's business-like tone. He hadn't expected her to show the same vulnerability in front of her peers that she had with him earlier that day, but it

didn't mean he was happy about it. "Are you free? There's something I wanted to show you."

"Now?" Jade asked, her eyes widening in surprise. Surprise that was mirrored by her friends.

"Tonight, if that works better for you," he answered. His reassuring smile did not seem to have its intended effect on most of them, but the small smile he watched Jade struggle to hold back was worth it.

"I think I can find some time," she said,

"Jade, are you sure about this?" Desert asked, only to be ignored.

"I'll meet you back here in a couple of hours," Jade continued. Darren couldn't help the satisfaction that rolled through him and his wolf at the frown on Desert's face.

"Works for me," he said, and just like that, it was over. Pulling her away hurriedly, Jade's friends tugged her along with them, the redhead already starting to question her. Desert and Chris hung back long enough to cast doubtful glares his way before following the others. The fact that rogues weren't fond of him shouldn't have been an issue. In fact, he hadn't met a single one that had liked him, or that he had liked for that matter, until recently. Winning Jade over wouldn't be an easy task, but if he could earn the trust of her pack too, then it could go a long way to earning her trust as well. Plus, it would make his father extremely happy to have some of her friends as new additions to their warriors.

More importantly, though, it could mean the difference between having a strong partner to help him lead his pack, love, and grow old with. Or ending up completely alone, with no Luna to guide them.

Either way, at least for the night, he had a date.

Chapter 17

Jade

"Kacen, if you don't get your hand out of Malcolm's bag right now, you won't have a hand anymore," Jade said, not bothering to watch as the other wolf's hand retreated sheepishly. As annoying as it was keeping the group in check, at least it gave her a reason to ignore Desert's pestering, even if it was for just a moment.

"Are you sure this is a smart move? I really don't think it's safe for you to be out there alone, with *him*," Desert said, as he trailed behind her as she made her rounds through the warehouse.

"I didn't know you thought so little of my basic survival skills," she answered, her tone taunting as she attempted to relieve the worry lines breaking out on his forehead from frowning, but they were only deepened by her reply.

"I'm serious. This could be a trap, a way to retaliate for the meeting with Alpha Power, or just because they can. They know how important you are even if you don't."

"And I appreciate your concern, but this is something I have to do on my own. Besides, I think I can handle one packwolf," she said. Not that Darren needed to be handled, but Desert didn't need to know that. She couldn't explain why she trusted the future Alpha. Maybe it was just the mate bond clouding her head, but she was sure that Darren's desire to keep the peace between their people was genuine, and that was enough to pique her interest.

"That's my whole point, though; packwolves are never alone," Desert said. Jade wasn't sure if it was the seriousness of his tone or his words, but she had to push away the shiver that rolled its way down her spine. He was right; there was no way for her to know for sure that it all wasn't some ploy from Alpha Power, the only way she would know if what Darren said was true or if he was just as brainwashed as the other packwovles were.

"I'll be back after dark; don't wait up," she said, avoiding Desert's eyes and ducking out of the door. Desert wouldn't understand why she needed to do this; none of them would. If she was honest, she didn't even completely understand it herself.

Darren was in her sights before he noticed her presence. He was too comfortable; even in his own territory with strange rogues around, it was dangerous for the Alpha's son to be on his own.

But he's not alone. He's with you.

True, as long as he was with her, she would make sure that no rogue harmed him. Would he say the same thing about her, though?

"Hey," she said, walking into the courtyard and finally into his sight. The grin that lit up his face sent sparks through her fingertips.

"Hey there, trouble," he said, ambling over. She had to crane her neck back to see his face once he stood in front of her. He was a head taller than her, but it was enough to make her feel small in comparison. For a moment, they both stood there, sizing the other up, not as a potential opponent, but really seeing the other person in front of them.

Out of the corner of her eye, Jade saw Darren's hand twitch at his side, as if he wanted to reach out for her but held himself back. It was probably for the best, yet there was still a part of her that wished he would have bridged the gap between them. There was a deep, deep need inside of her that wanted to feel his skin on hers, to let him feel the goosebumps trailing up her arms, to hold him close until he understood what she felt until she understood it.

Instead, they both stood there, waiting to see what the other would do.

"I…I was thinking we could walk down to this ice cream parlor I know. Does that sound okay?" Darren asked, moving his hand up to rub the back of his neck in an attempt to hide his self-consciousness. It didn't work, but it made Jade smile.

"Sure, but I have to warn you, I might be pretty indecisive. It's been a long time since I had to pick a flavor of any kind of dessert," she said.

"Wait, really? Now that's just sad!" Darren said as they started walking into town. Steps blurred by as they talked about their favorite treats they had as pups, the last time they had enough free time to discover new music, and their favorite trainers from the center. Words flowed out of her without her having to worry if she was saying the right thing; they felt right. She could tell Darren noticed it also. His shoulders were more relaxed than the last few times she had seen him. The smile on his face looked genuine; his laughter sounded real. He didn't even seem to notice the strange looks thrown their way by wolves that passed them, the ones who recognized her for who she was, but if he did notice he didn't let it show. Everything about him was so authentic, so pure, unlike her.

It wasn't that she didn't mean the jokes or that her ease with him was unreal. In fact, it was too real. It was all she could think about as she watched him eat another spoonful of his rocky road, wiggling his eyebrows at her when he caught her looking. They were still practically strangers, on the worst days; enemies, begrudging acquaintances at best. How could she feel safe around him, was it enough to trust him? The easy answer was that she couldn't, but she could enjoy one night.

"How's that fudge brownie treating you?" Darren asked, bumping her gently with his elbow to bring her back into reality.

"Honestly, I don't think I can go back to normal food after this. You've completely ruined my taste buds," she said, and she meant it. Roguehood had made her forget just how good some of the finer things in life could be, like chocolate.

"I told you that was the one for you. Next time you'll have to try this chocolate cheesecake that is downtown. They put fresh raspberries on it and-. Why are you making that face?" he asked, stopping mid-sentence, his eyebrows pulled down in a concerned frown.

"It's nothing; I just hadn't realized you were thinking about a next time," she said, scrambling to wipe the surprise from her face. The thought of seeing him again made her stomach flip in all different directions; she wasn't sure if she liked it. Was anything that could make her heart pound that hard really be a good thing?

"Well, I mean-" Darren stammered before he paused, glazing over his eyes, eyebrows furrowed as he focused on something far off, something Jade couldn't see. She wanted to ask what was going on, but the moment felt personal, one that shouldn't be interrupted. "I'm sorry, it's my dad; he needs me to

make a stop by the packhouse," he said, coming back to reality. "I hate to cut this short-"

"It's no problem; I understand. It's on my way. I can walk with you," she said, pasting a smile on her face, dismissing the disappointment that settled in her chest. It was eased when she saw Darren perk up at her words. Eyes gleaming, he offered her his arm.

"Shall we?" he asked, letting a grin sneak onto her face, sliding her arm through his.

Chapter 18

Darren

Walking arm in arm with Jade should have cleared his mind of any other thoughts; shaking away his father's voice in his head wasn't that easy. It wasn't just his father's voice either; there was a low hum through the pack link that evening. Tension, fear, and pure energy overflowed his packmates' minds and into his own, crowding out any thoughts of his own.

"I almost forgot what it's like having a pack link. What is that like still having one?" Jade asked, breaking through the white noise, her face turned upwards at him expectantly. He didn't miss the wall that was still in her eyes, only allowing little bits of her true thoughts to come through. Not that he minded. If her life in his territory was even half as bad as it was when she was roaming around, he couldn't blame her for being guarded.

"Honestly, a little invasive," he said, letting out a sigh he hadn't known he was holding inside. "Don't get me wrong, I know why we have it, and it's part of what makes us a pack, but sometimes I wish that it was just me up here," he said, tapping his temple. If he hadn't been watching her eyes, he would have missed the pain that flashed through them; regret filled him almost instantly. "I'm sorry, I wasn't thinking when I said that. I don't mean to sound ungrateful; I know there are lots of wolves out there that would kill to be part of one-"

"No, it's okay, you're right. Sometimes being on your own is easier; I imagine it's hard to keep anything secret for long with

everyone in your head like that," she jumped in, saving him from any further embarrassment.

"Not every thought is open to the whole pack. Any strong or sudden emotions are hard to hide, especially for younger wolves who just receive their pack marks. Over time it gets easier to block out the ones that aren't yours, and I've learned how to put up a wall around mine most of the time."

"Walls are something I understand," she said, nodding sympathetically, but there was something deeper in her eyes that Darren couldn't quite read. He wanted to ask about it, to see if she would open up and allow him to see her thoughts, her real ones, not what she allowed everyone else to see. Opening his mouth, he tried to speak, unsure of what he would say, but he couldn't ignore the urge.

"Jade, what do you-"

He was interrupted by the packhouse door opening, his father's booming laughter carrying out into the courtyard where he and Jade stood. The sound of Luke Power laughing was rare enough, especially considering who caused him to make that sound. Stepping out of the open door was his father and another young male wolf. Even from where he stood, Darren could smell the scent of the wilderness on him, the scent of rogues. Hair so light it almost appeared white in the dimmed lights topped his head, which was right in line with Luke's, who was not a small man. His damaged packmark wasn't clear to Darren, but the few scars along his arms were clear enough. He was either new to life as a rogue or had been lucky to have been in so few battles. Even Jade had more marks of a warrior than this new wolf. Catching sight of them, his father waved a hand, directing Darren to come to them, but they would have to wait.

Turning back to his mate Darren was surprised to see her openly staring at Luke and the new wolf, her face drained of its color.

"Is everything okay?" he asked, placing a hand on her shoulder when her eyes didn't move away from the other wolves. She flinched at the contact, and her eyes were wide when she did look back at him. He removed his hand quickly, unsure of what she needed from him.

"Y-yes, everything's fine. I think I should head back now; it looks like your dad needs you," she stammered.

"Are you sure? You look like you're about to be sick," he said, taking a step closer only to have her retreat two steps back. He tried and failed to hide the hurt from showing on his face, but his confusion was stronger. They had connected so well earlier, what could have changed so quickly to cause her to distrust him?

"I'm fine. I just need to get going; the others will be needing me," she said, her eyes not looking at him but past him to the packhouse behind him. "I'll see you tomorrow," she said before turning and walking away, her steps sharp and hurried, as if she was holding herself back from running away.

Whimpering within, his wolf tried to push forward, wanting to follow their mate; it pained him to see her run from him. Darren held him in place. They didn't have time now to go after her, not when his father needed him.

Forcing himself to turn back to the packhouse, he dragged himself forward, shoving his disappointment and frustration down as he faced his father. It would only cause problems if Luke thought he was getting too emotional.

He tried not to stare at the stranger as he drew close to them, but it was a difficult task. Something was…off about the other wolf, something Darren couldn't put his finger on. The stranger

was a few good inches taller than Darren, but his shoulders weren't nearly as broad. His eyes were an empty sort of blue with a silverish hue around the pupil; they were just as strange as their owner.

"Ah, here he finally is," Luke said, giving Darren a look that let him know he wasn't happy with his tardiness. "This is my son and future Alpha, Darren. Darren, this is Ash. He and his group just arrived. He came to introduce himself and let us know where they set up camp for the time being; he's been very courteous," Luke said, gesturing towards the rogue. Ash offered out his hand, shaking Darren's with a firm grip. He couldn't have been more than a couple of years older than Darren was, another young leader.

"Glad to meet you; we are anxious to do business with you. Was that another rogue I just saw you with? It looks like you are busy making friends," Ash said, raising an eyebrow in a suggestive manner, one that Darren wasn't sure he liked.

"Oh yes, that was one from the other group I was telling you about earlier. They've been here for a few weeks, but they have proved to be much more difficult to cooperate with, especially that one," Luke interjected, waving a dismissive hand. Biting his tongue, Darren kept his thoughts to himself. His father never appreciated being disagreed with in private; that annoyance would be tenfold if Darren dared speak his mind in front of another wolf.

"Well, I am certain you'll find working with us much more pleasant," Ash said, offering Luke one final handshake. "I look forward to hearing from you soon. I'll have the pups report to the hospital tomorrow for exams before they go into your care if that is alright with you."

"Of course! I'll make sure they are prepared for them. I'll look forward to the next time we speak," Luke said, sending Ash off with a warmer goodbye than Darren was used to receiving. "Isn't he wonderful? Much better than that other girl they trail behind. These were the kind of rogues I was hoping to deal with."

"Are you sure? I'm not sure he's one that we can trust," Darren said, watching Ash fade into the forest, the last light of day fading along with him.

"Of course not; you can never trust a rogue. I'm saying that if we can show him the benefits of his people being here, they'll be more likely to listen. That's why packs work, son. If we didn't offer something that they can't find out there in the world, then they would have no reason to stay,"

"I know. It's just that you barely met him, and I'm worried about letting our guard down around someone we don't know yet."

"You mean like that girl?" Luke asked, turning to Darren, his silent accusation shining through clearly in his eyes.

"I'm not letting my guard down. You're the one that asked me to keep an eye on her," Darren replied, fighting to keep his tone even as he walked back into the packhouse, to his father's footsteps and the click of the door as it closed behind them.

"I said keep an eye on her, not to be caught up in her spell like every other wolf she's tricked into believing she's worth following. They only listen to her because of her open defiance; it comes off as strength which they value. It is not something to be celebrated. Wolves that have clear contempt for the very foundations of our way of life have no place with us, wolves like her. Tell me you haven't fallen for her lies as well," Luke said,

grabbing Darren's arm, forcing him to face him. Roughly shrugging him off, Darren stepped back, his own anger rising.

"She isn't lying; she's just cautious, which she should be! What reason have we given her or any of them to trust us?" Darren asked, his voice rising with each word, just as the anger in Luke's eyes.

"Enough! I knew it was too much to trust you to see things clearly. You've always been too sentimental to see people for who they really are. If you can't do this task, then say so. I do not want you seeking her out until you can remove the fog from your eyes," Luke ordered, his voice cold as he stared in disappointment at his son.

"But-"

"Your Alpha has given a command!" Luke bellowed, his eyes glowing orange with his wolf, his power pulsing inside Darren's mind like a pounding hammer, beating down until he couldn't ignore it. That was the power true Alphas held, the ability to force others to bend to their will. You either accepted it, or you suffered.

Eyes cast down, he submitted to his father's dominance, the pressure easing almost instantly.

"I understand, Alpha," he answered, spitting the words out.

"Good. With the two groups here now, I believe it's time to move forward with the next stage of our plan. I'll arrange a meeting with both groups' spokesmen to move that forward. Also, Ash has agreed to accept our offer to house their pups while they are here. You will meet him at the hospital tomorrow morning. Those other rogues may have rejected our kindness due to poor leadership, but Ash is grateful for our assistance. I want you there to personally see that everything goes smoothly."

"I will be there. Is there anything else you need from me, or am I free to go?" Darren asked. His downcast eyes would have burned a hole in the carpet if he had been able to. Letting out a sigh, Luke pinched the bridge of his nose, closing his eyes as if Darren was a cause of pain for him instead of the other way around.

"You may go," Luke said, turning away. Taking his chance, Darren started bounding up the stairs. He needed to get away from his father now. Of course, his father had to have the last word. "But Darren," he called out, making Darren freeze in place. "I know she comes across as innocent; just remember that all rogues are rogues for a reason. Promise me you'll keep that in mind?"

"Goodnight, father," Darren said before continuing his way up the stairs. He knew his father wouldn't accept the idea of him and Jade together, and now that fear had been confirmed before he even had uttered the words. It didn't matter. His father could give him as many orders as he wanted; no matter what he said, Darren would see Jade again. No one was going to keep him away.

It was rare that Darren held onto any bitterness; he found that the longer he gripped it, the heavier the weight on his shoulders became. It wasn't always easy, but it was usually worth the effort it took to cleanse his soul from the darkness that anger stained it. He wished he had the strength to do the same that night. The anger festered, bubbling, and spreading through him until his hands shook with it. How could his father still command him around as if he were still a pup and yet expect him to lead their

people? Everything his father did contradicted what he said he wanted from his son, and Darren was beyond tired of it.

A soft rapping of knuckles on his bedroom door did little to quell the raging storm within, but it did pause his pacing. Even without his invitation, the door creaked open, a head of blonde hair poking in through. Gently closing the door behind her, Darren's mother, Heather, slipped into the room, her eyebrows dipped in a concerned frown.

"Why is he like this?" Darren asked, not giving her a chance to start her own inquiries. "He never listens, but I'm supposed to obey his every whim without question? I'm not a complete idiot. I know how to handle myself around a few rogues," he ranted, his mother's eyes never straying from his face. She watched quietly for a moment before gliding across the room to perch on the edge of his bed, patting the open space beside her. Sighing, Darren found himself trudging over to sit beside her. It was difficult to stay angry when she was near. Maybe it was some not so forgotten instinct that lingered from puphood. Or perhaps it was simply something that Heather carried all on her own that gave her the ability to soothe the most distraught souls. It was one of the traits that made her a perfect Luna.

Tucking her legs underneath herself, Heather brought her hands up and began to gesture with them.

You know he loves you.

That's not the point. Darren responded with gestures of his own. *He doesn't trust me.*

It was a language that was all their own, shared between the two of them. Darren had never heard his mother's voice, not out loud at least. No one had. Born without a voice, Heather had always relied on her packlink to communicate with her packmates. Even Luke opted to use it when she spoke with him.

She had believed it was her only option until her son had been born. What had started as a game between mother and child had soon grown, giving Heather a unique voice of her own. Even if it was one that only her son understood.

Crystal blue eyes that reflected his own softened, and Darren could have sworn he saw a hint of sadness pass over them.

He doesn't trust anyone. When he looks at the world, he sees enemies at every corner. That's the price that Alphas pay. They see the evil so that we don't have to, she explained, placing a comforting hand on his shoulder as he shook his head.

That sounds…lonely, Darren replied, to which his mother nodded. *Will I have to be like that when I'm Alpha?*

No, not if you don't want to be, Heather answered, her face taking on a firmness that rarely possessed it. *Your father followed the path his father gave him because it was what was right for him. But you aren't your father. Whatever Alpha you choose to be will be the one this pack needs the most.*

Darren could only muster an absent nod, his throat clenching around his mother's words threatening to bring tears to his eyes. She was right; he wasn't his father. If he was anything like him, then he would have had the courage to tell her all about Jade in that moment. He wouldn't have hesitated to tell her about his feelings for the rogue and how every day he doubted everything he had been taught.

But as she had stated, he wasn't his father.

Rising to her feet, Heather pulled her son into a tight embrace, ruffling his hair affectionately before placing her hands on either side of his face. No gestures were needed for her next message.

I love you

I love you too, Darren signed before she slipped out of the room, leaving him to stew in his thoughts.

Chapter 19

Jade

She needed to get far away, as far away as she could get, now. Rough pavement tripped her feet as she tried to pace herself. They couldn't see her run away; that would give him exactly what he wanted, and she couldn't let Darren see her for the coward she really was in that moment. Blood rushed through her ears, making it difficult to hear anything besides the pounding of her heart and her shoes slapping the pavement. None of it was loud enough to drown out the screaming of her thoughts.

What was Ash doing there? How had he found her? Would he tell Alpha Power or the others the truth about her? Would he tell Darren?

Questions continued to push forward, each one screaming louder than the last, building on one another until she could hardly distinguish them. Once she was in the cover of the trees she broke into a run, allowing her fear to drive her limbs. Every instinct in her body screamed at her to leave the danger far behind her. Darkness already spread through the forest floor, cloaking obstacles from her human eyes as she leapt over some and stumbled across others, never letting them slow her. Driven on by pure adrenaline, it was impossible to tell how long she ran for or how far she had gone. She didn't care, her heart still beating against her ribs, and her shaking hands told her she wasn't safe yet.

Something else built in her chest with every step, something powerful and terrifying. The very force of it rising up caused her

to stumble on a tree root, collapsing to the ground clutching her chest with one hand, the other one bracing her so that she wasn't face down in the dirt.

It tore at her from within, fighting against every restraint she had in place, feeding off of her panic as it pushed forward. A scream ripped through her as pain radiated through her chest all the way to her fingertips. Every wall she had built within was slowly starting to crack from the internal battle that raged. She wasn't sure how much longer she could keep them in place.

No!

Now was not the time. She was the one in control, she had to be, and that would not change just because of one insignificant man. Placing her second hand on the ground, she dug her fingers into the dirt. Squeezing her eyes shut as she tried to focus all of her energy on repairing the wall within herself, her breath coming in short gasps from the pain still pulsing through her. The foreign power pushed back on the wall, sensing her attempts to keep it caged just a little longer, but she was stronger. Another scream escaped her as she pushed it back inside, back to the farthest, darkest place within, where it couldn't bother her until finally, the pressure eased up, and the pain faded into a dull throb in her fingertips.

Sucking in gulps of air, she crawled slowly to the nearest tree; propping herself up against it, she held back a strangled sob. Why did Ash have to show up now? After all this time, and of all places. And of course, he made his appearance after she had found her mate. It shouldn't have made a difference; it's not as if things between her and Darren were going to work out anyway. But she found herself aching at the thought of the pain in his blue eyes being the last thing she saw of him.

It wouldn't be the last she saw of him. Maybe it was the cool air that was helping clear her mind, or maybe it was simply the fact that she had slowed down enough to have a coherent thought. Sitting under that tree, Jade realized that she couldn't just run away, not this time. This time there were other people involved, people who trusted her, people that she owed more than to disappear in the night without an explanation. No, she wouldn't run away as she had in the past, but she didn't know how she would face Darren again, let alone Ash, if it came to that.

Bushes rustled nearby; someone or something was close. Pulling herself to her feet, Jade leaned against the tree for support, staring into the darkness around her. She cursed herself for wandering out alone, the exact thing she was warning everyone back at the warehouse against. And now, she was going to wish she had listened to her own advice. The rustling stopped, but Jade didn't find any comfort in that as a twig snapped close by a moment later, and she could hear soft footsteps getting closer. She pressed her back into the tree, hopefully, whatever was out there couldn't see much better than her own human eyes in the dark.

There was movement to her right; whipping her head around, she looked just in time to see a wolf with reddish fur step out from the bushes, his ears upright in attention. Letting out a sigh of relief, she sank back to the ground, resting her forearms on her upright knees.

"You scared me half to death! Don't sneak up on me like that," Jade said. She didn't have enough energy to muster the frown she wanted to give him. Letting out a huff of exasperation, the wolf hunched his shoulders, joints popping, bones breaking and healing as a new shape was built. Within a second, Desert's

human body was crouched in front of her. He didn't seem to have any problem plastering a frown across his face.

"I scared you? Really?" he asked, clearly not wanting her answer, though, he continued on. "Jade, you were supposed to come home hours ago; I've been looking everywhere for you. The others have been as well. Was that you that screamed? What if I hadn't been the one to find you? What if you had-"

"But I didn't, so don't even go there," she said. "I'm the one who has to live like this; I have been living like this for years. I don't need you to remind me." Desert brought a hand up to cup his face, closing his eyes in what Jade assumed was frustration. When he opened his eyes again, his face was clear of its frown, concern replacing it.

"Are you alright? You look like you're about to be sick," he asked. Jade let out a humorless laugh.

"That's not the first time I've heard that tonight, and no, I'm not alright," she answered, letting her head fall back against the tree, allowing the exhaustion to sweep through her. "He's back, Desert, the one I told you about. He's back, and I don't know how to keep him away this time." She fought back the tears that wanted to pool in her eyes; now wasn't the time for tears, and they wouldn't solve anything. Desert sucked in a breath at the news, cursing quietly to himself.

"That's why you came out here alone. You were going to leave again?" he asked, his hurt distinct in the question. It was the same hurt she knew the others would feel as well if they knew how close she had been.

"Honestly, I thought about it, but I just needed some space. I wasn't really going to leave," she said, moving over as Desert came and sat beside her, his leg resting on hers, his own way of offering her what little comfort he could. "I couldn't abandon

you all like that, not after everything you've done for me. I just...I don't want anyone to get hurt because I didn't leave when I had the chance," she whispered, staring at the ground. This was why rogues were meant to be alone. It was easier to move on when you didn't have others to hold you in one place, like friends or a mate.

"We don't know that we would be any safer if you did leave. What I do know is that we are all better off with you here. Whenever we have a choice of being on our own or sticking together, that shouldn't even be a question of which is the right choice. We always choose family; that's why we are together in the first place. You know the others feel the same, don't you?" he asked. Before Jade had a chance to ignore the question, they both heard something crashing through the brush towards them. Springing to their feet, they stood just in time to see Kacen burst through the bushes, his breathing heavy, eyes wide with fear.

"Thank the Goddesses I found you," he gasped, sweat dripping from his brow. "You need to come quick; he says he only wants to talk to you. They have Kyler-"

"Who has Kyler?" Desert interrupted, but Jade didn't need to hear the answer. She knew who Kacen had seen.

"I don't know, but he said he would only talk to Jade. He said she would know who he was," Kacen raced on, his eyes darting back and forth between Jade and Desert in panic. Jade couldn't fault him for it as she felt panic of her own rising up once again. Jade didn't wait for either of them to say another word. Taking off in a sprint for a second time that night, she raced through the forest, branches pulling at her as she broke through them. Desert and Kacen crashed along behind her. Both of them opting to run in their human forms to not leave her in their dust. Ash hadn't been in the territory for a whole day, and

he was already making sure that she knew he was there and he knew how to find her, no matter where she went.

Bursting through the last of the trees, her feet faltered to an unsteady halt, dread forming a pit in her stomach at the scene before her. Most of her friends stood just barely inside the open double doors of the warehouse, hushed voices and anxious stares betraying their restlessness. Chris, Lola, and Chelsea stood a few paces in front of the others. The grimness plastered on each of their faces was a concerning enough sight; what stood before them was even worse.

Five strange men stood in front of the warehouse, three in their wolf skins, snarling and flashing teeth, clearly ready for a fight. Two others stood in their large human forms and just as intimidating as their wolf companions. Each one had a hold on one of Kyler's arms, placing him directly between them, making it impossible to get to him without the wolves noticing. Besides the dried blood crusted beneath his nose and down his chin, he appeared to be uninjured. Jade would save her thanks to the Goddesses until after the night was over. In front of all of them stood Ash. His relaxed stance was out of place for the situation, his light hair almost glowing in the moonlight. At the sight of Jade, he flashed what would have been considered a charming smile on any other face.

"There she is! Didn't I tell you all she would make it? I knew she couldn't leave without at least saying goodbye," he said, spreading his arms out in an inviting gesture. Jade's shoulders stiffened in response; hands clenched at her side as she sucked in a steadying breath. Head held high, she walked over to stand beside Chris and the others. Desert and Kacen were on her heels, the stench of fear rolled over her as she approached, causing a wave of nausea to pass through her. It wasn't unnatural

for wolves to feel uneasy in a standoff situation, but if she was able to sense their fear, then Ash and his wolves had as well. His foul grin confirmed it.

"You didn't waste any time, did you? Last I heard, you were in Redwood Pack's territory, stirring up trouble there. How did you get out here?" Jade asked, her voice steadier than her heartbeat. She could only hope that she was far enough away that he couldn't hear it for himself. He gave a halfhearted shrug, shoving his hands into his front pockets, his smile never faltering.

"I got bored dodging Redwood wolves every day. They are not the most welcoming pack in these parts. Unlike Alpha Power, now that's an Alpha who knows how to make a wolf feel at home. Besides, I heard that a certain she-wolf had found herself some friends. Even some wolves that were willing to call her their interim Alpha and was causing some problems for the local Alpha. Imagine my surprise when I found out it was my long-lost Jade!" he said, taking a step forward. Chris let out a menacing snarl which Ash didn't acknowledge, but his advance was halted. "I shouldn't have been surprised; I always knew you were a special one. I'm glad you've finally seen it for yourself."

"You didn't come here to give bogus flattery tonight, so let's skip over that. What do you want?" Jade asked, folding her arms across her chest, her fingernails digging into her arm, the only thing keeping her hands from shaking. Clutching his chest, Ash feigned a look of pain as if her words could ever make any kind of impact on his black heart if he even still had one.

"That stings, Jade. I come all this way to see you, and this is the welcome I receive? This is why the packs think we are so brutish and uncivilized. Use some of those manners I know that you have."

"Funny, I didn't think it was customary to welcome in thugs that kidnapped your friends," she said, nodding to where Kyler was still held by Ash's goons.

"That's fair, I suppose; how else was I supposed to get your attention? The last time I traveled this far for you, you were gone within the hour, and I couldn't risk that again. Not when you've had so much time to reconsider my offer," he replied, a smile slowly creeping back onto his face. Jade wondered how a face so beautiful could hide so much darkness underneath its surface.

"My answer is the same as it's always been; I will never come with you. There is nothing you can offer me that would make me change my mind," she said, arms falling to her side. She meant it; nothing he had said before had enticed her into following him before, and now that she had her own people to take care of, he couldn't convince her to leave them. Breathing out a disappointed sigh, Ash shook his head.

"I'm sorry you still haven't seen the light, but I'm confident that you will soon," he said. Turning around, he closed the gap between him and Kyler, slowly he paced around him until he stood directly behind him. The two wolves holding him shoved Kyler to his knees. Jade couldn't help the breath she sucked in. Taking a single step forward, she held out a hand cautiously.

"Don't drag them into this Ash. This is between you and me," she pleaded, not allowing her voice to break. Beside her, Desert and Chris leaned forward on the balls of their feet, ready to spring into action. The anxious whispers of the wolves in the warehouse grew louder; everyone knew what was coming next, and they were all too far away to stop it.

"I'm not; you're the one that brought them into this. The answer is so simple, Jade. I just need to hear one little word from you, and all of this can go away, but until then, your friends are

as much a part of this as you are," he said, placing his hands on Kyler's shoulders. Jade caught the shudder that went through Kyler; his wide eyes stared up at her.

"Are you deaf? She said she's not joining you!" Desert yelled, grabbing Jade's arm as she tried to move forward again. Ash's eyes narrowed as he looked back and forth between Jade and Desert's hand where he held her, his hands tightening on Kyler's shoulders for a moment. Lifting one hand, Jade could only watch in horror as he shifted it partially. Vicious claws sprouting out of his nails, his eyes darkening until they were completely black.

"Have it your way," he said before swinging his arm down onto Kyler's chest. Screams filled the air, some from Kyler and others from wolves in the warehouse, holding tight to their loved ones. The scent of fresh blood filled Jade's nose as she rushed forward, charging towards Ash. Desert, Chris, and Kacen all shifted into their wolves, along with Aiden and a few of the other rogues who flew from the open warehouse doors. The three wolves Ash had brought met them with savage snarls. Dodging around the fighting wolves, Jade was aware of more wolves joining in. Many were her own friends and followers, but somehow Ash's numbers were growing as well as wolves charged out of the darkness around them.

Howls, snarls, and snapping of teeth filled the night around her as Jade watched in horror as her people jumped into the fight, a fight that should have been hers alone. Desert and Kacen battled back-to-back while Chris battled two wolves on his own. Even Chelsea held her own against a snarling wolf as she jabbed at his face with a sharp stick to keep him at bay. Other wolves were locked in similar battles of their own. Most were experienced fighters; they knew how to take care of themselves.

But even the most skilled warriors could be caught unaware, and Ash's wolves had clearly come prepared for a fight.

Strong arms caught her by surprise, wrapping around her from behind, pinning her arms to her sides. Throwing her head back, she slammed it into her attacker's nose; crying out he dropped her, giving her a chance to throw in a couple more hits before turning to face her next foe. Coming face to face with a wolf, she tried to throw herself to the side but was too late as he crashed into her, throwing her to the ground. Snarling above her, he had one paw on her chest, pinning her to the ground and knocking the breath out of her. He snapped his teeth but didn't go in for the kill; that was his mistake. Bringing her hands up, she grabbed onto either side of his head, digging her thumbs into his unprotected eyes. Crying out, he thrashed away from her, bringing a paw up to wipe away the blood now sliding down his face giving her the chance to roll back to her feet.

Scanning the fight, she struggled to not get sucked into any one fight; she couldn't allow herself to be distracted, not before she found him. Moonlight flooded the field as a light breeze blew clouds by it, bathing everything in its ghostly hue as they tore into one another. Standing in the middle of the chaos as if he was oblivious to the violence around him, Ash met Jade's stunned gaze. Kyler lay unmoving at his feet, blood pooling on his torn shirt. Eyes frantically darting, she searched the faces of those fighting and felt her heart sink. The element of surprise had worked in Ash's favor. Everywhere she looked, all she saw was another friend with fresh injuries, struggling underneath assailants or hiding behind whatever cover they could find. It wasn't worth this. She wasn't worth this.

"Stop it!" she yelled, calling out to where Ash stood still, silently watching her every move. "Just make them stop!" she

cried. Ash cast one more glance around them, absorbing the result of his handiwork with satisfaction before giving his command.

"Enough!" he said, his voice rising above the sounds of battle. At the sound of that single word, his wolves drew back, slowly sinking back into the darkness, their yellow eyes the last part of them to disappear. Just like that, it was over.

The exhaustion of the day washed over Jade as she watched the danger finally fade away. Her legs buckled underneath her, and she fell to her knees, staring mutely at the grim scene in front of her. Quietly, her friends slowly started to get to their own feet, evaluating each other's wounds and coaxing younger ones out of hiding. She told herself that it could have been much worse as she soaked it in. Ash's wolves had gone easy on them, avoiding any strikes that could kill. She should have been grateful, but she couldn't help the hopelessness that filled her in its place. It was her fault that they had been placed in this situation in the first place. Would Ash have even found her if she hadn't allowed these people to place their misguided trust in her?

In the midst of the aftermath, Ash stood still as a statue. Even after his own wolves had disappeared into the night, he stood without words, watching the havoc of each new emotion that swelled within her. Slowly, he walked to where she was still kneeling in the dirt. Refusing to give him the satisfaction he was seeking, she stared at the ground, avoiding his eyes and the arrogant smirk that would be on his face at that moment. She watched his knees bend as he crouched down beside her; taking her chin in his hand, he firmly lifted her head up, forcing her eyes to meet his. The blackness of his wolf's eyes had faded, leaving his steely human gaze staring back coolly at her.

"I suggest you reconsider my offer to join my pack one more time before someone actually gets hurt. Leaders make tough decisions for their people. Stop being a child and be the leader these people think you are, the one I know is hiding in there," he said, his voice soft as if he were chiding a child that had disappointed him. Leaning in close, he placed his cheek beside hers, his lips brushing her ear gingerly, sending a shiver through her; she tried to lean away, but he held her face firmly in place with his hand still on her chin. "Thank you for the entertaining welcome, darling. You have no idea the plans I have for us now that we're together again," he whispered. Releasing her chin, he stood and followed his wolves, not sparing a glance for the other wolves around him, casting death wishes at him with their gazes. He had no fear of retaliation from them, and he didn't need any. He walked away from their camp just as polished and unnerved as he had walked into it, his face unburdened by the fear or somberness he left behind him.

A numbness flowed through Jade's limbs as she watched his back fade into the darkness. It was unclear if it was due to relief or simply the shock settling in. Slowly rising to her feet, she stumbled to where Kyler still lay on the ground, his blood staining his shirt and the ground beneath him. She allowed herself a sigh of relief as she inspected him. His wound was already beginning to heal at its edges. A few manageable drops of blood still trickled out, but the flow was slowing. His breathing was even and strong despite his being unconscious. He would have a nasty scar to show off, but he would live.

Her eyes searched the group frantically until she found who she searched for. Desert stood above the crowd as he helped old Malcolm stand. A mixture of dirt, sweat, and blood coated both of their faces, the group's weariness reflected in their eyes. When

he met her gaze, he paused, his face as sober as they shared a silent moment. She knew what he was thinking because it was the same thought running through her own mind. This was just the beginning of their problems.

Chapter 20

Darren

Beep!
Beep!
Beep!

Eyes still closed tightly, Darren rolled over and fumbled around with his alarm, the offensive blaring bringing him into an even more irritating state of consciousness. There was no moment of peace to be shattered by the foggy memories of the night before. He would have had to actually sleep to forget any of it. His father's words danced around in his mind all night, playing on an endless loop, popping up at every twist and turn his mind took to dispel them. Luke had his reasons for believing the way he did. It was part of an Alpha's duty to anticipate and prepare for danger at every turn, to see potential enemies in the faces of everyone. Darren supposed that's why he wasn't ready to be Alpha yet; he still saw loyalty and friendship where Luke saw anger and deception. Maybe he was naive, but he wasn't ready to let go of the hope that the rogues just wanted the same things he did, to be safe, well-fed, and surrounded by loved ones.

No, his father had to be wrong about Jade. He just couldn't look past the fact that she didn't bend to him the way other wolves did, the way Darren did. Not this time, though. It didn't matter what his father said, Darren knew that he had to see her again.

Rolling out of bed with newfound determination, he readied himself for the tasks ahead of him. Talking to Jade would have

to wait until later; first, he had to manage the new rogue pups being sent to the hospital. Rushing out without breakfast to ensure he avoided his father, he found himself quickly approaching the large building dedicated to the pack's health. Standing in front of the doors stood a familiar figure, causing Darren's feet to pause. His confidence for the day slowly depleted as his heart sank.

Spencer hadn't noticed him yet as he talked with two other young warriors, laughing at something one of them said. It wasn't long ago that they had been talking carefreely together. After the fight with Jade and her friends, Spencer had been standoffish with everyone. He had even gone as far as to outright refuse to speak to Darren after they had gone to meet with Jade's group. It wasn't just Darren he had pushed away. Darren had noticed him isolating himself on his breaks as well, watching over Valery from afar as she ate with the rogues.

When he did glance up, eyes locking on Darren, the smile faded from his face, replaced by a slight frown as he kept his anger reigned in. Wincing, Darren suppressed the urge to turn around and walk away, now wasn't the time to run from his own packmates. He would have to get used to their anger and frustration if he wanted to pursue any sort of relationship with Jade.

Striding up to them, Darren made sure to hold his head high. He didn't allow his face to reflect his disappointment when Spencer looked away, his cold eyes void of any kinship that they once would have held.

"Are you guys here to help with the rogue pups?" Darren asked the two other wolves. They both nodded in response, standing at attention as a sign of respect for his rank, but he noticed how they both avoided his eyes. It seemed Spencer

wasn't the only one that had issues with Darren's presence. "Alright, let's get to it," he said, stepping past them, leading the way inside.

Fluorescent lights buzzed softly in the ceiling, but they weren't needed as most of the room was lit from the sun pouring in through the expansive windows that lined the wall. Chairs with worn padding lined the wall on either side. In the middle was a large desk with two nurses manning it. Darren supposed it was welcoming enough for a place that was rarely in use since most of the population had supernatural healing abilities.

Excusing himself from their small group Darren made his way to the front desk, one of the nurses smiling pleasantly as he approached.

"Hello, Mr. Power, how can I help you?" she asked. Glancing over to where the other nurse sat, Darren lowered his voice so that only they would be able to hear him, aware of the eyes that bored into his back.

"I need to see the ones in the coma," he whispered. The nurse's smile dropped, her wide eyes looking nervously around the waiting room. When she was satisfied no one had heard his request, she leaned in close, her voice no louder than a breath.

"Follow me." She led him down a narrow hallway to the stairwell. They jogged up three flights of stairs before they made it to the door she wanted, holding the door open for him. Darren found himself in a dimly lit hallway, ten doors lining it on either side. Many of the doors were closed, a small window the only view through them, but a few were propped open. Darren chose one of those giving him a perfect view of the disheartening sight before him.

A young woman lay in a hospital bed; her hair and face shone from the scattered sunlight that came through the open

curtains. Pink flowers on the bedside table were cheerful. The girl would have appeared to be in a peaceful sleep if it wasn't for the tubes sticking out of her nose and mouth, a surge of air going through them every so often. Besides the steady beep of the monitor beside her, there was no sign of life. She was like a storybook princess waiting for her prince. Except there was no prince and no kiss that would wake her or any of them this time.

"They all are like this," the nurse whispered from the doorway, hands clutched at her chest as she stared at the lifeless girl. "We are getting more and more of them admitted every day. We're trying to keep it quiet like Alpha Power asked us to, but it's getting more difficult the more that come in. The pack is starting to ask questions that we don't have the answers to."

"Have we lost any?" Darren asked, clearing the lump from his throat. Even knowing what to expect going in, he found himself unprepared for the emotions wrestling within him.

"Not yet, but it doesn't look good for any of them waking up either," she replied, her voice breaking at the end. Darren felt for her, for all of the staff. It was his first time seeing his packmates in distress from a danger that he had no power to defeat. He couldn't imagine what it was like for the wolves that had to watch over them every day, slowly watching the life drain from them.

"You should probably get back downstairs; the rogues are supposed to be arriving with their pups soon," the nurse said, shaking Darren from his bleak thoughts. He could only nod in response; any words he could think of would fall flat.

It was strange, Darren thought to himself as he followed the nurse out of the room and back to the stairs, to find himself wishing for an enemy or a battle. Something physical that he

could fend off, anything besides this invisible foe wandering the halls, taking his packmates one by one.

They didn't have to wait long before rogues began to slowly fill up the waiting room. Parents held onto their wide-eyed pups; the pups that seemed to be without parental figures huddled together, for the most part. Their darting eyes and little hearts fluttering in their chests reminded him of a cornered rabbit. Pushing the bleakness from the fourth floor out of his mind, Darren tried to focus on the figures in front of him. He couldn't do anything for the she-wolves upstairs, not yet at least, but he could help these ones. He could hardly imagine the horrors these children had seen in their young lives. If they were lucky, his pack would be able to help them avoid any of their usual daily troubles for the next few weeks, forever if they chose to remain with them.

Hospital staff remained on the sidelines as the rogues continued to fill the room, their own wariness displayed in their furrowed brows and soft whispers. No one made a move to cross the invisible line that was forming down the room, rogues vs. packwolves.

A small cry and clatter of chair legs hitting the hard floor near the front of the divide drew everyone's attention. A young girl was sprawled on the ground, tears filling her dark eyes as she noticed everyone's eyes on her. Darren's feet moved of their own accord, striding over to kneel beside the girl he offered out his hand. Sniffling, she placed her hand in his, allowing him to pull her to her feet. She was young, no more than three or four

years old, far too young to be guilty of any crimes placing her into roguehood. Meeting her hesitant gaze, he offered a smile.

"Hi, my name is Darren, what's yours?" he asked, wiping her tears away with one of her tiny hands, the other still gripping his hand tightly.

"Lily."

"That's a pretty name, just like the flowers," Darren replied. "Where is your mommy or dad?" he asked, glancing around the room, ignoring the watching eyes he found glued to him. No one moved forward to claim the child. Uncomfortable glances were exchanged between the few adults that were in the room.

"They aren't here anymore; they went to be with the Goddesses in the sky," she said, pointing at the blue sky visible outside of the window. Darren's heart clenched in his chest at the girl's matter-of-fact words, declaring herself an orphan. How could anyone allow a child to not only live life without a home but to suffer through it without her parents was unthinkable?

"You must be a very brave girl, Lily. It just so happens that I am looking for a brave girl to be the first one to get her check-up done. Do you think you could be that girl?" he asked, giving her hand a gentle, reassuring squeeze. He tried to ignore how he could feel each of the bones in her hand, the evidence of hunger apparent on her face and arms as well. She thought over his words for a moment before slowly nodding her head, a small smile appearing on her lips.

"That's great news!" Darren said, standing up. His eyes widened with surprise when the girl stretched her arms towards him in a silent request. He scooped her up as delicately as he could, fearing any sudden movements would hurt her fragile frame. Walking up to one of the nurses still standing on the sidelines, he ignored the alarm in her eyes at his approach.

"Nurse, this is Lily. She was very nice to volunteer to go first. Do you think you can help her?" His words came out as a question, but the intention behind them was clear. There was no room for refusal. Thankfully, the nurse recovered herself quickly, painting a sunny smile on her face as she reached for the girl in his arms.

"Of course! And I think I might just have a lollipop stashed somewhere for my bravest patients," she said, whispering the last part to Lily as she was transferred to the nurse's arms.

It was as if a switch was flipped in the quiet observers. Hospital staff that had been standing on the sides sprang into action, smiles lighting up their faces as they greeted pups and the adults with them. Soon the room was filled with shaking hands, gentle questions; a few wolves even cracked jokes causing giggles to erupt from the pups nearby. An unknown weight began to lift itself from Darren's shoulders at the sight. It was a small victory, but a victory, nonetheless. Maybe there was hope for his people to accept the rogues into their ranks, even accept one as their Luna.

Gaining the attention of one of the guards, Darren asked him to run ahead and instruct the daycare facility to prepare extra food. None of the pups or the adults that had brought them in would be going hungry tonight. Watching the guard weave his way through the hustle and bustle of the room now alive with action, Darren stood back and surveyed the group. The smile that settled on his face was as genuine as they come. A firm hand on his shoulder interrupted his happy thoughts. Turning around, he was met with a pair of silverish blue eyes.

"Your father is a lucky man to have such a capable heir. It looks like you have everything under control here," Ash said, his own eyes scanning the room. Darren wasn't sure if he was

reading too much into his tone or if it was the emptiness of Ash's eyes, but he could have sworn that it was annoyance that he felt coming from the other wolf.

"Pups are easy; their needs and desires are simple enough. It's the adults that often hide their motives," Darren replied, earning a grin from Ash.

"I suppose you're right. Still, it is impressive, though, being able to inspire this kind of cooperation, but you have been busy building allies wherever you can from what I hear. Based on seeing you interact with that she-wolf last night, I would say my sources are correct."

"I'd rather find allies where I can than see enemies where there are none."

"A noble idea, but I suspect it's not one your father agrees with," Ash said, meeting Darren's gaze once again. Any hint of displeasure Darren thought he had seen earlier had disappeared and was replaced with curiosity. Shrugging his shoulders, he looked back out on the group, which was slowly growing smaller as pups were taken in the back to the exam rooms. Ash's observation was accurate, but it was one that Darren was hesitant to speak aloud. Especially to a stranger.

"Alpha Power knows what battles are worth fighting and which ones are opportunities for peace. That's why the Northwind Pack is so strong," he replied, giving the answer he knew his father would have expected from him if he had been standing there.

"What a very safe answer," Ash said. Darren didn't bother trying to respond; sometimes no answer was better than an unthought-out one. Instead, he turned his attention back to the room before him. Everything was still running smoothly, everyone where they needed to be. Among the hustle and bustle

stood a lone, grim figure on the other side of the room. Spencer's crossed arms and tense shoulders made him stand out from the rest of the group, which had become more relaxed once they had found their flow. His eyes smoldered with a silent anger. They would have burned a hole through Darren's head and into the wall behind him if they had been able to.

Darren felt the weight from earlier partially settle back onto his shoulders as he met his friend's glare. They may have been able to convince everyone to work together that day, but there were others who felt the same as Spencer. Their fierce hatred still burned strong, and Darren feared that it was a fire that would continue to spread.

Chapter 21

Jade

The pounding in her skull was relentless, hammering with each step she took down the brightly lit halls of the Training Center. She shouldn't even have been there, not after what had happened the night before, but she needed to see Darren, to warn him. Restless energy had filled the warehouse since Ash had pulled his men from the fight, licking their wounds and whatever egos were still intact. Kyler had sustained the most severe injury of the group. It would be a few days before he was back on his feet and weeks before the wounds faded to scars he would carry for the rest of his life. They should have found some solace in the fact that no one was more seriously injured, but the cloud over the group proved that they already suspected what Jade knew to be true. They had escaped with minor cuts and bruises because Ash had allowed them to; next time, he may not decide to be so gracious.

It surprised Jade that Ash had bothered with the politics involved with playing nice with Alpha Power at all. The violence he displayed was much more his style, but he had always been a fan of games. Winners always seemed to be. This game was one they would all be players in for a while, and Jade did not want him to get his hooks in Darren the way he already had them in his father.

The afternoon sun glared down on the yard behind the center, the rough circle of warriors in training sweating beneath it. Jade had a perfect view from the third-floor window to watch

the wolves pair up to practice hand-to-hand combat. The instructor stood off to the side, calling out instructions, where Darren usually would have stood. Scanning the yard, Jade tried to calm her pounding heart as she scrutinized each of the fighting wolves' faces. Darren was nowhere to be seen.

Maybe his father gave him a different assignment for the day, she reasoned. There were hundreds of explanations as to why he would have missed training for the day that didn't involve Ash. Unfortunately, she was having a hard time believing any of them.

"What are we looking for?" a lighthearted voice asked just behind her shoulder, their breath tickling her cheek. Whirling around, Jade held back a snarl as she came face to face with the owner of the voice, a horrifyingly familiar voice.

"What are you doing here, Ash?" she snapped. She had avoided the man for years, and now it seemed as if he was everywhere she turned. He shrugged his shoulders innocently as if he was having a normal conversation between friends.

"I mentioned to Darren Power how confusing the territory can be to newcomers, and he offered to give me a tour of the place. I gotta say I'm a little surprised at your behavior. I didn't think you were one to gawk at the brainless, shirtless brutes, but I guess there are new things everyone can learn about you, isn't there?" he grinned, peeking over her shoulder to the wolves below. "I understand your fascination, though; I mean, just look at those biceps-"

"I don't have time for this," Jade said, making it two whole steps before she was halted by Ash's hand landing on the window behind her, successfully boxing her in. Craning her neck up, she twisted her face with the most withering glare she

could muster, praying that he couldn't hear the blood racing through her ears.

"Get out of my way."

"Don't you know it's rude to walk away from a conversation? And we are just getting started," he said. "Besides, I have some questions for you. You surprised me last night. I thought for sure with your little friends in danger that you would have tried a little harder to fight back. I mean, after all, it's not as if you're entirely defenseless. Why are you still holding back?" he asked, his eyes boring into hers. The silver ring around his pupils slowly darkened to black as his wolf came forward. Veins of black spread through the blue in his eyes, not completely taking them over but joining the two perfectly; wolf and human worked in harmony with each other. They could have been called beautiful if they had belonged to anyone else.

"Don't try to put that on me. I wouldn't have had to defend anyone if you had known where you weren't wanted," Jade said. "You're the ones who hurt my friends, not me." Clicking his tongue, Ash waved a finger in front of her face.

"Everyone's actions impact everyone else in one way or another. Do you really think that your friends would still be living as outcasts of our society if we didn't continue to allow the packs to make us outcasts in the first place? Alphas only have their power as long as we allow it. They've created their own demise and don't realize it yet, but we can make them. The Council has always gone to what they believe the root of their issues are, us, and they are right. Our only way out is to find the root and choke it out.

"The longer you stand by and allow them to call us criminals, outcasts, or rogues the longer your friends will have to live life as such. We are the ones that control their fates. If

you continue to deny your destiny, you will continue to place them in danger." The blackness of his eyes deepened as he spoke, threatening to swallow Jade in their darkness if she let them. His wolf's power throbbed between them like a true Alpha's.

"Being exactly who they think we are won't improve our situation with the packs. Not all of the packwolves are afraid of us. The longer we stay out of their way, more of them will start to realize that we aren't the ones they need to be afraid of," Jade argued, slapping his hand away from her face. Her words were in complete opposition of everything he had said, but she couldn't pretend she didn't understand it. She couldn't count the number of sleepless nights she had laid awake wondering what life would be like without the packs. How different her life would have been if her Alpha hadn't had the power to banish her, a child from the only home she had known.

"You mean like the young but promising Darren Power? I'll admit he does have an unusual sense of optimism for a future Alpha, but he's no different from his father. They all end up the same, power-hungry, control freaks. But maybe you're right, maybe I can convince the young Alpha to join my cause; it would go a long way having the son of Luke Power as a supporter."

"Leave him out of this," Jade snarled, shoving Ash back as hard as she could. He stumbled back a single step; his eyes widened in surprise, mimicking her own shock at her outburst. She knew she had made a mistake as she watched the emotions drain from his face, a frosty stillness settled in his eyes. Bridging the gap between them, he placed both hands on the window beside her head, pressing her back into the frame to put any

distance between them that she could, but she could still feel the heat coming off of his skin.

"What's it to you? He's just another packwolf, right? It's not like the great Darren Power cares about what happens to you," he said, leaning his head down so that he was eye to eye with her, his nose nearly touching hers.

"He doesn't. I'd just hate to see any innocent wolf mixed up with you," she answered, the lie flowing out effortlessly. She knew her face was blank, free of any clues that Ash searched for. Her face may have been easy enough to control, but her body still found a way to betray her.

"Liar," Ash breathed, his eyes scanning her face almost wildly, his brow drawn together in confusion. "Want to know how I know?" he asked, not waiting for her to answer, "Your heart speeds up every time I say his name."

He was right. Even then, Jade could feel her traitor heart hammering away in her chest as if it was trying to escape her ribs, betraying her own thoughts at the mere sound of her mate's name. She needed to say something, anything to throw Ash off before he connected the dots himself, but her mouth was dry, her tongue unwilling to form the words she needed.

"You haven't been here long enough to actually befriend any of them, even if you do hide your anger towards them well enough. Especially Alpha Power's only son. You don't just think he's different from them; you actually feel something for him," Ash mused aloud as if he had a view directly into her mind. She wanted to look away, but his eyes sucked her in, making it impossible to look at anything else. Which gave her a perfect view to watch the realization light up his face, his mouth forming into a smile once again. "Well, who would have thought, lil' old Jade found her mate, and not just any wolf at

that but a future Alpha! Color me impressed," he said, his satisfaction growing as the blood drained from her face. "I do have to wonder what his father thinks about the whole arrangement, though. I can't imagine he was too happy when he found out. I wish I had seen the look on his face when he heard. What a wrench that must have thrown into the mighty Alpha Power's plans. He does know, right?"

"That's none of your business," Jade hissed, glancing over his shoulder to the empty doorway. She was uncertain if she was happy that no one had been there to hear the bombshell Ash had dropped or if she had hoped someone would be there, anything to get her away from him.

"Everything is my business, especially when it directly impacts our plans."

"I am not part of any plans with you!" Jade yelled, catching herself; she lowered her voice again. "It doesn't matter what you say, I'll never follow you."

"You don't have to follow me because I have a new offer now," Ash said, looking far too happy at whatever new idea he had hatched. One that Jade was sure she would like even less than his previous 'offers'. "The one wolf that an Alpha has no control over is their own mate. So become my mate, lead by my side as we create a new world for people like us, people like the ones you're trying so hard to protect now," he offered, his eyes serious as he gauged her reaction. If anyone else had suggested it, Jade would have burst out laughing, but she knew Ash meant every word of it, and it was no laughing matter.

"You find out I have a mate, and your first instinct is to ask me to choose you?" Jade asked incredulously, raising a brow, "Why would I ever agree to be your Luna?"

"Oh, heavens no, you're no Luna. You would never be happy standing to the side silently supporting someone as they lead. No, you're an Alpha just like me, but that's why we are the perfect pair to lead them together. And because you know as well as I do that he won't want you forever, not once he knows who you really are. Goddess-given mates aren't the only option out there. More and more wolves live happy lives with a chosen mate.

"You want the packwolves to change their ways just like I do; together we would be unstoppable. Think about it. Never again would you have to stand by as the Alpha Council made decisions for you. Your friends could stop looking over their shoulders wherever they go. I know you've thought of it before. We can create that world together; just come with me; become mine," Ash said, the seriousness of his words seeping in, filling her mind with unsavory thoughts. Of course, she had thought of a world where the Alphas' word wasn't law, where the word 'Alpha' meant nothing, a world where packwolves ate every single word they spoke unfairly against her. Where scared whispers didn't follow her every step because of what they thought they saw in her, but because of the power within her. Every rogue dreamed of a day where they were accepted, a world of second chances. But Ash would not be the one to create it, not without sweat, tears, and lots and lots of blood.

"Even if Darren doesn't want me, I would never choose you," she snapped, steeling herself for what would come next. "I may want the packs to accept us, but I would never kill over that dream. That's the difference between us."

"Are we really different, though? I used to think like you did, that one day if we did as we were asked, they would see that some of us were worth saving, but they haven't, and they never

will. All they see when they look at us is their failure to control us. That's why they will never be able to let us live in peace. Why else do you think we were all called out here? It's not about tracking us or getting us to fight their battles for them. It's about showing us that they still have power over us, even after they rejected us.

"I know you've seen it too, and once you're ready to accept that fact, then you'll see that I'm right, and you'll stop fighting your true desires and make the Alphas pay for throwing us away. We can make them regret ever looking at you and seeing something weak and disposable."

"You're wrong about me. I don't want anyone to pay for making me a rogue; I just want to be left alone. You're the one that's chasing a fantasy," she said, hating the way her voice shook when she spoke, but something in Ash's words scared her, the thought that maybe there was the slightest possibility that he might just be right. Ash was already shaking his head before she had a chance to finish, something similar to pity reflecting in his eyes.

"You're wrong, Jade. I'm the only one that sees you, the one who really sees who you are, and I accept you. Even your so-called friends encourage you to dim the power you hold within because it intimidates them. But I know who you could be if you learned how to harness it, what you could do if you accepted it and how you could shake this world. Can you really say the same thing about him?" Ash asked, his fingers locking onto her chin when she tried to look away, forcing her face back up to his. "He would never be able to look at you if he knew everything you hold inside. But I see it, Jade, and I can help you unleash it in a way that makes you more powerful than you could ever dream of being. All you have to do is stop fighting

yourself." As he finished his words, he turned on his heel to stride towards the door, leaving a stunned Jade watching his retreat, his words swimming in her head.

"What if you're wrong?" she called out, finding her voice before he disappeared through the doorway, his steps pausing. "What if the packs will be ready for us? Maybe not these Alphas, but the next ones could be different," she said, unsure if she believed herself even. But she needed to say it, needed to speak the idea into existence as if that would make it closer to reality.

"Tell you what, let's test that theory," Ash said, not turning around fully but peeking over his shoulder. "You have three days to tell your mate the reason your last Alpha banished you in the first place. If he thinks he can love you despite that, then I'll leave him and his pack alone. If he can't, then you give him up forever." Swallowing deeply, Jade struggled to keep her breathing even, fighting the rising panic from within.

"And if I don't?" she asked, already suspecting his answer. Only part of his face was tilted towards her, but it was enough for her to see a small smile on his lips, his eyes black as night.

"Then I'll make sure he and every other wolf in this territory knows."

Chapter 22

Darren

Where is that wolf? Darren thought as he weaved through the halls of youths, cursing himself for letting Ash out of his sight. He had no reason to be concerned about the fact that Ash had somehow gotten lost or given him the slip, depending on his motives, but for some unexplained reason, the pit in his stomach grew the longer he searched for the missing rogue. Giving tight smiles to those he passed in an attempt to hide his concern, it had already been such a long day, and it was far from over.

"Darren!" a voice called out from behind him, whirling around Darren let out the breath he had been holding as Ash's white hair bobbed through the crowded hall towards him. "Glad I found you; this place is bigger than I expected," he said once he had reached Darren, his eyes roaming the faces of the wolves that passed them.

"I was starting to get worried. I looked up, and you were gone," Darren said, glancing wearily over Ash's shoulder, but there didn't appear to be anything amiss. "Where did you want to go next?" he asked.

"I actually need to be getting back. Thank you for all of your help. You can't imagine how...informative this little trip has been," Ash replied, giving Darren a handshake in farewell. "I'm sure I'll be seeing you again very soon."

He declined any assistance with finding his way back out, leaving Darren to stand in the middle of the hall, watching his back as he walked away.

What a strange wolf, he thought to himself as the rogue disappeared from his sight, leaving him with nothing but goosebumps and growing dread. His day was not over yet, though. His father would expect a report on how the morning at the hospital had gone, and he would need to find out if the most recent border patrols had found anything of interest, but most importantly, he still needed to talk to Jade.

With thoughts of Jade swimming in his head, he felt the hair on his arms rise. His wolf purred from within at the thought of their mate. No, it was more than just the thought of her that had his wolf prancing happily in his mind; she was close. The mate bond gently tugged him forward as if a string was attached to his chest. It guided him closer to the one his wolf desired more than anything in their world, the one he found himself smiling at the mere thought of seeing her again.

Following the timid pull from his chest, he was led away from the crowded halls and classrooms, away from the watchful eyes of his peers until he found himself wandering an empty floor. She was in one of the vacant classrooms, her head down as she braced herself against the wall; as he drew closer, he could see her frame shaking, hands clenched into fists. With a scream, she slammed her fist into the wall, plaster, and wood cracking beneath the force of the blow.

Steps faltering, he stood a few paces in the room, the smile falling from his face at the sight of her…anger? That didn't seem right. They may not have gone through the mating rituals that would join their minds and souls as one, but even without it, Darren didn't feel anger coming from the girl in front of him. He stared silently at her, his thoughts running a mile a minute to identify the emotions coming from her, uncertain of how to move forward until he understood.

Withdrawing her hand from the hole she had made, blood sliding down her wrist from scratches running along the back of her hand, Darren was sure it was riddled with splinters as well. It was then that she sensed him. He knew by the way her shoulders stiffened, her stormy eyes going wide as she turned towards him, only relaxing slightly when she recognized him. His feet moved on their own as he strode towards her, no longer able to hold himself back. Wrapping his arms around her, he pulled her against his chest. There was no need for her to explain the emotion spilling out of her, no need to give it a name. It didn't matter what they called it; his reaction would have been the same. He needed to hold her, if not for her, then for his own sake.

Jade was stiff within his embrace, the scent of her blood creeping up, nearly throwing his wolf into a frenzy, but Darren soothed him easily enough. This was not a battle that could be won with fang and claw. Gradually, Jade's body began to relax against his own. Her shoulders trembling, her arms remained at her side, but she made no move to escape his embrace.

Darren didn't know how long they stood there together; it could have been minutes, it could have been hours, the time didn't matter. All that mattered was that she was in pain and who had caused it.

An eternity later, and much too soon, Jade pulled herself away from his chest. Eyes avoiding his face, she took a step back out of his reach, letting out a sigh as she steadied her shoulders.

"I'm sorry about the wall," Jade said, gesturing behind her to where her fist had gone through. "I'll make sure it gets fixed."

"Jade, you don't need to worry about that. What happened?" Darren asked, grabbing her injured hand gently in his own. Jade shook her head, brushing a loose strand of hair out of her face.

"It's nothing. I just got a little overwhelmed with everything is all; I'm fine now," she answered, but it was a lie. The longer Darren watched her, the more certain he was that everything was not alright. There were dark circles under her reddened eyes as if she hadn't slept. In addition to her bleeding hand, her arms were littered with tiny scratches, a bluish bruise on her chest peeking out the top of her shirt. All were new injuries.

"You're not fine; just look at you," Darren argued, his hand locking onto her wrist when she tried to withdraw her hand. "Who did this to you? I'll make sure they are punished; I can make sure they never touch you again," he said, his voice coming out harsher than he had intended, his own anger combining with his wolf's. She had just been with him the night before. He had been right there, and he had failed once again to protect her.

Yanking her hand from his grasp, she backed away from him, her stormy eyes darkening.

"I don't need your protection, Darren; you know that I've been doing this long before I ever met you. I know what I'm doing," she snapped. Withdrawing his hand, Darren tried not to let her words sting, which was easier said than done. He must have failed miserably at hiding it as guilt washed over Jade's face, replacing any anger there had been. "I'm sorry, I didn't mean that," she said.

"I just hate to see you like this, especially if there's something I can do. You don't have to carry it all on your own," he said, his voice nearly a whisper.

"Don't I?" she asked. "You may be here for now but for how long? What happens when your father is done with us and turns us all out into the wild again? I can't leave my people,

Darren, not now, not after they've placed so much trust in me, and your pack would never accept me."

"They will," he interrupted, forcing himself to believe the words as he spoke them. "They will accept you because I do. They'll learn to love you for who you are."

As I do.

The words he really wanted to say stuck in his throat. Could he really love her after such a short time? Love was a foreign language for him, one he was unsure of how to speak, let alone feel. Yet his wolf's feelings were clear enough; his wolf loved her without a drop of doubt, hesitation, or fear. But every wolf knew that the beast's feelings were not the man's, and wolves weren't always the wisest of creatures. Jade must have had the same uncertainties as she shook her head, Darren's heart already pounding before her words left her mouth.

"You don't know who I am. The mate bond makes your wolf and you blind to what everyone else sees. Look at me, Darren!" she said, baring her arms out, giving him a full view of every scar that marked them, as well as the damaged fang on her right arm. "How do you think I earned these? Innocent wolves don't carry this many. I'm not what you think I am. I'm no Luna."

"I don't care about any of that. You can call yourself Luna, rogue, villain, or Alpha for all I care. They're just words. They all mean nothing if you throw this away now," he pleaded, unwilling or unable to process what she said, not if it meant what he thought it did. "Tell me any stories you want for each scar. Say you won them by saving a litter of innocent pups; say you were forced into each battle and that you had no choice to defend yourself. Tell me your Alpha was an evil man, corrupt with power, and he was cruel for abandoning you. I don't care if they

are all lies, but say whatever you need to so that you can stay." He reached for her arms, gripping them gently in his hands as he tugged her towards him, but she didn't yield a single step forward. The pain coursing through her eyes throbbed weakly through the mate bond, Darren's only warning for what her next words would be.

"I may be used to the lies that come with this life, but there isn't a bone in your body that isn't repulsed by the idea. If the Goddesses really meant for us to be together, do you think we would still be hiding it from everyone?"

Darren didn't have a response, not one that would help. She was right, there he was, begging her to consider him, to let him protect and defend her, and he hadn't even found the courage to tell his own father about who she was to him. Gently, Jade brushed his hands away from her arms, eyes downcast, sparing Darren from having to see the emptiness he was sure would be filling them.

"It's time we both stopped chasing a future we know can never happen, before anyone gets hurt," she whispered, her hand brushing his as she walked past him. Catching her hand in his, he turned her back to him, unsure if his actions were his own or if they belonged to the beast inside. No matter who they came from, he couldn't hold the words back, even if he had wanted to.

"What if I want to get hurt? If we can't live on the lies, then we'll show them the truth and let them think what they will. I don't care anymore. You've fought long enough; I can fight for us now, and I will, even if you can pretend that it's not what you want."

He meant it, every word of it. He would fight for them, he would face his pack's judgment, he would even face his father's

wrath if it meant she could stay near him if she could even consider that at this point.

But it was impossible to tell what she thought as she kept her face turned away. Yanking her hand away from him, the sound of her retreating footsteps echoed in his ears long after they should have faded. Unable to find the will to move his feet, he stood in the emptiness that surrounded him, watching the sunlight filter through the window, bathing the room in a warmth that couldn't reach him.

Not only was one of his worst fears becoming reality, but he felt it spinning away, further and further out of his control. How had it gone so wrong? Wasn't it only that morning he had felt such hope that he could push past everyone else's fears, his father's fears, to earn her love and trust? Now that he was ready to face any foe for her, it seemed the one thing that would defeat them was Jade's own doubts.

Amidst the darker thoughts swirling around his mind, there was one single light that Darren held onto. He focused all his energy on the one thought in an attempt to drown out the despair that could have swallowed him.

She hadn't rejected him.

Yes, in her words, she had told him to back off, had said that they didn't belong together, yet the mate bond still pulsed faintly. The invisible cord that tied them together was still intact. Even if Jade herself didn't realize it, she was still holding on to the thought of them together, still leaving the possibilities open, and that was enough to give Darren reason to hope. He couldn't force her to change her mind, to be blind to the challenges they would face if they were together, but he could make sure she knew he hadn't given up.

Chapter 23

Jade

It was impossible to escape. Everywhere Jade looked, there seemed to be one more thing thrown her way, adding to the never-ending list of things for her to worry about. No matter how she looked at it, there was no way out of the torture that lay ahead of her.

"What's that about?" James asked, peeking over Jade's shoulder at the piece of paper one of the guards in front of the Training Center had shoved into her hands just before she entered the building. The edges of it crumpled in her clenched hands.

"Just Luke Power's attempt to ruin another day," Jade sighed. She allowed Desert to pull the summons out of her hands as they trudged forward, her shoulders sagging in defeat.

"You have been recognized as one of the official spokesmen of the rogues willing to continue coexisting with the known packs under the Council's protection. As such, your presence has been requested at the Northwind Packhouse at two-o-clock to further the discussion of the peace between our people."

"Huh, that was a little nicer than I was expecting," Desert said, handing the note back.

"I don't care how nice it sounds; I'm not in the mood to deal with any pompous Alphas today," Jade grumbled as she shoved it into her pocket. Of course, she would be called in front of Alpha Power just hours after she had told his son to take a hike. With her luck, Darren would be in attendance as well, and she

would spend the entire meeting thinking about the blue-eyed gaze she was avoiding. What could she possibly have done to anger the Goddesses so much that they would want to torment her? Or perhaps they just found it entertaining to watch the problems pile on her. Either way, Jade hoped they would take pity on her, at least for one day.

"Do you think Alpha Power is ready to let us know why we're here?" Kacen asked, popping up right behind Jade's shoulder. Somehow, the summons had made its way from her pocket into his hands as he scrutinized it.

"How many times do I have to tell you not to do that?" Jade snapped, snatching the paper from his grip. The young wolf shrugged, utterly oblivious to Jade's glare as he danced up the stairs beside her, his dark locks bouncing with each excited step.

"Sorry, force of habit. But seriously, do you think he's ready to tell you what's going on? It's been weeks, and all I've learned is how quickly I can fall asleep during History of the Packs," he said, bounding up the steps backward as he turned to face the rest of the group.

"There's no way to guess what goes on in that wolf's head," was Jade's only reply, but it clearly wasn't a satisfying answer as Kacen continued his train of thought.

"I mean, it's not like they like having us here. I heard some of the Northwind wolves saying that they should stop giving us the ration chips so that we'd have to find our own food again. Maybe that's what he wants to talk to you about."

"Or maybe he just wants to try to steal more of our pups," Chris added, his words settling on the group like a dark cloud as they exchanged brief but concerned glances.

"Well, whatever he wants, I'm sure we'll find out soon enough. Besides, it can't be too terrible. If the Council had

wanted to get rid of us, they would have done something already," Desert reasoned, perking the group up a little. Jade didn't bother to respond, but she knew her thoughts were written across her face as Desert's eyes found hers. She hoped he was right, but a small voice in the back of her mind whispered that they had much to fear from Alpha Power and the rest of the Council.

It was official; the Goddesses hated her. Jade contemplated exactly what life decisions she would need to go back in time to change to help her avoid the empty chair in Alpha Power's personal office. The chair that was located directly across from Darren and his too observant gaze, and the same chair that happened to be located beside Ash as he sprawled in his own. Standing at the head of the table, Luke was flanked by two guards who stood at attention behind him. On his right sat the Beta of the pack, and on his left a beautiful blonde woman, her eyes the same striking blue as Darren's; she had to be Darren's mother, the pack's Luna. Like most wolves, Jade had heard the rumors whispered by rogues around their late-night fires of the voiceless Luna. It wasn't that the condition was unheard of. It was common enough. It was odd, though, for an imperfect wolf to be in a position of such power. Looking at her in person, Jade would never describe the she-wolf before her as lacking anything. She looked like a Luna. With hair the color of warm honey and eyes that matched the sky itself, she was the embodiment of everything warm and inviting.

Everything Jade was not.

The sound of someone clearing their throat brought Jade's attention back to the room to find everyone's eyes on her, much to her chagrin.

"Once everyone is seated, we can get started," Luke said, giving Jade a pointed look. Ignoring the heat that rose to her cheeks, Jade kept her head high as she picked up the empty chair and walked it towards the other end of the table, as far from Ash as she could get. Unfortunately, it meant she found herself directly across from Luke. Sliding into the seat, she looked up to see wide eyes staring back at her. "Are you *comfortable*?" Luke asked, his eyes taking on a flaming hue as he watched her from across the table.

"Very," was Jade's only reply. She kept her eyes locked on Luke's as his glare intensified; she didn't care, though. She'd risk his wrath any day rather than willingly sit next to Ash while he found ways to torture her as Darren watched her every move. Luke must have decided the small power battle wasn't worth the effort as a small huff escaped him as he took his own seat. Jade knew that it shouldn't have mattered, but she couldn't help the satisfaction that bloomed in her chest as Luke looked away first. It may have been a small win, but it was a win nonetheless, and she couldn't be entirely sure, but she thought she saw Darren hide a smile behind a fake yawn. Jade's lips twitched as she held back a smile of her own until she caught Ash's eyes darting between her and Darren, successfully killing any amusement she might have felt.

"I've asked both of you here today since your people have chosen you to represent them during your time here. Before we begin, though, I'd like to officially introduce my Beta, Johnathan Pike, and my mate, Heather," Luke said as he gestured to the wolves at his side. Johnathan gave a slight nod as Heather gave

a wave to the group, a gentle smile that seemed genuine danced across her lips. "First and foremost, I'd like to thank your people for their patience. I know everyone has been anxious to find out why the Council has requested your presence," Luke said, scooting his chair forward. His eyes flicked back and forth between her and Ash but gave no clues as to what his true thoughts were. When neither of them spoke, Luke continued, "I know that as rogues, it probably seems as if us Alphas are very removed from your plights, but that is far from the truth. Over the last few years, we have not been blind to the rates at which your people have grown, which I'm sure is as concerning for you as it is for us."

"Why would the Council think that?" Jade spoke up. "I understand why it's a bad thing for you. The more rogues there are, the higher the chance of some crossing into your territory, hunting on your land. But why would we care if the packs are kicking out more of their own?"

"Packs aren't the only ones that get into skirmishes with rogues. And in my experience, criminals don't tend to get along even with their own," Luke replied coolly, causing Jade's shoulders to stiffen in response. "As your numbers grow, life will continue to become more difficult for each of you.

"I'm assuming this is where the council comes in with a solution," Ash said, the mockery in his tone was well hidden, but Jade could swear she heard a little leaking through each word. If Luke heard the same, he chose to ignore it, nodding his head in response.

"One that will benefit everyone."

A scoff almost escaped Jade's throat before she turned it into a cough. Somehow, she was doubtful that the rogues would agree with him.

"Not only does the number of packless wolves increase every year, but the spaces you normally inhabit are becoming more and more crowded. Which has resulted in more shelter and food issues, and it is adding to the deaths of your people. Instead of having the rogues wander aimlessly once they have left their pack, we would have a set place for them to go, a place with plenty of territory and hunting grounds for each of you," Luke said. His voice was confident, but Jade watched warily as a shadow crossed Heather's face. Luke may have mastered the art of lying to people's faces, but his mate hadn't. She wanted to let her eyes slide over to Darren to see if he had a similar reaction as his mother, but she resisted. The ever-growing pit in her stomach was the only other proof she needed.

"Where did you have in mind?" Ash asked, feigning a look of interest passable enough to earn him an approving nod.

"Here," Luke answered as Johnathan stood and moved towards a map hanging on the wall. Jade watched as the Beta pointed towards the top of the map, her heart plummeting as she saw where his finger landed.

"You want to dump us in The Pits?" Jade blurted out the words before she could think better of it. "Yeah, I'm sure the Council doesn't have an issue abandoning all of their problems in a territory that is so undesirable that even you won't fight over it."

"What are you insinuating?" Johnathan asked, taking a threatening step forward, but Luke waved a dismissive hand.

"I would be offended by your accusation if I had expected anything else from you," he answered coolly. His tone fueled the flame beginning to burn within Jade's chest.

"It would only be offensive if it was an empty accusation, which it's not," Jade replied, doing her best to keep from

snapping. "There's a reason none of the packs made their home out there. It's literally as if the plains tried to turn into a swamp that freezes over every winter. We're all survivors, but how do you expect us to live in a place that has little to no shelter? Do you even know if there's anything to hunt out there?"

"Each pack sent scouts to ensure that the land would sustain the number of wolves that would potentially be living on it. Now that we have even a better idea of how many rogues there truly are, we are confident that it can become a new home for each of you," Luke said, but his attempt to reassure fell on deaf ears. It wasn't that what he said was a lie. In fact, Jade was certain that Luke meant every word he had said in the Council's defense, but that didn't mean it was true.

Against her better judgment, her eyes slid to where Darren sat. Unsurprisingly, his guarded eyes were already trained on her as he took in her reaction. Had he known about this plan? How could he not have warned her about it? She tried not to let the betrayal sink in too deeply; it didn't matter now. Besides, it couldn't really be a betrayal when it meant he had respected her wishes and left her alone.

"So, your plan would be for all the existing rogues and future ones to all live together? That could cause its own issues," Ash spoke up, drawing everyone's attention back to him. "After all, you were the one that brought up that even rogues don't always get along amongst ourselves."

"One of the many reasons we chose that territory was due to how spread out it is. We would allow the rogues' territory starting here," Johnathan said, pointing to the beginning of The Pits. "And we would include where it expands out to here," he said. Motioning his hand, he drew their eyes over the section above The Pits, where the land was broken up by water, turning

each section into its own tiny island. "We believe that by giving this specific territory that it will give rogues that have formed groups such as each of yours a chance to divide the area up amongst yourselves and still allow room for the lone wolves."

"In addition to the territory, I am willing to make an offer that the rest of the Council isn't providing," Luke said, holding out his hand as one of his guards handed him a plain-looking folder. "You may have wondered why we asked you all to be involved in our training or work alongside the pack, especially when it's a struggle for our people to get along. But it's all come down to this," he said, letting a dramatic silence descend on the room as he slowly opened the folder and withdrew two pieces of paper. His eyes locked on Jade's once more as he handed the documents to Darren, who stood and gently placed both in front of Jade. Their eyes met for the briefest of seconds, but in that second, Jade thought she saw something flash across his face as the papers settled on the table, but Jade couldn't distinguish it before he turned back to his chair. Shame? Sorrow? A warning? It was impossible to tell.

Jade didn't have time to wonder long. As she scanned the papers quickly, her mind became consumed with what filled them; each paper contained two columns listing its contents one after the other. With a sinking heart and bile stinging her throat, Jade tossed the documents onto the table again, unable to continue looking at them.

Names. They were a list of names, and she knew every single one of them.

"What is this?" she asked, the bile in her throat making her voice come out raspier than intended.

"That is a list of wolves we have observed during your group's stay here that have impressed us. We would like to offer

them a place within the Northwind Pack. We also have listed what position they will hold if they accept our offer. I trust you'll be able to pass along the message to each of the individuals listed there?" he said, raising a quizzical brow in a silent challenge.

It took everything within Jade to hold her tongue, one of her hands dug into her leg, but it gave her the will to choke out the necessary words.

"Of course."

"Great. Ash, with your group having just arrived, we will need more time to evaluate them, but I am certain we can work with you to narrow down a list for you as well," Luke said, turning his attention to Ash. The smile the rogue gave him sent goosebumps rising all along Jade's arms; his eyes grew a shade darker as his smile grew.

"I look forward to it."

Chapter 24

Darren

After his father had dismissed the rogues, Darren had followed suit, hurrying after them. If he was quick enough, he could reach Jade before she made it back to the Training Center. He'd seen her face when Luke had told them about the Council's proposal. She had tried to hide it, but he hadn't been blind to the betrayal she had felt. He couldn't blame her. He would have thought the same if he had been in her shoes, which is why she had to know the truth, even if it didn't change anything between them.

"Oof!" Darren grunted as he rounded a corner only to collide directly into Spencer, causing him to stumble back.

"Hey, watch it! You're not the only wolf walking here, you know," Spencer grumbled, recovering himself.

"Sorry, I was in a rush; I guess I didn't see you," Darren apologized, moving to go around the other wolf, but Spencer took a step in the same direction, successfully blocking his path.

"Whoa, slow down. What's chasing your tail? Today was the meeting with the rogues, right? That was all Dad could talk about last night. How did they take it?" he asked. Darren tried to not let his annoyance show; he didn't have time to waste. Even if it was the first time Spencer had willingly spoken to him without a hint of animosity. In fact, he was almost buzzing with excited energy. "They have to take the deal, right? I mean, they would be stupid not to. It would be an insult to just ignore the fact that the Council is willing to literally give them their own territory."

"I don't know what they'll decide yet. We just presented them with the offer today. They'll need time to think about it and talk with the rest of the rogues. I'm not sure all of them will be open to the idea of moving to the middle of nowhere," Darren answered before brushing past Spencer's shoulder to continue his mission.

"Yeah, but it's not like they have much of a choice. If they refuse, we can just force them to go. It will take a few extreme examples to convince the rest of them to listen, but it will be worth it," Spencer shrugged as he followed Darren's path. Darren's steps halted; his feet frozen in place as he turned his head to look at his friend.

"I can't believe you would say that," he said, slowly shaking his head, but he couldn't shake the cold dread that had seized his chest. "These are other wolves we're talking about. We are asking them to uproot their lives and maybe leave homes to move out of our way to make our lives easier, and you're ready to harm them over a little bit of land. Do you think we'd be jumping at a chance for the same offer?"

"Of course not!" Spencer exclaimed, indignation coating his words. "But this is about making sure our pack is safe! They're not like us. You keep acting like they are normal, but they're not. That's why no one wants them anymore. Everyone knows life as a rogue is hard, but they're the ones that chose to live that life. Whether they abandoned their pack or did something to get themselves kicked out," he finished with another casual shrug, as if they were discussing nothing more than the weather. He wasn't the first to think it, let alone say it out loud, but his words washed over Darren like an icy wave, knocking the air from his lungs while waking him up all at once. Had he sounded so callous when speaking of the rogues only

weeks ago? Maybe it was worse with so many rogues in their territory, or maybe he had just been deaf to it before. This time Spencer's words burned his own tongue as if he had swallowed a mouth full of acid.

"They didn't ask for this Spence, and if some of them did, it was probably because living with people like us was a more terrifying thought than being on their own," Darren choked out the words. He was unsure of where the words came from, but they continued pouring from his lips. Every doubt that had crossed his mind the last few weeks, every realization that had gone unspoken, was being pulled from him. "Did you ever think that maybe they aren't the ones that are screwed up? We're not better than them because we have a pack to support us. In fact, maybe having a pack is what holds us back. Everything we do is supposed to be about this pack and making sure that every choice we make strengthens us somehow, and it's exhausting! Maybe they don't have a home anymore, but they have more freedom than you or I ever will have," he said, the truth of his words lifting an unseen weight from his shoulders while sinking his heart at the same time. He had pitied the rogues for all they had lost. He'd thought his life a far more desirable one compared to theirs, but he saw the truth now. Yes, their life was difficult, probably more than he was even fully aware of, but they were free to live life away from other wolves' expectations, to live life for themselves.

Something he would never be able to do.

"What happened to you?" Spencer asked, staring at Darren with wide eyes. "You're the future Alpha, the future of this pack. You can't say things like that. You can't even think like that." A humorless laugh escaped Darren; the sound rose out of him of its own accord. There was a dark bitterness to it, something he

hadn't even known was within him. If he was honest, it scared him a little because he knew that once it was out in the open, once he acknowledged it, there would be no going back. Spencer must have heard it too. He took a step back, his eyes widening fearfully as if he didn't recognize the wolf in front of him. To be fair, Darren wasn't sure he recognized himself either.

"It's a little late for that now, don't you think?

Chapter 25

Jade

Fuming didn't even begin to express the torrent of emotions raging through Jade as she stormed out of the Northwind Packhouse, the papers crumpled in her clenched hand. It didn't help that Ash followed her step for step, his eyes boring into the side of her flushed face.

"I hate to say I told you so, but…." Ash trailed off with a casual shrug.

"Shut up," she snapped, drawing a chuckle from him.

"Your anger is misdirected. I'm not the one trying to banish our people to the middle of nowhere while stealing the best among us for himself," he said. "I bet you're not even on that list. He handpicked wolves he deemed worthy enough and is having you deliver the news, all while reminding you that you're worthless to him."

"I said shut up!" she yelled, her knuckles turning white as her grip tightened.

"Go on, prove me wrong. If your name is on that paper then I'll be quiet and leave you alone. Well, at least for the rest of the day," he said, prancing down the stairs beside her. Sunlight streamed in from the windows above flashing along his blonde locks, turning them a pure white. If only it could cleanse his black heart too.

She couldn't give him what he asked for. He was right. Not a single name listed on either paper was her own. It shouldn't have surprised her. Nothing Luke Power did should have at this

point, but even that thought couldn't erase the sting that blazed through her every time she thought of that stupid list.

"You can't do it, can you? Once again, Alpha Power has shown his true colors," Ash practically sang as they stepped through the double doors into the bright afternoon sun. Its warmth doing very little to cool Jade's boiling blood.

"As if you're any better, sitting there hanging on his every word. You licked his paws more than any of his own underlings ever could. I don't know how you can stand to look at yourself," she snarled as she stalked around the corner of the building. "No, I take it back; you're worse than he is. At least he's honest about what sick thoughts go on in his head. Hey-!" she let out a grunt as her back slammed into the brick wall, Ash's fingers digging into her arms like silver cuffs. Black tendrils snaked their way from his pupil through the rest of his empty blue eyes. That same darkness seemed to seep its way into Jade's veins, bathing her in its icy grip as it sent a shudder down her spine.

"Don't you dare compare me to them. Ever," he said, his usual icy eyes burned with anger as he stared into hers. "I'll admit my methods may not always be within the realms of what others might consider reasonable. But everything, every single thing that I've done, everything I'm about to do is so people like us can stop hiding. So that *you* can come out of hiding," he said, letting his arms fall to his side as he took a step back, allowing the breath Jade had been holding to tumble out of her. Running a hand through his hair, Ash closed his eyes and let out a sigh of his own, the dark tendrils retreating back to their place once he opened his eyes, but the tremble in his voice betrayed how close he was to losing his composure.

"You may hate me right now, but I'm just playing the game they created. The game that they are still running. You can either

be a pawn for them or become your own player, and I think we both know that you're no one's pawn."

"Stop acting like you know me! I'm not a pawn or a player in your stupid game. I'm not playing games with anyone. Not you, not Luke Power or any of the other Alphas," Jade said, pushing off of the wall to come face to face with him again. This time it was her eyes that were lit with an angry fire. "All of you sit around and lie to each other's faces. You act like you're willing to work with him, and he pretends to have a shred of respect for you; then the rest of the Council pretends to care about living peacefully with each other. But really, all of you are just waiting for the next chance to screw the others over. If that's what it means to be an Alpha, then I don't want any part of it," she said, but she had to pause as a harsh laugh burst out of Ash, his head rearing back with the force of it.

"But don't you see? You're already a part of it; we all are. You judge me for my deception, but I'm only as good as my teacher, and I learned from the best," he smirked, sending heat rising to Jade's face once again. "You can avoid it all you'd like, but we have more to lose than they do if we don't come out on top. Speaking of which…" he started, his usual calm demeanor settling over him once again as he began a slow meander, forcing Jade to trail along to hear him. "Have you told your *soulmate*?" He said the word as if it left a sourness behind on his tongue, "about your little secret?"

"Last time I checked who I've spoken to about my life isn't any of your business," she snapped, speeding up her step to catch up with him. Ash continued as if she hadn't spoken at all, maintaining his leisurely stride.

"Only two days left, and those will fly by. I'd think about spending some one-on-one time with him soon if I were you.

You wouldn't want something unfortunate happening before you have a chance to tell him yourself."

"Is that a threat?" Jade bristled. Darren was already in too deep when it came to her troubles; she didn't need Ash centering his crosshairs on him too.

Ash lifted his shoulders in a casual shrug, his hands sliding into his front pockets, looking as undisturbed as always.

"Take it however you'd like. The truth is that you need to figure out where you stand with him, without any of the lies you both keep telling yourselves. I'm just here to help you get there a little faster," he said, as his eyes slid to the side to glance down at her. Jade opened her mouth to whip out another retort, but she found herself biting her tongue. It didn't matter what she said or even how she said it. Whatever words she could come up with would only stoke the fire Ash was trying to spark, and she had zero doubts he would find a way to make her own words burn her.

They continued their path in tense silence. The only sound was their feet pounding into the pavement, each step dropping another weight on Jade's stiff shoulders. There was too much going on for her mind to wander beyond the issues in front of her, the crumpled papers in her hand and the foreboding presence that walked beside her. But her thoughts did wander. Each thought meandered down its own dark path. The Alphas' plan to remove the rogues, Ash's deception and manipulations, and her constant failures to the people who needed her the most. Each path would have been a worthy one to spend time going down. Each still required more from her, something that she was missing with them. But no matter how she tried to concentrate and keep her thoughts in check they all weaved their way to the same destination.

Darren Power.

Without him, Ash wouldn't have his newest form of ammunition. Without him, she would have been spending more time planning on how to handle Luke and anything he could throw her way. Instead, she caught herself wondering what was going through her mate's mind; could he truly be an ally, or was he all part of one of Luke's master plans? Could there ever be a real future for them, or was that a fantasy that she continued to entertain?

The sound of laughter broke through the dark cloud that had found its way into her head. She had been too deep in her own thoughts to notice that they had reached the courtyard outside of the Training Center. Morning classes were finished, which meant the trainees found themselves with an hour to spare. Most days, they entertained themselves by having lunch in the courtyard.

She could have found her friends even if she was blind and standing in a blizzard; their laughter rang off the bricks around them, drawing her eyes to their ragtag group. It didn't matter how many times she saw them; the pride that rose in her chest surprised her each time. Their original group of seven had swelled until the tiny corner they once had claimed was now overflowing with jokes, laughter, and games. And not just from their own wolves. Valery's sunny smile frequented the group every afternoon, and somehow, slowly but surely, she had convinced some of her own friends to join in the fun.

Luke Power may claim that he wanted peace between packs and rogues, but he had no idea what that looked like. But she did, and it was right in front of her.

"They almost look like they belong, don't they?" Ash spoke beside her, his own gaze drawn to the group. "But they don't. If

you don't show them where they belong, they'll be sucked into the lies the Council spews, just like everyone else. Don't let them take one more thing from you."

She didn't bother to turn as the click of Ash's shoes on cobblestone faded, his words haunting her more than his presence had.

Chapter 26

Darren

Feet pounding into the ground, Darren tried to not think about Spencer's stunned face or his father's inevitable disappointment when he discovered Darren's brief lapse of composure. In that moment, any possible consequences seemed insignificant, although Darren was sure he would regret not pausing to consider what he was about to do.

He didn't have to wonder where he would find his mate. Even if he hadn't had the light tug of the mate bond in his chest pulling him towards her, he still would have known where she would have gone to find her peace of mind. All he had to do was follow the sound of boisterous laughter.

There she was, standing just at the edge of the courtyard, with her back to him. She stood there, watching the other rogues as they laughed and joked with one another, but she didn't join them. Darren wanted to go to her, but something held him in place. Maybe it was the guilt slowly eating away at him that froze his feet to the ground, or maybe it was his father's voice in his head that screamed at him to forget the girl. Or maybe it was the light-haired rogue that stood at her side, whispering in her ear that made him hesitate.

Darren had been so focused on his relationship with Jade, or lack of it, that he hadn't stopped to consider that he might not be the only one vying for her attention. A surge of jealousy nearly knocked him off his feet as he watched Ash's hand flitter forward as if to latch onto Jade's, but at the last second, he pulled

back. The rogue stared down at their hands and the space between them for a single moment before turning away.

He should have stepped behind a tree, or at least looked away, but all of that was an afterthought as Ash's eyes connected with his. Darren wasn't sure what he expected from the other wolf, but it wasn't the slow smirk that crept up Ash's face or the playful wave he directed at Darren before casting one last glance at Jade.

Much to Darren's relief, Jade didn't turn to watch as Ash retreated. What could be going through her mind? He tried to reach out through the mate bond, but it yielded nothing to ease his or his wolf's anxieties.

All he could do was watch as Jade shook off whatever thoughts weighed heavy on her in that moment and steel herself as she moved forward, placing herself among the group, smiling as if she hadn't just received soul-sucking news. It was a perfect mask, well, nearly perfect. Darren didn't think that Jade was capable of real relaxation. She put on a good show for those around her. But every mask has its cracks, and all it took was an observant eye to find hers. Even with the worry lines in her face relaxed, there was still a wire of tension that held her spine in a stiff line, one hand still fisted around the crumpled papers.

As much as Darren enjoyed basking in the glow of his mate's smile, even her fake ones, he was starting to feel like some kind of stalker just standing on the sidelines. Forcing one foot in front of the other he found himself steadily moving towards her, his steps exuding a confidence he didn't possess.

"So, then he says, 'I always thought brutes of your size lacked the basic intelligence to comprehend anything but dismantling the tranquility of those who are unfortunate enough to endure a conversation with you.' And I said, 'Sorry sir, I'm

going to have to ask you to slow down. You had me until you said intelligence," Chris finished his story, laughter bursting from his lively audience. Even Jade allowed a chuckle to escape as well as a roll of her stormy eyes.

The joyous laughs died one by one as his presence was noticed. Light and mischief faded from their eyes and was replaced by a wariness all the way to open hostility. He tried to hide the wince he felt creeping up on him. After all of his efforts to win Jade over, he neglected to build any kind of bond with the crowd she surrounded herself with. A mistake he would have to attempt to rectify.

"Hey everyone," he greeted, cringing as his voice cracked at the end. "It should be a crime to have classes on a day this beautiful," he said, trying to recover whatever he could.

"Too bad there isn't someone who could make a law against it," a young red-headed male replied, giving Darren a pointed look. Darren would have laughed if he wasn't afraid of offending the rogues further. Did any of them really think he held that kind of power or any kind of power for that matter? Not as long as his father was Alpha.

He opened his mouth to reply, unsure of what he could say to ease the growing tension, but thankfully he didn't have to find the right response.

"Maybe one day," Jade answered for him, finally meeting his gaze. Whatever sharpness her words lacked, her eyes made up for. Lightning crackled through their storm cloud grey, sending shivers down his spine. He had thought on an occasion or two of how unfortunate it must be for any wolf that ended up on the receiving end of her wrath. Darren suspected he was about to discover just how unfortunate those wolves really were.

Just as quickly as she had summoned the electricity between them, Jade severed that connection by turning away. Her eyes darted over the group, her brows drawing together in confusion.

"You know what's strange…I haven't been pounced on yet. Where's Valery?" she asked, directing the question towards her friends.

"Don't know," Desert shrugged as he threw a glance around the group. "I haven't seen her at all today, actually."

"She's probably at the hospital," Darren blurted out before he had time to think better of it. "Her and Spencer's mom hasn't been well for the last few days, so she's in the pack hospital until she's back to a hundred percent. Valery probably wanted to be close to her." It wasn't a lie; their mom really had fallen ill and was at the hospital. They didn't need to know she was just one of the many that were currently under the pack doctors' care. Darren found himself swallowing the lump that formed in his throat from the thought of his ill packmates. It had only been days ago that Valery's mother had stood in the Training Center teaching trainees the local plants and herbs, and now all she could do was lay in a cramped hospital bed and hope that the pack doctors found a cure.

"Do you think she needs anything? I can bring her some fresh clothes," the small red-headed female, Lola, said, nothing but sincerity filling her wide eyes.

"I'll check up on her today and let you know. I'm sure she'll be happy to know that you guys were asking about her," he answered, plastering a reassuring smile on his face. The chime of a nearby clock signaled the start of a new hour, its high-pitched melody sending wolves pouring back into the building. Jade made a move to head towards the double doors, but the thought of her turning her back to him one more time was nearly

too much. Before he could stop himself, Darren's arm shot out, his hand latching onto her free hand.

"Wait- "he said, his voice dying in his throat as her eyes shot back to his, nearly swallowing him in the tempest that rage within them. "Jade, can I talk with you?"

A few of her friends paused their progress to hang back, their eyes laser-focused on where his hand was latched onto Jade's. She didn't need their protection, though, not around him at least. Jade must have had the same thought because she dismissed them with a small jerk of her head, not bothering to take her eyes off of Darren's as her friends' hesitant footsteps faded.

"I think we've both said enough at this point, don't you?" she said, but she didn't shake his hand off. That was something, at least.

"Not nearly enough," he answered. Even with his eyes focused on hers, his skin still burned from the heated stares from his lingering packmates. "I'm sorry I didn't have time to warn you about my father's plan. I only found out just before the meeting started. He likes to be the one in complete control, which means keeping everyone else on their toes."

"It's fine, I get it. I don't need you to run and tell me everything your daddy does. You don't owe me anything," she said, but her eyes flashed with a fire that threatened to scorch Darren and the very stones he stood on. "It's not like I expect you to stand up to an all-powerful Alpha; that would be far too much to ask of anyone. I mean, it's not like you have your own conscience to worry about," she continued, finally jerking her hand out of his hold.

All Darren could do was stare in shock for a moment, letting her words wriggle their way into his brain and settle in. Then he did something that he definitely should not have.

He laughed.

It wasn't a chuckle or giggle, although those would have been embarrassing enough on their own. No, this was a full-body, tears leaking out of the eyes, impossible to hold back kind of laugh.

He knew how crazy he must have looked; it felt insane even to him, but none of that could quell the laughter that continued to bubble up. He didn't have to wonder about what Jade must have thought about his outburst; her confusion was written plainly across her face.

"I...I don't understand what's so funny?" she asked, narrowing her eyes as he doubled over with a final chortle. Standing up straight, he ran a hand through his hair, wiping away the last stray tears that found their way out of his eyes.

"I'm sorry, it's not funny; none of this is. I just..."

"You just what?" she snapped, not bothering to mask her growing irritation.

"I'm happy. I'm happy that you're angry with me," he said, the words sounding bizarre even to him.

"You're happy that I'm angry?" Jade repeated, raising a skeptical brow. "Why in the world is that something to laugh about?" she asked. Darren shrugged, not trying to dim his smile even slightly.

"I guess because if you're angry, it means that you still care about what I do. Maybe about me even," he answered. The fire in Jade's eyes dimmed, and her face softened.

"Just because we're not right for each other doesn't mean that I don't care," she said, lowering her voice and her eyes,

some of her dark hair falling loose from her braid. Darren was unsure if it was him or his wolf that led his hand forward to brush the loose hair back. It didn't matter which one directed it, not when they both wanted the same thing. Her eyes shot back to his at his touch, causing goosebumps to rise along his skin as Darren held back a shudder.

"Can I show you something?"

Chapter 27

Jade

Afternoon sunlight filtered through the evergreens' branches and danced off of the head of blonde hair that walked just ahead of her, his hand still gently cradling hers as he guided her through the dense forest floor. It was times like this that Jade could almost forget that she was far from home, surrounded by enemies.

Almost.

"Where are we going?" Jade asked, allowing Darren to help her over a fallen tree, ignoring the electricity that zinged through her fingertips every time his hand brushed hers.

Darren brought a finger up to his lips, signaling her to be quiet, a playful grin lighting up his face.

"Shh, you don't want to scare them off," he whispered, nodding towards the top of the hill they were working their way up.

Jade wanted to ask what exactly she was in danger of scaring off, but she decided against it. Darren's eyes sparkled with an excitement that Jade hardly remembered feeling for herself. Simply watching his anticipation filled her with a kind of anxious buzz, that kind that made her want to see what would happen next.

They continued walking up the nonexistent path, away from Darren's packmates and her friends, away from the whispers and stares, away from Ash and Luke Power with their games and threats. The higher they climbed, the taller the trees grew, the

space between them growing thinner and thinner. For the first time they were completely alone.

"Just a few more steps," Darren whispered as he pulled himself up the small wall that a rock created in front of them. He pulled himself up in one swift pull, gracefully swinging his legs up as well. Turning around, he leaned down and offered her his hand once again. This time she ignored his offering. Finding her own handholds, she leapt off the ground with enough force to bounce off the boulder to her side and swing herself up beside him. She gave him a playful smirk as he looked her up and down.

"Show-off," he muttered, rolling his eyes forcing a small laugh from her. Looking back down their path, Jade let out a breath; the view was beautiful. They were just above the treeline, giving them a view down the whole valley.

"I see why you like it up here," Jade said, surveying the view before her.

"Yeah, it is pretty breathtaking up here, but that's not why I come up here," Darren said. Placing his hands on both her shoulders, he turned her completely around. "This is why I come here."

A breath caught in Jade's throat at the sight before her. Maybe twenty feet below them, Jade watched as sunlight sparkled off of a lake of water so clear Jade could see the bottom of it. Moss-covered boulders lined its edge just beneath where they stood. Across the lake, on the opposite shore, a large moose walked out of the forest, delicate vines dangling from his antlers, nature's way of crowning the magnificent creature. Waterbirds flitted across the lake's surface, ducking their heads under the water to nibble on the occasional plant or two.

"It's incredible," Jade whispered, watching the scene before her in awe.

"We can go closer if you'd like," Darren said. Jade nodded and followed him down a careful path to the mossy rocks below. The moss was spongy under the soles of her shoes and a little damp as she found a seat on it, but she didn't care; it gave her the perfect seat to watch nature unfold in front of her. Darren took a seat beside her at the water's edge, watching closely as the moose made his way into the water, undeterred by the cool temperatures or their presence.

"They seem happy, don't they?" Darren asked as they watched the moose wade. "Life is so simple for them. They don't have to wonder about tomorrow or where they will end up. They're enough just as they are. They don't' have to pretend to be anyone they aren't. Kind of like you," he said, turning his head to look at her. Jade let out a scoff and kept her gaze on a pair of geese that decided to drift closer to where they were seated.

"You hardly know me."

"I know that you don't pretend to be someone you aren't just because it might make others uncomfortable. If you did, you wouldn't have been in that meeting today. You wouldn't have had so many wolves see you for what you are, a leader," he said, sounding a little too much like Ash the longer he spoke. Darren shook his head, turning back to the lake. "I wish I was more like you."

"No, you don't. There's so much you don't know about me. Things that aren't…good," Jade said, tossing a loose pebble into the water. She watched as the water rippled out from the disturbance, each ring growing bigger and bigger, just like her. Everywhere she went, pain and confusion seemed to just spread to anyone who came in contact with her.

"But you aren't pretending like those parts of you don't exist. That's what makes you a good person," Darren continued his thought, resting his hand behind him.

A long silence stretched between them, each of them wrapped up in their own thoughts. It was peaceful, but it wasn't meant to last.

"Did you know Ash before you came here?" Darren's question shattered any kind of serenity that she had gained during their hike. "It's okay if so," he quickly followed up as he watched the color drain from her face. "It's just that you two seem…familiar with each other. The way he looks at you makes it seem as if you're not strangers."

Of course, he caught on. Her mate was too observant for his own good.

"We have…history," was all she could choke out.

"You don't seem to get along with him."

"We don't," she nearly snapped. He wasn't the one she was annoyed with, though. It wasn't really his fault. None of it was.

"Does he want to get…along with you?" he hesitated as he asked the question as if he were uncertain if he wanted to even speak the words. She wished he hadn't. Somehow, even when Ash wasn't there physically, he had found a way to infect what could have been a perfect moment with his presence. Sure, it was only a shadow of him, as easily banished as he was summoned, but that wasn't the point. The point was that he was there at all. The point was that her mate had noticed his advances, forcing Jade to relive memories she would have rathered kept under lock and key.

"There was a time when we were close. I trusted him more than I should have. It was before I'd met the others, back when I was truly alone. I think there's a part of him that misses that

time," she answered honestly. Silence stretched between them, wrapping its tendrils around Jade's tongue, holding back the words she really needed to say.

Now was the perfect time. She could tell him about her past, about what she really was, before Ash had a chance to. Maybe he wouldn't want to run screaming; maybe he could look past what no one else could.

"I'll try to talk to my father when I get back; I should have stood up to him earlier. I'm sorry," Darren said, finally breaking the silence. His eyes bored into the side of her face, but she couldn't bring herself to look at him. Instead, she watched as low flying birds dipped beneath the trees and wondered what it would be like to fly away from it all.

"There's nothing to forgive, Darren; like I said, you don't owe me anything."

"Maybe not, but I owe it to myself. I don't think I'd be able to look myself in the mirror again if I didn't at least try to help," he said, looking back out over the water.

That was where they were different. After today Darren would go out into the world and try to make a difference. He'd rise up like the hero in a fairytale and save the day, or at least try to. And she'd still be here, wrapped in the dark secrets and lies that had haunted her for years.

Jade didn't try to respond. She didn't have the words left in her to, not the right ones at least. Ash had won. He had known that she would never be able to be honest with anyone again, not even her mate.

Chapter 28

Darren

The halls of the packhouse seemed unusually long as Darren strode down them; perhaps it was because he dreaded who or what he would find on the other side of it. Nothing good ever came from emergency meetings with Luke Power.

His father's office door was already propped open as other members of the Northwind Pack council filed in one by one until each seat in the room was filled and the door shut behind them. Looking around the room, Darren saw many familiar faces, which would have been comforting in any other scenario. Here, it meant something big was going down. He tried to mask his unease as he surveyed the room, trying to gauge the group's emotions. One by one, each wolf met his gaze, his dread reflected in each of their eyes. As always, Luke's chair was at the head of the table. He stood as he watched the group find their seats. His very stance was commanding; it demanded respect from any who laid eyes on him. There was no doubt in anyone's mind that he was the epitome of strength, a perfect picture of a true leader, an Alpha. But not even that strength could hide the heaviness that weighed on the room, Luke's gaze stern but tired as he looked over the group he had gathered. Something was wrong, and they all knew it, but no one raised the question. Instead, they sat in silence, watching their leader for a sign.

Luke let them stew in the quiet unrest, watching them shift uncomfortably in their seats before finally standing. Resting his

hands on the table in front of him, his eyes narrowed as he scrutinized the group before him.

"I've called you all here with urgency today, an urgency that I have not felt in many years," Luke began. If he hadn't had the complete attention of every wolf before, he certainly had it with his following words. "What I am about to say is of the utmost secrecy. No one must breathe a word of it outside of this room or with anyone not in this room now," he said, the weight of his command washing over them. Even if they had wanted to, it would be nearly impossible to break the order. Luke paused for a moment, waiting for a murmur of, 'Yes, Alpha,' to escape their mouths before continuing.

"Our pack is in great danger, a danger I fear that I may have invited into our midst. Many of you who haven't heard it directly from me have already begun to hear the rumors circulating among our people. Our she-wolves are under attack. Every day more and more of our females are falling ill, and until this moment, we had very little information to go off of. Dr. Brown is here to explain our findings," he said, gesturing to the pack doctor, a thin man with silver hair who looked as if he rarely saw the sun. Taking his cue, Dr. Brown stood and faced the group, his hands clutching a clipboard so firmly that his knuckles paled. It would not be good news that he brought them.

"Currently, we have nearly twenty-seven females ranging in ages from fourteen to forty-five that have been admitted with varying levels of the following symptoms. Headaches, nausea, vomiting, exhaustion, and ultimately unconsciousness that we are unable to wake them from," Dr. Brown said. His matter-of-fact tone grated on Darren's nerves as he spewed out the numbers. Was it that simple to really condense a person into nothing more than lists and numbers? He pushed his anger

down. The doctor was simply doing his job, was what he told himself, but he kept the image of the girl from the hospital close in his mind's eye as he listened.

"We believe those numbers will continue to grow as we are unable to determine how it is spread. But we figured out a crucial piece of information today," he continued, pausing for dramatic effect. "We have discovered the origin of where all of them have fallen ill so far. The Training Center."

A murmur went up among the group, and Darren felt his breath catch in his throat, his mind racing with his own thoughts and his packmates' anxiety that leaked through the packlink into his own. There wasn't a single wolf in the pack that didn't send their children to the Training Center. It was one of the most guarded buildings in their territory. If their she-wolves weren't safe there, was there anywhere they could protect them?

"How long has this been going on?" one of the seniors asked, his voice cracking with either age or fear, Darren was unsure of which.

"The first case was nearly three and a half weeks ago," Dr. Brown answered, his eyes darting towards Luke uncertainly as if he was unsure if he should continue. He didn't need to question, though, as everyone knew what his next words would have been. Four weeks, that's how long the rogues had been in their territory, training alongside their wolves. How long Jade had been there.

Darren knew it was true the moment his father's eyes met his. Their blue had turned steely as he watched the realization cross Darren's face. He didn't need his father to speak to know the message he wanted his son to understand, that once again Luke had been right, and Darren had been the fool.

"But none of the rogue she-wolves are sick, right?" one of the warriors asked. "Are we sure that they have anything to do with our own falling ill?"

"They are the only common link between all of the patients," Dr. Brown answered. "It's most likely some disease that they carry from the wild, one their bodies may have found some resilience against. Whether they know it or not, I am certain they are what brought this fatality to our people."

"Fatal?" I thought no one had died from it, just continued to sleep?" Darren asked, finding his voice.

"That was true, until this afternoon," Luke said, stepping forward, once again taking control of the conversation. "Only an hour ago, we lost two of the she-wolves that were battling it. Dr. Brown and I will inform their families after this meeting is over."

Darren could hardly fight the bile that rose up in his throat, coating his tongue in its stinging acid. He had just been there. He had walked by their doors, looked in on them, and sat beside beds. How could any have taken a turn for the worse in such a short time?

"With this new information, we will be closing down the Training Center until further notice," Luke continued, his voice breaking through the dark fog that had settled over. "I have a meeting with the Alpha Council tonight; we will decide what to do with the rogues in light of this new threat."

"And what of the sick wolves?" another elder asked. His face twisted in pain shared by all in the room. Sighing, Luke let his features soften for a moment as he took in the uncertainty around him. He seemed to be at a loss of words for a moment before his mate, Heather, took his hand in her own. Looking down at their joined hands, Luke's thumb moved gently over her

knuckles. It was such a simple gesture, one that Darren found himself aching for after he watched his parents together.

"Pray for them. Ask the Goddesses to grant us the strength to overpower this enemy," Luke finally answered, his words a comfort to neither him nor the rest of the wolves in front of him.

Slowly, almost cautiously, the room's occupants began standing from their chairs and paying their respect to their Alpha and Luna before trudging out of the room. Each carried a new weight on their shoulders that had not been there earlier. Darren remained seated and waited for the other wolves to shuffle out of the room, leaving him, his mother, and his father. Pushing up from his chair, he found himself standing in front of his parents, his mouth dry and his tongue empty of any of the words he had rehearsed a thousand times.

Sensing his hesitation, Heather rose from her seat. She brushed softly by her son, resting her hand on his shoulder in passing, an offering of her silent comfort before disappearing from the room as well, the door clicking closed behind her. At last, only he and Luke remained in the room, but Darren found himself wondering if it was his father or his Alpha he would find there.

Letting out a long sigh Luke allowed himself to fall into his chair, gesturing for Darren to take the seat nearest him. They both sat in the silence for a moment allowing their thoughts to run rampant in the only quiet moment they might know for the rest of that day.

"I said that girl would be trouble," Luke said, his voice gruff from a full day of speaking. "I don't know how she is involved in this, Darren, but there is little more that I've been certain of. Somehow she is killing my pack, and I won't allow it."

"You don't know that," Darren said, the sound coming out weaker than he had intended, earning a scoff from his father.

"You're still allowing your desire to see good blind you to the reality in front of you. That girl holds some kind of power, a darkness that allows her to gain the allegiance of our enemies. I can sense it within her. We need to find out what it is. She will be the key to ending all of this, and you need to be more vigilant than ever. I hear she's taken a liking to you. That's good. We can use that as long as you can maintain your wits around her," Luke said, a plan already forming in his mind.

"I thought you wanted me to stay away from her," Darren replied, reigning in his frustrations. They would only serve to make this conversation more difficult than it needed to be. But even with his efforts, based on Luke's narrowed eyes, he must have let enough of it seep into his words.

"I know what I said before we had wolves under our protection dying, but things change. Now I need you to find out whatever you can, do whatever it takes to get what we need from her."

"You don't know what you are asking of me," Darren said as he stared at a water ring on the table near his hand, focusing on anything to avoid having to see Luke's reaction.

"What I'm asking of you? Son, all I'm asking you to do is do your part to save your pack. All I want you to do is grow a backbone and stand up to those strays. It's not like I'm asking you to kill the bitch; just use her infatuation with you to get me some information. This pack is your priority, Darren, not whatever sense of honor you think you're protecting. You will find out what she knows, do you understand?" Luke asked, but they both knew that there was no real question in there. Darren knew what he wanted from him, and any other time, for any

other request he would have given it but not when it came to Jade. Not this time.

Luke's gaze bored into the side of his face as he continued staring at the tabletop, his jaw clenched shut. He wasn't able to give his father the answer he wanted, but he wasn't about to open his mouth and dig himself a grave. Silence couldn't save him from the anger either, though; it rolled off of Luke in waves, slamming into Darren, but it only encouraged him to hold his tongue.

"I never would have guessed my own son would have been taken down by a few insignificant rogues. And without so much as a single wound to show for it," Luke sneered, his hand gripping the back of Darren's chair, supporting himself as he leaned in. His hot breath washed over Darren's cheek, droplets of spit clinging to his skin. Still, his eyes remained unflinching and steadfastly forward.

A snarl escaped Luke's teeth, pushing off the chair making it rock slightly. He towered over where Darren remained seated; the composed Alpha from before had completely disappeared.

"Pathetic," he breathed out the word as, striding for the door, his anger surpassing anything Darren had seen before. He should have kept quiet. He should have held his tongue a little longer until his father's footsteps had faded. Until he could no longer feel the coals of his own anger smoldering in his belly.

But he didn't.

Listening to his father's footsteps snap across the wooden floor as they took him further away from the truth. At that moment, something inside of him rose up, and whatever walls Darren had in place cracked.

"She's my mate," he called over his shoulder, and the footsteps paused.

Chapter 29

Luke

For the first time in days, Luke Power's mind was blank. All the thoughts dancing around non-stop were emptied out by three little words.

She's my mate.

"What do you mean, she's your mate?" he asked, each word enunciated as they were dragged from his lips. He didn't turn around, but he imagined his son's eyes were wide as saucers as they bored into Luke's back.

"I think you know what it means," Darren said, nearly whispering his response. Spoken like a coward.

"No, I don't understand," Luke said, finally turning to face his son. "I don't understand how my son could be stupid enough to get caught up in some pretty girl's web. Not only that but that you would be foolish enough to believe that you would mean anything to her beyond just another way to humiliate me."

Luke had known the girl was manipulative, but clearly, he had underestimated her skills. She must have had her hooks in deeper than he had thought to convince Darren there was a cosmic connection between them.

"I know you don't trust her, but she hasn't done anything to take advantage of our bond. Plus-"

"Of course, you're defending her. I don't know why I would expect anything else at this point. Tell me, do you pull these stunts just to punish me, or is there some other satisfaction you gain from it?"

"How do you make me finding my mate into an attack against you?" Darren asked, finally finding his voice. "In fact, how do you find a way to make everything I do about you?"

"Because it is!" Luke yelled, embracing his wolf's anger along with his own as they rose together. "Everything you do impacts this pack, which means it impacts me. Just because you refuse to accept your responsibilities doesn't mean they don't exist. Every wolf that you open yourself up to is not only a potential threat to you but to the safety of this entire pack."

"Jade isn't a threat to you!" Darren replied, his own voice rising to a yell which caused Luke's anger to smolder in his chest. "You're the one that brought the rogues here, and you're the one that said you wanted me to find the ones that could help strengthen the pack. Well, I'm telling you Jade could be one of those wolves."

Luke didn't try to hold back the bitter laugh that escaped him, but he did choose to ignore the way his son flinched at the sound.

"Let me guess, you think she'd be a perfect Luna? Just because she's shown a strong front a couple of times and convinced a few flea-ridden brutes that she's a leader does not mean she has what it takes to be your Luna."

"How would you know? You're hostile every moment that she's around. Why would she trust you enough to show you what she's capable of?" Darren said, his knuckles white as he gripped the back of the chair. "You're the one that is creating your own enemies."

The smoldering anger turned into a raging fire that blazed away any restraint Luke had held onto. His wolf surged forward, stopping just beneath the surface.

"If you still believe that, then you are more naive than I thought. Maybe I was wrong; maybe she should be the Alpha, and you can be her Luna," he sneered before turning on his foot and storming out of the room, leaving Darren to stew in the mess he had created.

Where had it all gone wrong? Had Luke not been present enough in his son's life? Too soft or too harsh? Either way, it was clear that Darren was not the person he had thought he was, and Luke was sure of one thing.

It was that girl's fault.

Luke hardly noticed anything as he strode through the hall until he reached his private room, the door slamming behind him as he entered his safe haven.

His shoulders shook with a rage that he could barely contain. His vision blurred along the edges as his wolf's fury bled into this own. Without a single thought of what he was doing, he grabbed a vase off the dresser and threw it across the room, the sound of shattering glass doing little to soothe him.

His head whipped to the right as a soft rustling broke through his senses. With just that look, he felt the haze lifting from his mind as his eyes locked on the blonde hair and wide blue eyes that stared back at him. With a grace he had only seen her possess, she glided slowly across the room to him, a silent question in her eyes.

"I don't understand that boy, Heather," he said, his voice not entirely his own with his wolf still close to the surface. "He has been raised in one of the most powerful packs on this continent. He's grown up with some of the best training available. One day he'll be handed this pack on a silver platter and all the power that comes with it, and yet he's willing to

throw it all away over a girl. Oh, and not just any girl, that rogue mutt that has found every way possible to be a thorn in my side."

Heather's confused frown drew a sigh from him, his shoulders releasing some of their tension as her hand landed on his arm.

"Maybe you just need to have more faith in him. He's not a child anymore, you know," Heather said, her voice playing in his mind, but he was already shaking his head.

"But he is a child, and he's proven that today. I thought I knew my own son, but I'm not sure I do anymore."

Chapter 30

Jade

Once again, far too soon, Jade found herself putting as much space between herself and Darren and his perfect, gentle soul. Only this time, her instincts screamed for her to turn around, to go back to his embrace. Back to where, even if it was only for a moment, she could pretend everything was going to be alright.

In reality, everything was far from alright. She had two days before Ash made good on this threat to reveal her past, which she had little doubt he would most certainly do, despite the fact she had already sent Darren packing. She had no doubt that it had been a necessary move, if not to protect him, then to at least keep his rose-tinted view in place a little longer. Just because she saw the unspeakable around them didn't mean that he needed to.

There should have had plenty to occupy her mind away from thoughts of Darren and everything that came with him. Especially since Alpha Power had announced that the Training Center would be closed until further notice, leaving all the rogues free to congregate together, their anxious speculations filling the air around her.

"The whispers among the packwolves are growing louder; soon, they will be tired of waiting for us to give them what they want. We need to get out of here before Alpha Power, or the rest of the council does something drastic," old Malcolm said, his words causing others to nod their heads in agreement.

"Why are we always the ones to run? I say we strike them before they have the chance. If we crush them now, then they

will think twice before following us," Aiden countered. "Ash and his followers certainly aren't tucking their tails between their legs and cowering down. I say we fight with them." A small cheer went up amongst some of the younger males, the energy in the room taking a dangerous turn.

"What about our pups?" a she-wolf asked, her mate pulling her in close. "They still have all of the pups that we handed over. We have to get them back before we do anything."

"It's not our fault if you were stupid enough to put your children in their hands. There's no time for the rest of us to wait for you to fix your mistake," Aiden sneered, stoking the raging emotions of the group.

"No one is doing anything yet," Jade said, her voice lost in the uproar.

Their anger and panic swirled around her like water rising within, seeping into the cracks she hadn't guarded enough. They spun around and around, threatening to sweep her away as they mixed with the memories of the past two days.

He would never be able to look at you if he knew the truth.

What even was the truth anymore? Lies had been her bread and butter for nearly her entire life; would she even know the truth when she needed it?

Run!

They should run; it was an art all of them were versed in. It was the one thing that kept them alive. But there had to be more out there than just running from one enemy to the next, right?

Our only way out is to find the root of it and choke it out.

Find the root.

Something in Ash's words struck her, dulling the roar of voices in her ears as if she was submerged underwater. Her body moved forward on its own, her limbs not her own yet her mind

was as clear as it had ever been. Calmly, every step deliberate she moved her way to the center of the room. Wolves moved aside as she came close to them; their eyes went wide, and arguments halted with one look at her. As she reached the thickest part of the crowded warehouse, the bickering had subsided to a soft buzz, easily silenced with a single word.

"Quiet!"

Anyone who hadn't had their eyes trained on her already moved them to her then, a hush falling over the group. Their words had died down, but the electrifying energy still crackled around them, coursing through each of their bodies into Jade, fueling the fire that was smoldering in her belly.

"No one, and I mean no one is doing anything yet," Jade said, her voice low enough that everyone had to remain silent to hear her. "I'm going to go talk to Alpha Power and get us some answers. Once I get back, *then* we can decide what to do. Desert will come with me; Kyler and Chelsea are in charge while I'm gone. Everyone stick close for now; the pack has been antsy lately, and we don't need any unnecessary brawls right now."

A murmur of understanding went up from most of the group except for a few individuals whose glares deepened. Aiden was one of them, his lips pressed firmly together, his hands clenching and unclenching at his side.

"You know Power isn't going to give anything away. Why are you wasting your time with this?" he asked, towering over her. "If you're not willing to go on the offense, at least get these people out of here."

"And what about their children we would be leaving behind? At least let me find out what I can; I will make sure that everyone is safe," Jade replied, holding his gaze as he glared down. His eyes turned yellow at the very edges but not quite

making the full change. There was a lot of anger underneath the surface, waiting to bubble up and over until it filled him completely, and there were few things more dangerous than an angry wolf.

"Will you, though? When I first came here, I stayed because it was clear that you not only cared about these people but that you were actually capable of helping them. But I've gotta say, lately you seem distracted. And a distracted Alpha is a weak one. So, are you going to continue letting pack mongrels distract you, or are you going to save these people?" Aiden asked, his eyes scrutinizing every blink of her eyes or twitch of her cheek. Judgment shone through clearly, but what that kind of judgment would he cast on her?

"I don't take the trust you've placed in me lightly, Aiden, but we need to do this before any decisions are made. Give me two hours, and then if you want to leave, I will personally help each of you and everyone else get out of this place," she said, holding firm even when his eyes remained hard, but their yellowish hue faded away, leaving behind the man, a man that could hear reason.

"Fine," he snapped. "You better send a prayer up to the Goddesses, though, that you know what you're doing." Spinning on his heel, he strode away, allowing Jade to relax her own shoulders. His words threatened to haunt her as they still echoed in her ears, but she banished them before they could nestle into her brain permanently. He was right, a distracted Alpha was a weak one, and her people needed to see strength in that moment.

Walking up beside her, Desert watched Aiden's retreating back alongside her, letting her sit with her thoughts for only a few seconds before breaking the silence.

"You ready?"

"Let's get this over with," she sighed, painfully aware of the eyes that followed their advance to the doors, like tiny pinpricks all over her skin. Aiden wasn't the only one who thought she was wasting precious time. Maybe it would be wise to retreat at the first sign of unrest, but she couldn't leave without giving Luke Power one final chance, to give Darren another chance to prove all of them wrong.

Desert was quiet as they walked side by side down the dirt path, probably consumed with his own thoughts, leaving her unsure if she was grateful for the silence. It meant that she had a moment free of his probing. But it also meant she was left nearly alone with her thoughts, which were too many and too few all at once.

How in just a few short weeks had her life come to this? Where was the quiet, lonely life she'd once had? Now it felt as if she couldn't turn around without seeing another friendly face or a new enemy. Everything about her life had become...full. Full of new friends, nights overflowing with laughter, back-breaking responsibilities, and ample amounts of headaches and heartache. Was that how it was for the Northwind Pack as well?

"You know Aiden is right about you being distracted lately. It seems as if you're far away, and there's little that can bring you back, and it's not only the issues with Ash or Luke Power. What's going on, Jade?" he asked, finally shattering the silence between them. Of course, he was right, but it didn't soothe the sting behind his meaning. She was failing, not only as their leader but as a friend. She had accused Darren of being ashamed of the bond between them, yet those closest to her were still in the dark about the turmoil she faced.

"Do you believe in soulmates? I mean for everyone, not just for people like Lola and Chris," she asked, watching poofs of

dust swirl around her feet with every step. Much like the thoughts that flew away from her every time she got close enough to touch them. "Are they really the one and only perfect match for you? If that's true, would you do whatever was needed to be with them, even if it meant giving up who you were?"

"I don't know if I've ever thought much about it," Desert said, mulling over her questions, a seriousness clouding his face. "I suppose that if we were really meant to be together, then they wouldn't ask me to sacrifice any part of myself. Or maybe I wouldn't mind giving up those parts, not if we were truly made for each other."

"I see," Jade said, watching the dirt turn to pavement under her feet. There most certainly would be sacrifices for her to choose Darren. Ash had been right; she could never be a Luna. That was who Darren needed at his side, and that title encompassed all the parts of her that would be impossible to let go of.

Desert didn't press for any clarification even though she had ignored his initial question, which she was grateful for as they came upon the packhouse. Now was the time to put all thoughts of soulmates, fickle Goddesses, and future Alphas in a dark corner. She only had room for what she would say to Luke Power to convince him to give up his secrets.

Jade should have known something was wrong when the loud knock on the front door of the building was received with no answer besides the door creaking open at her touch. Greeted by an unexpected emptiness, Jade exchanged a wary look with Desert before stepping over the threshold. The windowless hall was just as silent as the rest of the house; a few lights lined it, giving it a much more ominous aura than it should have had for it being the middle of the day.

Unwilling to break the stillness, Jade made her footsteps as soft as if she were creeping up on a deer on the forest floor. Somehow, the low creak of wooden floorboards seemed far louder than any snapping of twigs or rustling of fallen leaves. When they reached the familiar wooden door leading to Alpha Power's office, Jade wasn't surprised to see it cracked open, allowing more light to filter into the hall. What she was surprised to hear was voices coming from the room.

Although it may have been amoral, Jade found herself signaling Desert to slow his pace as they drew closer to the voices, close enough for them to become clear.

"And what news of this epidemic do you have for us, Alpha Griffin?" an unfamiliar voice asked, static crackling at the end of his words. Creeping closer enough to peer through the sliver of an opening, Jade saw Alpha Power sitting with his back to his desk as well as the door. The large windows behind him no longer reflected the outside world. Instead, seven screens displayed the faces of seven different men, all varying in age and appearance. Even through the screens, they held the same authority in every flick of their eyes and breath they exhaled.

The Alpha Council

"It is the same for us here in the Stonehill Pack," one of the faces said, "the number of ill increases daily, and so far, there has been a zero-recovery rate."

"That's three packs now that have reported the exact same disease," another one growled. "How can it spread from pack to pack with the limited contact these packs have had?"

"The only logical tie is the rouges. I knew something like this would happen by inviting them into our lands, and now they will be the death of us," an older wolf snarled, banging a hand on the desk in front of him. A few of the others chimed in their

agreements as he continued. "This is unlike anything we've ever encountered before, and it's fitting that it should happen when we are conducting the most unheard-of experiment in our history."

Illness? Perhaps that's why the packs had been so on edge as of late, but Jade hadn't seen any sign of sickness among the other rogues. How had she missed something so vital that it would have the whole Alpha Council in a tizzy?

"Whether this is the doing of these criminals or not, it's clear that this idea of ours has failed. It's time to bring it to an end. I trust that you all are prepared for the next step?" a silver-haired Alpha asked, his voice sending chills down Jade's spine.

"Are you certain it's time for that, Alpha Archer?" Luke spoke up, his voice gravelly from his silence. "Northwind suffers as much as anyone in these times, but do we not fear the repercussions of this plan? No reasonable wolf parts with their own child without a fight."

"Since when do we describe rogues as reasonable?" a young dark-eyed Alpha scoffed, earning a few chuckles from the others.

What an odd thing, Jade thought as she viewed the gathering, *for Alpha Power to be the sound of reason within any group.*

"We don't, but the rogues have not been quiet and are hardly cooperative. I fear anything involving their pups at this point will only strengthen their bonds unless we break those first," Luke countered, wiping the smiles from their lips as shadows fell over their faces again.

"You may be right, Alpha Power, but I fear we no longer have time for that. We've each handled unruly wolves before; these will be no different," Alpha Archer said. Their words

slowly sank into Jade's bones, fearing that she knew what plan their words hinted at. If so, it would be far worse than any whisperings that could have been uttered.

"We've wasted enough time. I call for a vote," Alpha Griffin said.

"Fine, all-in favor of moving forward with the plan show so by raise of hand," Alpha Archer said, his own hand going up. One by one, six hands were raised, only two remained at their sides, Alpha Power's and a quiet middle-aged wolf the odd ones out.

"Alright, starting tomorrow, we move forward with the plan. All of us," Archer continued, a clear jab at the opposed ones. "Alone we are strong; together we will prevail."

"Together we will prevail," was echoed by the rest of the group. Blackness claimed each monitor until none were lit, leaving Luke with his thoughts and Jade still in the dark.

"You can't tell me that you seriously plan on doing this," another voice spoke up in the room, the small opening keeping them hidden from Jade's view. She didn't need to see their face to know who the voice belonged to.

Darren

"I'm not left with a choice; the vote is final," Luke answered, but his voice held no apology or sorrow. He may have voted against whatever their plan but not for any sense of compassion on his part. "We move forward along with the rest of the council."

"How can you tear children away from their parents? If we do this, we'll be worse than anything we've ever feared from them. If you do this now, we lose any chance of peace between us. This might as well be a declaration of war," Darren argued, his voice rising until he was yelling. Jade felt the pressure of

Desert's hand on her shoulder, trying to pull her away, but she couldn't move. Not yet; she needed to hear what was being said.

"We will be doing them a kindness, even if they are too arrogant to admit it! Do you really think their life will offer what those pups need? How many do you think will die out there if we don't intervene? Those children will grow up in the safety of the packs with food, shelter, and loving families. They will thank us for this one day." Luke was also yelling, he had stood while he spoke, facing where she assumed Darren stood, still hiding behind the door. Their words sent Jade's stomach roiling, her heart plummeting as everything came into place. This was far worse than the manipulation she had anticipated. Darren was right; this plan would be an outright declaration of war between the council and rogues.

"Then give them a choice like you did when they first arrived," Darren continued. "Show them what you are offering their children, or better yet, let the parents follow them into our ranks. That would grow our numbers even more than the other packs without tearing these people apart even further."

"Haven't you learned anything these last few weeks?" Luke asked, but he wasn't looking for an answer; he had already made his judgment. "Not only would we still be inviting death for our she-wolves right onto our doorsteps. But we would also be bringing in wolves that we can't guarantee will follow our laws. We don't waste time on the hopeless. We save who we can and let others live out the consequences of their choices. Tomorrow morning, we will take all of the warriors and collect the rest of the rogue pups that aren't already in our possession. Then we will remove the rest from our territory with as little bloodshed as possible."

Desert had both hands on her shoulders, pulling her away from the door, and this time she didn't fight him as she backed slowly away from the door before taking off down the hallway. She should have quieted her steps, should have maintained the same quiet caution she'd had entering the packhouse, but her feet held a new urgency, one that couldn't be ignored. It seemed Desert felt the same urgency as he followed on her heels, never once urging her to slow down or remain silent.

Hot air filled her lungs as they burst through the doors, the late morning sun nearly blinding her for a moment, black spots filling her vision as her eyes adjusted, but she didn't stop moving. Stumbling over the pavement, Jade continued moving forward. They needed to put distance between them and the packhouse in case anyone had heard their retreat. Only slowing once they reached the shadows of the nearby forest did she allow her feet to stagger to a halt, her lungs burning with more than the physical exertion. When no sounds of pursuit followed them, Desert leaned his back against a tree, hands propped on his knees as he shook his head in disbelief.

"I always knew that Alpha Council was afraid of our numbers, but I never thought they would go this far," he said; his words were quiet as if he was speaking to himself. Whether they were meant for Jade or not, she hardly heard them over the blood roaring in her ears.

For weeks she had sat in front of Alpha Power and listened to his lies. For weeks she had watched her friends endure countless insults, the hundred moments of abuse and all for what? So that once again, a few Alphas could decide that they were the ones who should take control of everything around them, no matter who it hurt or what consequences followed in their wake. None of that mattered as long as everyone knew that

they were the ones with the power, and if they were kind enough, they might let you have a taste of it only to snatch it away again.

She was used to their shows of dominance, but their cruelty had gone too far this time. The burning in her lungs had shifted, no longer focusing itself inside of her. Instead, it spread along her skin, a fire crackling along every hair and cell until it felt as if she could burn the forest down just from standing beneath its canopy. Just like any untamed fire, it burned out of control, unable to find anything within herself to soothe its raging.

Her hands moved of their own accord, her fist finding its way to the nearest tree, its bark rough on her bare knuckles. Over and over again, her fist connected with the thick tree trunk. She could hear the splintering of wood with every hit, but it did nothing to cool the fire that blazed on, threatening to consume her completely.

"Jade, stop it!" Desert called out, but his voice was far away and dulled by the pounding of her fists and heart. With a final crack, the tree snapped its heavy top crashing down to the forest floor, leaving the broken stump in its wake.

Strong hands gripped her shoulders, spinning her around to face a wild-eyed Desert; his eyes darted frantically over her face to the damage behind her.

"Your eyes, Jade, your eyes! Come back; it's okay; just come back to me," he said, his voice barely breaking through the haze clouding her brain. But his face was what broke through. Enlarged pupils in wide eyes, breath coming in short pants, beads of sweat dripping down the side of his face, colorless cheeks. All coming together to form one singular emotion, one Jade had hoped to never inspire in anyone ever again.

Fear

The fire eating away at her died down to a slow simmer as her anger was choked out as if a blanket had been thrown over it, not killing it completely but dulling it enough to see what was in front of her, to really see it.

"We need to get back to the others," she said, her voice shaking almost as much as her hands. "We need to all get away from here, now!"

"Slow down for a second," Desert said, surveying her face with more intensity than usual. "Are you sure you're okay? We can take a minute-"

"No, we can't. They are going to take their children! They all wanted to leave, but I'm the reason they are still here. I'm the one that told them to wait, to trust me, and now it might be too late. I have to get them away from here now before Power notices what is going on," she said, already jogging away. She didn't look back to see if Desert was following behind her; she knew he would. Right now, she had more important things to worry about.

Chapter 31

Spencer

There was little that Spencer found surprising these days. Not after his Alpha had willingly brought flea-ridden scum into their territory, and especially not after his best friend had gone soft for the mutts.

So, he certainly shouldn't have been shocked when he watched Jade and the scruffy stray that was always following her around burst through the doors of the packhouse. Stepping back so that he was covered by the corner of the building placed him just out of their line of sight. Not that it seemed to matter. Neither one appeared to be aware of anything around them as they ran for the cover of the trees as if all of hell were on their tails, never once sparing a glance behind them. Yet no one followed through the doors. In fact, it didn't seem as if anyone else had even seen them.

Spencer entertained the thought of running inside, finding whoever he could, and raising the alarm, but what good would that do? Even if he did prove that the rogues had been in the packhouse unannounced, Darren would find some way to justify them being there. And there was no telling how Alpha Power would react without any proof.

It was that thought that drove Spencer forward, his steps more cautious than the steps of those he pursued. He had been on plenty of hunting trips with his father, which served him well as he crept through the forest floor. Carefully avoiding the twigs that could snap or bushes that would move too much if brushed

by, but hunting deer or elk was one thing. Hunting a fellow predator was an entirely different matter.

They were easy enough to track, not bothering to cover their pathway or scent. Even if they had, it still wouldn't have taken Spencer long to find them as they had only run far enough to not be seen or heard by anyone on the road. Even from where he watched them, he could catch a few words here and there, unable to piece together complete sentences, but one thing was clear, they were angry and scared, especially Jade. In what he could only describe as a fit of rage, he watched in awestruck horror as the she-wolf plunged her clenched fist into a tree. Her fist came away bloodier with every hit until the tree gave out, crashing to the ground. Her anger must have surpassed anything Spencer had seen before for it to give her that kind of strength. She-wolves were stronger than the humans they looked so much alike, but even the strongest she-wolf was nowhere near as strong as their male counterparts, and to snap a tree like that took immense strength.

Her friend seemed just as shocked by her outburst as he dragged her away from the havoc she'd created. The stench of his fear drifted on the breeze, stinging the inside of Spencer's nose.

Spencer had never feared the rogues, even with their violent tendencies, such as the one he watched before him. It was all that you could expect from wolves who gave up their families and homes. Yet, for the first time since laying eyes on them, Spencer felt a cold dread wash over him, goosebumps rising on his skin.

"Your eyes!" the other rogue yelled loud enough to ring clear in Spencer's ears, and Spencer had to swallow down his own cry. He tried to convince himself that his eyes were playing tricks on him. Something to do with how the light filtered

through the trees, or even his mind looking for anything to justify what he had witnessed. But nothing could explain away the blood-red eyes that glared out where her human eyes had been.

Unnatural

Enemy

Wolf

His wolf howled from within, clawing at his chest, demanding to be released as he sensed the danger that was before them, even if Spencer was unable to understand it, let alone give it a name.

As quickly as her terrible eyes had made their appearance, with a blink they were gone just as quickly. It would have been easy to convince himself it had all been in his head if the image of those eyes, those demon eyes, hadn't been branded in his mind. He should have continued to follow them, but all he could bring himself to do was watch in stunned silence as they sped off through the trees again. Whatever urgency that had possessed them from before was renewed.

The silence that settled over the forest after their departure should have been a familiar, even a comforting one. Instead, Spencer found it eerie and unwelcoming. He needed to process what he had just witnessed to understand what it all meant. How could he be expected to explain something that he couldn't even come to grips with?

"Disturbing, isn't it?" a voice asked from behind where he stood. He nearly jumped out of his skin, whirling around to see another rogue wolf leaning casually against a tree a few feet away from where Spencer stood. The wolf's white hair nearly glowed in the dappled sunlight. "And no, you're not crazy,

although I don't blame you for thinking it. Most people would doubt their eyes after seeing what you just observed."

"You're with that other group, aren't you? What are you doing here?" Spencer snapped, composing himself as best he could, a quick glance around their surroundings revealing that they were alone. The other wolf shrugged, flicking away a stray leaf that clung to his shoulder.

"Same as you, just a concerned citizen hoping to keep those I care about out of harm's way, even if no one else sees the danger surrounding us."

"You mean from people like you?" Spencer spat, "It's because of all of you that my sister is sick. What could you need protection from that you didn't bring upon yourself?"

He'd seen the rogue before around town and at the hospital with Darren; Ash was his name if Spencer remembered correctly. There were too many of them to know for sure.

"More than you would think," Ash answered, "and right now, one of the biggest threats to all of us that bear the title rogue is ourselves. That's why I'm here. My goal is to make sure that we don't make life worse for ourselves because of the choices of a few, but that seems a more difficult goal to obtain than I anticipated. I think that's something you can understand," he said, glancing up at Spencer with an inquisitive eyebrow raised. Spencer pressed his lips tightly together, pushing away images of Darren, and every time Spencer had been forced to watch him choose the rogues over his own pack. Over his best friend. He certainly could understand the other wolf's dilemma.

"Whatever. It doesn't matter what I saw anyway; no one will believe it," he said, not trying to hide the bitterness that tainted his words. This wolf was a rogue, just like any other. Even talking to him for this long could be dangerous.

"What if they did, though? And what if I could guarantee that after today not a single wolf would question you again about it?" Ash asked, taking a single step forward, his eyes alight with promises. "What if I could swear that this can all be over soon and that all it would take is one, teeny, tiny thing from you?"

They were just words, words filled with empty promises as far as Spencer was concerned. But then why did his heart leap into this throat at the simple declaration?

"Wh-what would it take?" his voice slipping out before he could think better of it. He wasn't sure if he liked the knowing smile that spread across the other wolf's face, as if he and Spencer were now part of an inside joke, only it was a joke that Spencer didn't understand.

"Nothing difficult; just make sure Darren Power makes it to the warehouse just outside of town at sunset. Not before, not after, it has to be at sunset. Do you understand?" Ash asked, his eyes boring into Spencer's so intently it made the hairs on the back of Spencer's neck stand up.

"Why? What is going to happen there?"

"It's better if you don't know. All that you need to know is that tonight will be the key to putting everything right," the other wolf reassured.

"How do I know this isn't a trap?" he asked, looking around their surroundings again warily. "I'm not sending my future Alpha anywhere he might get hurt."

Ash scoffed as if the idea itself was the most foolish thing he had heard that day, and Spencer swore he would have rolled his eyes if Spencer's eyes hadn't been trained on him.

"I have more important things to worry about than harming the golden boy of The Northwind Pack, but I respect your concern. I can promise you that no bodily harm will come to

your friend while he is there tonight. You can even come along to ensure his safety," Ash said, holding out a hand. Hesitantly, Spencer took it in his own, letting the other wolf lead the firm handshake between them. As soon as it was done, he yanked his hand away from Ash's grip as if he had been burned, leaving his fingertips tingling.

"I look forward to seeing you again," Ash said, throwing a wink in Spencer's direction before disappearing into the trees. Finally alone, Spencer felt the cold seeping through his jacket, causing goosebumps to rise along his arms. But it was more than the winter chill that sent a shudder through him. Standing in the eerie silence, he couldn't help but wonder what he had gotten himself into.

It was easier than expected to keep Darren at the packhouse for the day since he spent hours arguing with his father, their bellows echoing throughout the whole building. The slamming door finally signaled the end of the dispute, followed moments later by Darren's heavy footsteps thudding down the stairs. Spencer didn't move from where he lounged in a large armchair on the main floor as he watched his friend descend the stairs. He swore he could almost see smoke blowing from his nostrils.

"I take it your father won this round?" he asked. Darren only growled in response, heading straight for the door. Springing to his feet, Spencer caught up with him, following him step for step, his friend's eyes still never reaching his face. "Where are you headed off to?" he asked, stepping out under the burning sun. It was still too early.

"You don't want to know," Darren answered, his shoulders squared and jaw clenched in determination.

"You're going to *her*, aren't you?" Spencer asked, rolling his eyes as Darren let out a small huff, his eyes barely flickering towards where Spencer walked. "I've seen the way you look at her; I'm not a complete idiot. We've all been sucked in by a pair of pretty eyes and a sharp tongue before."

"You don't know the half of it," Darren mumbled, his shoes scuffing on the pavement, his face never slowing. He was moving too quickly; Spencer needed to find a way to slow him down.

"Hey, I may not know exactly what is going on, but I do know if you go out there now, then you'll raise more suspicions. They are already saying that you prefer the company of rogues to your own pack. Some are even spreading rumors that they must have bought a spell from a witch to make you like one of them."

"Well, they're wrong! I'll always care about the safety of this pack; what do you think I'm doing now?"

"I hear you; I'm not saying not to do whatever it is you're planning. All I'm saying is wait until dusk. There will be fewer people to see you, which means less people to tattle to your father about where you're going," Spencer reasoned. He hated himself for the relief that washed over him as Darren's steps slowed until they halted completely. Finally turning to face Spencer, Darren clearly contemplated the wisdom in his suggestion. "It will be dark soon enough; what difference will a couple of hours make?"

"You're right. I'm too wound up right now; I need to slow down and think this through. Thanks, Spenc."

"Of course, that's what friends are for," he said, hoping that the knot in his stomach wasn't a sign of what was to come.

Chapter 32

Jade

If the energy in the warehouse could have been described as restless before, then it was turned into pure chaos once Jade and Desert returned. Jade had sent a few wolves into town with their remaining ration chips to get whatever supplies they could, another group to gather whoever was left in town, and the rest to pack up their limited belongings.

"Let's hurry, everyone; I want to leave the second that it's dark out," Jade repeated as she walked up and down the rows of sleeping spaces, helping as she saw a need.

"Why at dark? We should leave as soon as everyone is ready," Chris said, shouldering a large bag of his and Lola's belongings over his shoulders. "It will give us a longer head start in case they decide to follow us."

"Because if it's still light, it's more likely that their patrols will notice a group this large leaving. We can cover our tracks better in the dark. With any luck, they won't notice that we're gone until morning," Jade replied without looking up from her task as she tied a rolled blanket together. She practically threw it to Maryanne as the she-wolf hurriedly threw her bag together while keeping her pup close to her side.

Chris's only response was a huff, but he hurried away. Jade watched silently as her friend placed some of Malcolm's belongings in his own bag when the older wolf tried to stand with a bag that hunched his shoulders and made his knees wobble. Jade feared it was harsh, forcing all of them to uproot

so quickly, but she feared the brutality of pack warriors even more. Most seemed to understand and even magnified her urgency, all except a few.

Aiden moved slowly through the crowd, casting doubtful glances everywhere he looked. He had argued again to take the fight to Alpha Power, many of the younger males agreeing with him. But Jade had shut down that idea before Aiden could waste any more time.

"Jade, pass me that blanket, will you? I need to wrap this in something," Maryanne asked, pointing out a blanket a few paces away. Lunging over to grab the blanket, Jade's foot caught another bag that was sitting on the ground, successfully tipping it over, its contents spilling to the floor. Swearing under her breath, Jade shoved the random assortment of food, clothing, and trinkets back in, her hand pausing on one item, a small leather pouch. It was light in her hand, hardly weighing a thing, but that wasn't what caught Jade's attention. It was the scent that wafted out from it as a breeze stirred the room. The sweet scent, overwhelmingly sweet, made her stomach churn. It felt as if it left a stickiness on her lungs as she inhaled it, still unable to identify what it could belong to. All she knew was that it was wrong, very, very wrong.

Hands shaking, she tugged at the string that tied it together, unsure of what possessed her fingers as they drew out its treasures.

Seeds.

Seeds barely smaller than her fingertips filled her palm. Their white skins didn't have a speck of dirt on them as if someone had taken care to wash them. A few stray petals fell alongside them, the source of the sickly sweetness. They didn't belong to any plant that Jade was familiar with, but there was

something dangerous within their tiny shells, her pounding heart her witness.

"Who does this belong to?" she asked, her words rising above the clamor. Something in her voice caused all of their wide eyes to turn to her, the air crackling around them. When no one spoke up, she repeated her question, holding the bag high. "I won't ask again," she warned, watching the faces of those around her, unsure if their sweaty brows and guarded faces were from her or from the thought of packwolves closing in.

"That's mine, it's uh...it's nothing really," Kacen said, but he kept his eyes away from her face.

"Where did you get it from?" she asked, her voice coming out sharper than she intended, but with her heart hammering in her chest and warning bells blaring in her ears, it was difficult to keep her own fear contained.

"Aiden gave them to me. It really isn't important; it was just for a prank," he said, his wavering voice betraying his lie, but only a partial lie.

"What are these, Aiden?" she asked, her eyes landing on where Aiden stood leaning against a wooden beam in the middle of the room, but he never had the chance to answer.

"Ah, I was wondering how long it would take you to find those. Honestly, I thought it would be sooner, but it seems I overestimated your instincts just a bit," Ash said from the doorway, turning all of their eyes to him. He wasn't alone. Jade watched as nearly twenty other wolves filed in behind him, her own friends retreating away from the door as far as they could.

"We don't have time for your games, Ash," she said, hoping he couldn't sense the panic that was rising within her.

"Then you better make the time," he said, moving forward. Jade hated the way his eyes lit up as wolves scrambled to get out

of his way. All of it was a joy to him. Their fear, the riddles, the manipulations were all just a game to him. Simply another way to amuse himself. "Besides, it seems as if I didn't come around now, I would have missed you completely," he said, throwing a glance down at the belongings scattered around the room.

"This has nothing to do with you," Jade snapped, resisting the urge to move away as well as he drew closer.

"Are you sure about that?" he asked, maintaining his lazy pace, surveying the room instead of her face. "It seems that while I continue overestimating your readiness, you keep underestimating me."

"What does that mean?" Desert asked, holding firm in his stance just behind her, but she heard the quiver in his words, as did Ash based on how his lips twitched in a slight smile.

"It means that after years of waiting, everything is finally falling into place the way I intended. I have spent countless sleepless nights putting all of the pieces together and tonight is the start of everything we've all hoped for and more."

Whispers filled the room at his words, at the promises of hope that they held. It took all of her strength to hold back her own promises, ones that would not be as rosy or comforting. Especially as his words came together in her mind, like pieces of a puzzle, she'd had the whole time but was only now seeing how they connected.

"You're the reason their she-wolves are dying," she choked out, her hand gripping the seeds tightly. "With these?"

"You wouldn't believe how long it took for me to find something that they wouldn't even know to look for. I even had to track down a witch or two to get my hands on those. The old Alphas made a worthy effort of eradicating it, much like they have with us."

"What are they?" Kyler asked from the side of the room, but Ash's eyes never moved from Jade's face, watching every blink of her eyes, every bead of sweat that formed on her skin.

"Lupinus, well, their seeds, to be more precise. The plant itself is mostly harmless, but the seeds are a very different matter once ingested. To be honest, finding wolves to slip it to them was the easiest part," he said, nodding where Aiden stood. Aiden bent his head in respect, the way he would have to his Alpha. His eyes flickered over to another wolf for the slightest second before slipping back to the scene unfolding before him, but Jade had seen who he had been searching for.

Kacen. The pickpocket's skillful hands weren't only useful for stealing items. They set him up perfectly to slip things in unseen as well. They hadn't joined Jade because they had seen something in her worth following; it had all been another one of Ash's plots. Maybe another game to see if she would be stupid enough to trust them. And she had lost.

"How? The whole council had females that were sick. How did you get to all of them?" Jade asked, her voice cracking.

"I've spent years preparing for this, do you really think that I would risk having all of my wolves in one territory?"

"But why? The she-wolves aren't any threat to you. Why would you want them dead?" Desert asked, speaking Jade's own thoughts.

"Not dead, awakened," Ash corrected. Any clarification he might have given was halted by a commotion outside.

"Jade!" a new voice called from outside the warehouse, and Jade felt her heart sink even further. He wasn't supposed to be there. He should have been with his father, his friends, anywhere but there.

"Ah, right on time," Ash grinned, sparing a peek over his shoulder. "Welcome Darren, we were expecting you."

There he was, standing in the doorway. The fading light made his silhouette dark, his face unclear, but Jade knew those blue eyes of his would be filled with confusion as he took in the scene. His breaths were coming in quick and deep gulps as if he had run the whole way there. He didn't bother trying to understand the sight before him as he strode into the bleak building, Ash's wolves stepped aside to let him and his companion, Spencer, through.

"Darren, you need to go," Jade said. She knew it was too late, even if he hadn't ignored her warning.

"You all need to get out of here now; my father-the council, they're moving against you tomorrow. If you leave now, they might not be able to follow you," he said, clearly not understanding the danger he was in.

"How heroic, the little son of Alpha Power rushing in to save the day. Doesn't that just give you all of the warm and fuzzy feelings?" Ash asked. Laughter rang out from his followers; it echoed off the walls making Jade want to shrink away. Darren's face twisted with confusion as he watched the sneering faces around him.

"You don't understand. They are serious this time. They mean to take your pups and-"

"And do as they've always done. Push us away from another home, condemn us to another harsh winter, and slaughter any who don't cower before them," Ash interrupted, but he wasn't speaking to Darren, he addressed the captive audience before him, his words stirring a murmur through the crowd. "We've stood by long enough and let them spew their lies. Lies that they have told you, saying that you don't belong,

that you are less than them because you don't bare their marks because you dared to question them. But the time for their lies is over; a new day is coming, and with it will rise the truth."

His words earned him a cheer of agreement from his men, a few more voices joining in, but Jade didn't look to see who he had swayed. The cold dread that had consumed her was replaced by something alive, taking hold of her heart and bringing her desperation to an unbearable level.

"The truth? Tell me this truth then, how much blood will be spilled for this new world of yours? How many of the people in this room are you willing to sacrifice to prove your point?" she shouted, the cheers dying down.

"Every good thing in this world requires sacrifice, something you'll understand once your life isn't cloaked in this fabrication you've built," he said. Jade tried to hide the shudder that passed through her as she watched his slow advancing steps. She could practically see the dark power that flowed from him. "I think it's time for all of these people to see your true face, don't you?"

Jade didn't have time to respond, let alone move a finger before Ash's wolves made their move. Two of them lunged forward, each one latching on to one of her arms, another threw Darren to the ground, twisting his arm back painfully. Others must have grabbed onto Desert and Chris based on the struggle behind her, but she couldn't turn around. It would have been easy enough to throw her captors off, to slam her foot into one's knee until it buckled and headbutt the other one but that would have taken time. Time that she didn't have.

As soon as the wolves' hands latched onto her, Ash was in front of her, a sharp sting in her neck causing her to cry out. Just as quickly as they had pounced on her, Jade felt their hands drop

away as she fell to the floor. Fire was running through her veins, its flames licking at her bones, burning its way towards something deeper.

"Wha-What did you do?" she gasped, one hand clutching her neck, the other barely holding her up, unable to stop the tremors that had taken over her body. Her vision was blurred, but even through her foggy gaze, she could see the empty syringe his hands toyed with.

"You see, the funny thing about Lupinus is that it impacts humans and non-shifters similarly, but for shifters...Well, it impacts us very differently," he said, pocketing the syringe. "And in this concentrated form, it's extremely effective, fast-acting too, I must say."

He barely had finished his gloating when the fire roared to life inside of her as it reached its mark. Taken by surprise she couldn't stop the scream that was torn from her as her chest burned with the invisible flame that had taken hold of her. Collapsing to the ground completely, she writhed on the floor, unable to stop her own body from thrashing about. Hands were on her, and she thought she could hear Darren and Desert calling her name, but she was too far gone, the pain swallowing her completely.

Her blood was boiling, surging through her veins, ready to bubble and burst through her skin. She felt the break before it happened, her arm twisting on its own in a sickening snap that pulled a shriek from her throat that didn't sound like her own.

Stop fighting, a voice whispered inside of her, a voice that sounded very much like Ash's. *It will hurt more if you fight it.*

She couldn't give in; she couldn't let it break her. The words repeated on and on in her mind; not even the sound of her screams could drown them out. There was too much at stake, too

much that would be lost if she didn't stay strong, if she didn't hold *it* in.

But no amount of words could save her when the wall she kept within herself, the one she had spent years building, strengthening, and perfecting, cracked.

Chapter 33

Darren

Jade's screams tore at his heart as she thrashed on the ground. If she could hear his voice, she wasn't able to respond. Her skin was hot to the touch, sweat coating her brow. Desert was also at her side, trying to hold her still, but whatever pain wracked her body was too powerful. Bile stung his throat and tongue as he watched helplessly as one of her arms twisted, the bone giving a sickening snap as it broke.

"Oof, that's gotta hurt," Ash said, wincing and bringing a hand up to his mouth for show.

"What did you do?" Desert yelled. He had to be yelling, but Darren's brain couldn't process it. He could hardly understand anything going on around him besides Jade's pain throbbing weakly through the mate bond. He wished they had already completed the mating bond, wished that he could feel the extent of her pain, and even more than that, he wished he could take it from her.

"I wouldn't stand that close if I were you," Ash said, ignoring Desert completely, his sing-song voice rising above another scream as he danced away. "Things could get a bit...hairy."

"You can fight this, Jade; don't give in now, not when you've come so far," Desert tried to reach her, but even Darren knew she was too far gone for words.

Almost as if he had said the magic word, Jade's screams turned into one long shriek. It started off high pitched but

quickly took on a deeper, animalistic tone as if something possessed her. More snapping came from her body as more limbs contoured themselves unnaturally, almost as if-

Suddenly her eyes flew open, and Darren had to suppress the urge to flinch away at the sight of them. The eyes that he once knew were gone, their beautiful grey replaced with an alarming red. It was the kind of red that haunted the nightmares of every warrior after his first kill, the kind that Darren had washed off of his own clothes after a border patrol had gone wrong. The bloody kind.

All around them were yells and people scrambling to move as far away as possible. Darren was aware of Ash's wolves blocking the entrance, trapping them all inside. He was faintly aware of Spencer's hand on his shoulders, trying to pull him away, but Darren stayed in place. He needed to be there, not just because she was his mate. Something deep inside, something almost ancient whispered that he needed to see what would come next, that whatever came, he was meant to be a part of it.

Flipping onto her stomach, Jade's hands clutched at the ground, but she found nothing to hold onto. She tried to speak, but only a faint rasp came out, which turned into another heart-wrenching, tired cry. Black fur erupted from her back, spreading over her entire body. The last of her bones creaking as they shifted to their new places; newly broad shoulders knocked Darren aside. Claws replaced her slim fingers, fangs shining in the fading light as her lip pulled back in a vicious snarl.

"Jade?" Darren whispered, but the girl was nowhere to be found. A towering, black, very angry wolf was in her place, her teeth snapping and eyes glowing.

"Blood Wolf," Spencer breathed out, his fear dripping from each word, tainting the ancient name. As if in a dream, Darren

found his eyes wandering the surrounding faces, Spencer's fear and horror reflected in most of them, but not Ash. A wicked smile spread across the young rogue's face; his silver eyes were nearly all black, white hair giving off a ghostly glow.

"There she is."

Chapter 34

Jade

Fear

Blood

Kill

Her wolf's thoughts were simple in her first moments of freedom, breathing in the familiar stench of fear that filled the space around them. It was the scent that always came before the danger, danger that Jade had faced on her own for too long. She snapped her teeth, ensuring the surrounding wolves took a few steps back, except one.

Mate

Familiar blue eyes met hers in the same wide-eyed, gaping stare that followed the monster everywhere. Their brain fought with everything it had to believe that it wasn't true, that nothing that horrifying could still exist.

That she shouldn't exist.

Jade tried desperately to take control, but her mental wall might as well have been demolished. Her wolf was powerful after years of saving her energy for that very moment. It took every ounce of strength left in her just to hold her new body in place, to keep herself from lunging forward and tearing all of them to shreds.

"Do you see now? Do you see what the Alphas have done to us? They have forced you from your homes, condemned your children to lives of solitude and danger. They convinced you to hide who you are, convinced us that we aren't strong enough to

withstand their power, but look at what's before you!" Ash's voice rose above the chaos, completely unwavering as he gestured towards Jade's dark form. "They told you that her existence was impossible, and yet here she stands, proof of the truth they have hidden from you all along. The truth that will soon become their demise."

A roar rippled through the crowd, their frenzy only fueling the creature's anger as she snarled, thrashing against Jade's slipping hold. This wasn't how it was supposed to go. She was supposed to keep them safe, not be the source of their fear. They should have left when Aiden suggested it, except he was just another one of Jade's many, many failures.

Ash was right; she had lied. Her whole life had been nothing but lies, and now she would pay for it.

Trapped within the body of a beast, Jade's mind was aware of Ash's wolves filing out of the building, familiar faces following them into the darkness. It didn't matter, though; she couldn't focus on any of their faces, not with the root of her fear standing so close, his dark eyes watching her closely. No gloating or words of rebuke slipped from his lips as he observed her; maybe he knew none were needed, her defeat and shame already an unbearable, crushing weight.

"Join us when you're ready," Ash said, his words directed to the entire room, but Jade knew they were meant for her. As suddenly as he had appeared, he slipped back into the night, leaving a shaken silence in his wake, the quiet sobs of those who remained breaking that silence. With danger nowhere in sight, the dark wolf's anger finally eased, allowing Jade to come forward once again despite her uncertainty of when Jade would allow her out again.

The shift back to her human skin was nothing like what it had been when her wolf had burst out. It was natural, no more difficult than slipping off one shirt to replace it with another. The floor was rough on her hands, a breeze from the open doors raising goosebumps on her arms and neck. Blurred vision hid most of the room from her gaze, not that she would have been able to understand what her eyes saw, not with the fog pressing along her mind.

Frantic hands were on her shoulders and arms, pulling her into a sitting position. She heard her friends' voices calling her name, but it was all she could do just to keep her eyes open, their every blink bringing the surrounding darkness closer. But no dark mental clouds could keep *his* voice out, not when he was the only one the creature inside yearned for.

"You need to leave. Go now; you might be able to get ahead of them before word spreads," he said, his words falling out of his mouth rapidly, unable to hold them back. Fear cascading off every word. It was expected; how could he not be afraid of her? But it didn't lessen the sting that pricked her heart at the sound of them. Oddly, she was grateful that her breath was still coming in quick, rasping gasps if it meant she didn't have to find it in her to respond.

"Consider us gone," Desert said as Jade felt her body being lifted. She could smell Chris's scent as she rocked gently in his arms. Lola whispered softly to her, stroking her hair as they carried her away from the nightmare that had unfolded before them. From the back of her mind, her wolf whimpered softly as the mate bond pulsed weaker and weaker in her chest. Was it from the distance that was slowly growing between them or because Darren had let the idea of them fade away? That was the

last thought she held onto as the darkness that had been lurking around the edges of her vision finally consumed her.

Mother always said not to let her socks get wet. Wet socks were how little pups got the sniffles, and no pup should be stuck in bed with the sniffles. She wondered what Mother would say when she saw her socks, standing in a puddle that surrounded her feet, the white fabric turning a queasy shade of red as they soaked up the liquid.

Unwavering hands were held out in front of her; she knew they were hers, but she wanted it not to be true as she watched the blood slip down her fingers. The droplets caused tiny ripples in the puddle. It was easier to focus on her hands, much easier than staring at the quiet body that lay on the floor, the warmth leaking from his body with his life-giving blood.

"What did you do?" a voice screamed, but Jade didn't answer, for it hadn't been her that had done it, not really. Yes, it was her hands stained red, but they hadn't hands when the deed had been committed. If it hadn't been her hands, could it really have been her?

"You killed him. Murderer!"

Murderer. The word echoed through her whole body, bouncing back and forth through her mind, stomach, and toes until it settled into her bones, becoming part of her very being.

Murderer

Murderer

Murderer!

Jade woke with a start with tremors shaking her body uncontrollably, a cry trapped in her throat turned into a strangled

sob. Memories of long ago danced in her head, twisting and turning with far more recent images until her head was spinning. Bile rose up, burning her throat and mouth as she retched up the few contents of her stomach.

She flinched as hands landed on her back. She would have turned around if it weren't for Lola's soothing murmurs as Jade recognized her friend's soft touch running up and down her back. It was hard to notice much when her stomach was heaving, but she was aware of filtered light, dimmed by cloth walls that surrounded her and the stuffy air that always came with too many people in a tight space.

"She's awake," Kyler's voice called out softly. A soft rustling followed his words and a quick flash of light as another person slipped into the makeshift tent. With some shifting of bodies, Lola's hands were replaced with Desert's, his voice just as quiet but lacking the softness their friend always embodied.

"You had us worried. Everyone's been asking when you were going to wake up," he said, helping her into a sitting position. She could feel his eyes boring into the top of her head, but she kept her face downwards. She couldn't bring herself to look him or any of them in the eyes. After what they had seen, she wasn't sure how they could look at her.

She wiped saliva from her lips, the hot stench of vomit filling the space. Whatever pride or dignity she thought she had gained from her time as their leader was completely and utterly shattered.

"Here," Lola offered a small dish of water which Jade sipped on gratefully, the cool liquid soothing her burning throat. But mostly, she was grateful because it meant she wouldn't be expected to talk for another moment or two. They were in a crude shelter built by throwing a sheet over a low-hanging

branch and staked into the ground. It was stuffed with the three of them in it. Lola was practically half out of it already; even so, Kyler's head poked through the opening, watching intently. Jade was used to their eyes on her, the way they filled with questions as they waited on answers she should have, but she didn't have any answers for them this time. None that they would want to hear.

"You are alright, aren't you?" Kyler asked, his wide eyes making him look younger than Jade. Perhaps that wasn't saying much, though, since Jade's body ached as if she had turned ancient overnight. Still unable to find her voice Jade only nodded, watching her still hands resting on her knees. If she stared long enough, would she see the same red from her nightmares coating them once again?

"Well, say something," Desert said, his voice making Jade wince, not only from the way it made her head throb.

"Hush Desert," Lola scolded, but she placed a gentle hand on his arm. "Give her some time. I'm sure you'll be sick of words once they come to her," she said with a small but genuine smile.

"It's alright, Lola," Jade said, her voice raspy and cracking on each word. "I suppose it would be asking too much to hope that it was all a bad dream?" she asked. She wasn't surprised when she watched their faces fall, all hesitant to answer her. A groan escaped her as her head fell into her hands. Everyone had seen her. Darren had seen what she was. The loss of her secret should have stung more, but she found herself surprisingly numb. "Where are we? Did everyone make it out?"

"We're a few miles south of the Northwind border. Don't worry, we're still following the mountains so that there are less packs to come across," Desert answered, but worry still creased

his face. Those hadn't been the words he was hoping for. "Almost everyone got out, well, everyone who was still with us."

"Ash?" she asked, but she knew the answer before his head nodded. "You said almost everyone, who stayed?"

Desert hesitated, his mouth opening, but no words came out right away, as if the names caught in his throat. Even Kyler and Lola stared at the ground, their cheeks tinted pink in shame. They had nothing to be ashamed of. It was Jade that should have feared their retribution.

"Who?" Jade asked again, her voice growing firmer, forcing Desert's eyes to hers.

"Aiden and his boys went with Ash, but there were a few of the others...their pups...they couldn't leave them behind," he said. A brand-new wave of nausea hit Jade's stomach as his words sank in. Letting her head fall into her hands, a moan escaped her. How could everything have gone so wrong?

"We need to get moving; Alpha Power could still send wolves after us," Kyler spoke up, only adding to her headache.

"We don't have to go just yet if you need more time to rest," Desert jumped in, but Jade was already stumbling to her feet, crouching slightly to avoid the short roof.

"I don't need to rest. You need to keep heading south towards the lake. You remember the one I'm talking about," she said, her mind already racing.

"What do you mean 'you'? You're coming with us," Lola said, but it came out more like a question, concern filling her eyes. Jade ignored her; she couldn't let them be distracted now.

"It will take you a few days if you use the daylight and don't get lost. It's crucial you get there before the first snow," she

instructed, mainly speaking to Desert, holding his gaze and only his.

"I don't understand. Why aren't you coming with us?" Lola spoke up again, annoyance and fear making her voice high-pitched. Still watching Jade closely, his eyes alight with understanding and mouth set in a frown, Desert finally answered her.

"She's going back. Back to Northwind," he said, a gasp escaping their other friends.

"You can't go back! Alpha Power will have heard about you by now, and Ash is still there," Kyler exclaimed, his voice already wavering at the thought.

"That's why I have to go back; I can't just leave them. I can't betray them like that."

Not like I already have

She needed them to understand, to know that she wasn't leaving them, at least not just to save her own skin.

"You can't save everyone, Jade. They made their choice. There are still plenty of us that are here and ready to follow you. Let them go," Lola said gently, as Jade sought for the words to make them understand.

"It's not just that…." Jade trailed off, unsure if she even wanted to utter the words aloud, to make them real once again.

"It's because he's still there, isn't it? Power's son," Desert asked.

"This isn't about him. This is about what I am and what I've done. Ash is there because of me, and every wolf who is still there is in danger until he is dealt with."

"Then let them deal with him. Northwind has some of the most experienced warriors of any pack; they know how to handle a few unruly-"

"Not like Ash," Jade cut Lola off. They didn't understand, and how could they when she hardly understood it herself? "He was right. I'm just as terrible as he is. I've lied to everyone, even after you all put your trust in me, just like a monster. If I don't go back now, that's who I'll always be," she yelled.

She meant it, every single word of it. Maybe it was the guilt that fueled her, or the wolf within was to blame for her newfound courage. The beast's presence lingered unmistakably in the back of her mind, much like the headache that was still pounding in her skull.

"Go, get everyone to safety like we planned, and I'll join you if I can," she said, shoving past Desert and Lola and forcing Kyler to step aside. The breath that was sucked from her lungs wasn't a result of the frosty air. Standing right outside of her shelter in the dim morning light were dozens of faces staring back at her, hope pouring out of every one of them as they gazed at her.

"You're all here?" she asked, the words escaping her before she could halt them.

"Of course, we are. Did you really think we would leave just because you're a little different?" old Malcolm said from the front of the group as he gestured around to all the sober faces. "Just look at us, we're all different. That's what brought us together; you helped show us that it didn't matter what everyone said about us, that we could be whoever we wanted. Do you still believe that?" Jade could only nod, the words catching in her tightening throat.

"We do too, which is why we could never abandon our Alpha," Malcolm said with a slight bow of his head.

Alpha

Like a spark, the title was whispered through the crowd, heads bowing in respect everywhere she looked. The word echoed through her chest and caused her wolf to stand tall within her. It was a word that had been used for her before, but never like this. Never had it been spoken as if it were the complete and utter truth. She was their leader, their Alpha, and not because she was stronger or better than any of them but because they saw her, the real her, and still chose her. Tears stung her eyes as she let a few slip down her cheeks. These were her people, beyond a shadow of a doubt.

"We haven't left you yet, and we don't plan to now, so don't give up on us. Let us help you," Desert said from behind her, Jade didn't turn around, but instead, she brushed away the stray tears and squared her shoulders.

"It won't be easy; there will probably be a fight like none other we've had before, and I can't promise the safety of anyone that joins me," she said. A grin spread over Chris's face as he let out a hoot.

"I've been beggin' you for weeks to let me rough some wolves up a bit. The Goddesses themselves couldn't keep me away."

"Me either!" Chelsea called out. Her cheer echoed through the group, and Jade couldn't stop the smile that lit up her face or the pride that swelled in her chest. Doubts and fears of loneliness that had plagued her for years seemed to slip away. How could she fear the future when she had her friends- no, her pack by her side?

Chapter 35

Darren

Slap!

The sound of skin hitting skin rang through Luke Power's office, Darren's cheek burned, but he didn't raise a hand in defense, not even when his father's palm connected with his face a second time.

"How could you be so stupid? I warned you not to let your guard down around them. I told you that you couldn't trust that girl and what do you do? Walk in there and hand a *Blood Wolf* our only edge!" Luke bellowed, nearly spitting out what Jade was.

His anger should have cut more deeply than it did. Maybe it had lost its sting because Darren had anticipated this reaction. Luke had been ranting for hours, only pausing when Johnathan cut in to add his own concerns about the newfound information. Their shock and disgust at learning Jade's true identity was understandable, but Darren couldn't find it within himself to mirror any of it.

Darren should have been more surprised. Blood Wolves were supposed to be gone, their darkness eradicated completely from their world, but somehow it all made sense. Jade had been different from the day he had laid eyes on her. The fact that it had taken him so long to learn that she was truly exceptional was more surprising to him. He only wished he had been able to hide it from his father a little longer, but that was nearly impossible with witnesses.

It would have taken death itself to hold the news inside of Spencer even for just an hour. Before Darren had left Jade in the care of her friends, Spencer had already run back to the packhouse. Word of what had taken place spilled out of him before Darren ever had a chance to stop it, and now he would pay the price. He couldn't help but wonder if it wouldn't have been better to leave with Jade, he had no doubt that Desert and the others would protect her, but he couldn't deny the longing that already ached in his chest at her absence.

"I know what I did, and I'm sorry if you are hurt by it, but I would do it again if I had the choice," he answered, aware of Spencer and Johnathan's eyes on him. It was bad enough talking to his father, let alone spectators, also judging his every word.

"Hurt? You betrayed your entire pack; you betrayed yourself and everything a true Alpha should stand for. I hope you can look yourself in the mirror after today because the Alpha I thought you could be clearly is gone," Luke yelled, his words hitting their mark. Darren had known what his father would think of him, but he hadn't expected the shame that washed over him. Maybe his father was right; maybe he didn't have it in him to be an Alpha.

"So, you would have me betray my mate instead?" he ignored the breath that Spencer sucked in at the revelation. He certainly didn't deserve any explanation from Darren, not after what he had done. "You're the one that always told me that a wolf should do everything he can to protect his mate, and that's what I did. Besides, it isn't Jade that we need to be afraid of. Ash is planning something, and we need to be ready for it."

"I'd say it's a little late for that," a new voice said from the open doorway.

Ash

He was right; Darren was too late. Whatever Ash had planned was already in motion. Darren's own alarm was drowned out by the hum of the packlink, suddenly alive with too many thoughts for any one of them to be distinguished.

"What do you think you are doing here? How did you even get in?" Johnathan demanded as Spencer let out a startled snarl.

"Much easier than you would think. You really should get your security checked out. It seems to be...lacking," he said, making a show of glancing around the room. "Unlike this room. Please tell me that isn't a portrait of yourself Luke; that's just tacky."

"I've heard enough," Luke said. With a wave of his hand, Johnathan and Spencer moved forward.

"Uh, I wouldn't if I were you," Ash said, a quick snap of his fingers bringing four other wolves into the room from behind him. Outnumbered, Darren and his packmates were forced back until Darren's shoulder blades came into contact with the wall. "Why don't we take this little talk outside?"

For a moment, Luke surveyed the wolves in front of them, calculating his next move, but even Darren couldn't tell what was going on in his mind, and with the packlink buzzing, it was impossible to reach out.

"Yes, let's," Luke replied, deciding to play along with whatever game the young rogue had concocted, and Darren feared they were all simply his new pawns. Without another word, Darren and the others followed Ash outside, careful of every step they took, knowing that they were being watched closely. Throwing open the double doors to the packhouse, Ash strode out into the faint morning light. Darren's stomach lurched at the sight before them. Nearly every Northwind wolf old enough to walk on their own was standing in the courtyard. The

stench of their fear crashed over him like a wave from the sea. Wolves surrounded their entire pack, vicious rogues, some of them already in their wolf's skin. Their teeth snapped at anyone who dared to meet their dark glares. It was impossible to tell just how many rogues surrounded them, but Darren was certain that there were far too many to get the she-wolves and pups out safely.

The chatter from the packlink increased at the sight of their Alpha making Darren's head swim. They were afraid, as they should be. Cold anger seemed to roll off the pale-haired rogue, the calm before a raging storm.

"Gentlemen, I'd like to introduce you to my friends. They've been very anxious to meet your pack," Ash said, wrapping an arm around Luke's stiff shoulders as if they were old friends. "This here is Glen," he gestured to a large misty-eyed man. "His pack decided they were tired of feeding a blind pup, and he found himself abandoned in unfamiliar territory. And dear Margaret was kicked out of her pack when her mate, the Alpha of their pack, was overthrown. She was forced to watch her mate and pup murdered in front of her before she escaped," he said, pointing to a glaring brunette with scars running across her face.

Stomach twisting, Darren held back the bile that threatened to rise up as Ash continued introductions. The stories couldn't be true, just another one of Ash's games, but even as Darren tried to convince himself of the lies, he saw the truth of Ash's words in the faces of every rogue. He had never seen so much anger and pain in anyone, and now he was surrounded by it. Was Jade's story as sickening as the others?

"You call us criminals, Luke Power; you and the Alphas like you have condemned us to lives that your own nightmares

can't fathom. Our Alpha's deemed us unfit for their world, called us rogues, monsters even. But how can we be blamed for our actions when we've become exactly what you created us to be?" Ash's question hung in the air, the weight of it pressing down on all who heard it. "We've paid a heavy price for your peace; it's time you paid it back."

"You're insane!" a young male shouted from the crowd; his teeth bared. "Do you know what we do to filthy strays like you?"

"That's enough-" Luke started, sensing the fight in the young wolf's words.

"I know too well what you've done to people like us and what I'm sure you'd love to do now," Ash cut in, something dangerous lighting in his eyes. "I've lost many good wolves to your pack. All you packwolves sit here in your homes, finding ways to grow your already large territories. Always picking fights with neighboring packs, punishing the weaker members of your own pack, nothing is ever enough for spoiled pups like you. It's mongrels like you that make packs weak with your empty, worthless-" Ash was interrupted by a snarl as the other wolf leaped forward.

"No!" Darren yelled, but strong hands held him back, and Ash moved faster than his words. Before any of the Northwind wolves could understand what was happening, Ash's hands were around the boy's head. With one quick movement and a sickening snap, his body collapsed to the ground. His neck broken, his body limp.

"He really shouldn't have done that," Ash said with a shrug.

"They attacked Ash," a rogue called out, and a yell went up through the rouges before all hell broke loose.

All Darren could hear was the screaming. It echoed all around him, ringing in his ears as the chaos unfolded around

him. He could only watch in shock as mothers snatched up their pups, running for any cover they could find. The fighting was everywhere; the scent of blood overpowered his nose as he searched frantically for familiar faces. He couldn't have called out for them even if he had wanted to, shrieks of terror and pain drowning out any attempts.

"You don't know how long I've waited for this moment." Darren whirled around to see Ash just a few feet away, perfectly calm in the midst of the turmoil. The eye of a terrible, bloody storm.

"I planned everything, every single tiny detail. I made sure it all lined up, and that I was prepared for anything that could have happened, except you," he continued, seemingly talking to himself, but he started to pace a predatory circle. Darren's feet shifted with every step the rogue took, careful to keep the other wolf in front of him. "Jade would have been mine by now, but she just had to meet her mate. You, my friend, have been more trouble than you're worth. You really had me thrown for a loop for a little while there, but it doesn't matter now. You pushed Jade away quickly enough. I hardly had to lift a finger to help you with that."

"I wouldn't get ahead of yourself; I haven't lost her yet, and I don't plan to," Darren answered, letting his wolf rise to the surface. Ash made a show of glancing around them, his arms spread in a questioning gesture.

"I don't see her here, do you? I don't know about you, but I'd say a wolf that has his mate run from him has lost. Now, just to make sure that you don't ride back in like the prince charming you're always trying to be, I'll have to get rid of you. Which might just be one of the most satisfying things I'll do. Well, besides the moment Jade becomes my mate," he said with a grin.

Darren's wolf let out a snarl as he let the beast take control. Shifting into his wolf's skin, he charged forward.

Everything seemed to slow down as he watched Ash's smile widen, his teeth lengthening into fangs as his own shift took place. Black eyes consumed his light ones and white fur sprouted along his skin, covering his entire body until a large white wolf was in his place.

Phantom Wolf

In the span of twenty-four hours, two extinct wolves made an appearance within the same territory; the Goddesses must have been laughing at Darren's foolishness going against one of their blessed ones.

With his mind moving a mile a minute, Darren knew he was in trouble before the collision happened. Ash's wolf was larger than his own, and Darren's initial shock of seeing the unusual white fur left Darren vulnerable. Ash's body collided with his own, knocking the wind out of Darren as they tumbled to the ground, snapping and snarling the whole way down. Somehow Darren found himself with his back on the ground, teeth aimed for his throat. Before he had a chance to push the larger wolf off, something flicked in the corner of his vision, and a familiar cord tugged at him. His nose was filled with the wonderful scent of falling rain and summer grass. Quick as he could blink, a huge black wolf slammed into Ash's side, throwing him and the other wolf to the ground. As soon as they hit the ground, both wolves shifted back to their human forms and faced each other.

She's here! That was all Darren could think as he watched his mate in place of where the black wolf had stood, crouched in a fighting stance. A low growl rumbled in her chest as she stared back at Ash's stunned face.

"No one touches my mate."

She had come back; Darren couldn't believe that she had actually come back. She wasn't alone, though. Darren watched as wolves poured out of the trees around them and into the fight that raged on. Warmth coursed through his veins simply at the sight of her standing there, dark hair flying around her face, her bare arms showing off every scar they bore. Beautiful, perfect, and the definition of power.

But Darren didn't have time to bask in the heavenly warmth long as it was sucked away as dread took over. She shouldn't have been there; she should have been miles away from the territory, safe from whatever horrors played out around them. Even the screams and battle cries seemed to fade around them as Jade faced Ash, Darren's watchful eyes glued to their every move.

"You don't want to do this, Jade," Ash growled, watching her with guarded eyes. He moved forward slowly as if she was a spooked animal. "Don't defy me again. Walk away now, and I'll forget this happened. I won't force you to be part of this cleansing. Turn around and ignore it, just as you always have," he said, drawing closer to her with every step.

"I have a different offer. Back off now, and I might let you and your pack leave in one piece," Jade snarled. Both wolves circled each other threateningly, growls rumbling from both as they gauged their opponent's movements.

"I didn't want this for you; don't force me to be your enemy," Ash said, his voice softening with his plea. Jade let out a mirthless laugh and shook her head.

"You think I want to be your enemy? Ash, I fear for anyone who has angered the Goddesses enough to end up on your radar. You're the one who has forced my hand when I didn't want any part of this," Jade replied, tired anguish cracking her voice. "I never wanted any of this."

"It doesn't matter what you want!" Ash screamed, his anger spiking unexpectedly. "Don't you see? It's never been about what you, or even what I want. It's about what is supposed to happen and who's willing to shoulder that burden." He spread his hands and gestured around them. "Open your eyes. If we ever want a new world for us and our friends, those who the packs have deemed inferior, then we have to make it ourselves. As long as these packwolves stay in power, the world can never change. I know you want this change too; isn't that why you came here in the first place?"

"Not like this! I will not have any part in this war you want. I refuse to have their blood on my hands." Jade growled, something dangerous flickering in her eyes.

"That is your destiny, and as much as you try to fight it, you know it deep down," Ash snarled. His eyes darted towards Darren for a moment before focusing back on Jade. "You still think your destiny is tied with his, but he still doesn't know the truth about you, does he? He doesn't understand what you are truly capable of, but you remember. You remember how your Alpha was so horrified by what you had done he had no choice but to banish you when you were just a child- "

"Enough!" Jade yelled, but Darren's mind was already racing. What could Jade have done as a child to warrant such a punishment? Some of his mind's inner workings must have slipped onto his face because when Ash looked at him again, a dark grin spread across his face.

"How about we show your mate the monster that you truly are," he said before shifting and leaping at her, anger burning in his soulless eyes.

Jade shifted just before Ash slammed into her, and they rolled together on the ground. The dust rising from the battle made it nearly impossible for Darren to see who had the upper hand. Without thinking, he leapt into the dust cloud, uncertain of which wolf was closest to him. He landed on top of Ash's wolf, knocking him away from Jade's darker form. Rolling to his feet, Darren found himself in the shadow of two snarling wolves, both of their wolves larger than his own. Perhaps deadlier.

Even more horrifying than the savageness that had taken over their whole beings was the power that emitted from both of them. It beat down on Darren, causing his legs to shake, nearly buckling under the weight. He was more than familiar with the power of an Alpha but trapped beneath their full strength; it was overwhelming.

Neither one spared him a single glance, as if he were no more threatening than a common field mouse or a flea, certainly nothing that they should fear. While Darren's wolf felt nothing but pride from the sight of their mate standing fearlessly in front of their enemies, Darren couldn't ignore the dread that began to tickle his own mind. The kind, tender Jade he had become so accustomed to was gone, and in her place was a vicious, bloodthirsty beast ready to kill. Which was the real one? And would this Jade even consider him?

Chapter 36

Jade

She could feel the mate bond throbbing in her chest, pounding, pulsing, and urging her to meet her mate's gaze, to run to him and find his embrace. Instead, she kept her eyes focused solely on Ash. He was the most important thing right now; she couldn't let him stand in her way any longer, in the way of her happiness anymore. As she allowed power to course through her veins, she wondered how she had ever allowed him to go this far, to instill such fear in her. Fear that was long gone.

She was tired of always running from him, tired of wondering what new dark secret of hers he would spill next. So tired of constantly worrying about everything that he would take from her one day. It was time for all those fears to rest.

Leaping over Darren's wolf, Jade pounced right onto Ash's larger wolf. Her skin burned as his claws raked over her side, just as her tongue was overwhelmed by the taste of blood as she latched onto his leg.

Ash was larger than her in human form as well as his wolf's, and stronger, but Jade was just as ferocious as he was, if not more. Both wolves fought mercilessly, each driven by a need that the other one couldn't understand. Both battled for their own need for inner peace and redemption. While Ash burned with the need for revenge, the need to bring justice back to their twisted lives, Jade was pushed forward by the cries of her own packmates as they fought and bled to defend the Northwind Pack. The bloodshed she could have-*should* have prevented.

Springing around, Jade lunged in for another attack, but a movement from the corner of her eye caught her attention. She looked just in time to see Darren in a bloody fight with one of Ash's packmates, and he appeared to be barely holding his own. Before she could make a move towards him, she was knocked to the ground. The air was pushed painfully from her lungs as she landed. She never had a chance to catch her breath before Ash placed his full weight on her chest, completely cutting off her airway. His teeth pressed down on her throat to pin her in place, her blood turning his white muzzle pink where his teeth met her skin. Desperately, she writhed beneath him, trying to throw him off. She clawed at his exposed stomach with her hind legs in an attempt to dislodge him, but he didn't budge. Her lungs screamed for air, and her head felt as if it were going to explode. Pure, animalistic terror seized her as black dots began to cloud her vision.

Had she really come all this way, found her mate, and built a pack from the ground up simply to have it all end in darkness? It couldn't be over so quickly; there was more she had to do! Yet even that thought wasn't enough to lift Ash and allow precious oxygen to flow freely through her. It wasn't enough to save her. Were the Goddesses really so cruel to play such a wicked game with her life? She'd come back; she'd finally come to end it all, to face her fear, and now she was going to die. It was all she could think about as black dots slowly clouded over what little vision she had left.

"Let us have the girl, Abby; we don't want to hurt you," the man demanded in an angry voice that made Jade cower back in fear.

He was scary, just like the others that stood behind him. Why were there so many of them? Why couldn't they just leave her mother and her alone? Jade peeked out through the crack in the bedroom door to watch as her mother squared her shoulders, her small frame blocking the scary men from the doorway.

"You can't have her; I won't let you. She's my pup, and she is entitled to the protection of the pack just like you," Abby argued, crossing her arms in front of her chest. Oh, how Jade wished those arms were wrapped around her instead. Maybe then she would stop trembling.

"She's a monster! Surely, you aren't so blinded by your maternal instinct to be unable to see what the child really is. If we don't do something now, it will be too late for our pack; now step aside!" Jade flinched back from the anger in his snarl. He shouldn't yell at her mother like that. Her mother was a former Luna; they should show her respect! She could feel the familiar heat of anger building in the pit of her stomach. The wolf within her called out for her to do something, to drive the men away from her home, but she smothered that desire. Her mother had told her time and time again that she could not heed her wolf's calls like the male wolves could. She always said Jade was special, which Jade knew now it just meant she was different from everyone else, and her packmates hated her for it.

"She is a child! You cannot touch her by our law. She hasn't hurt anyone." Abby said. Jade was amazed at how there was no trace of fear in her mother's voice, none at all.

"Not yet! We can't sit around and wait for her to harm someone before we do something about it. I'm sorry, Abby, but I have my own pups to think about. Now give us the girl, or we will take her." The man took a threatening step forward, but Abby stood her ground.

"*Over my dead body. Leave now, before I call the Alpha!*" Jade's mother yelled as she spread her arms, her tiny body the one thing that stood between the angry pack and the small girl hiding in the bedroom. Jade's heart pounded painfully in her chest as the man who had been yelling pushed her mother roughly to the ground. She could hear the blood rushing through her ears as her skin burned with hot fury.

"*Don't touch her!*" Jade growled as she threw open the bedroom door. Abby's eyes grew wide as she watched in horror as her daughter stepped out of her hiding place and into the open. All eyes were on Jade, but she didn't care. She could feel her wolf pushing forward, slowly taking the control Jade had so desperately been holding onto. Jade wasn't sure what she would do, but that didn't matter. All she knew was that she couldn't let these men hurt her mother while she hid like a coward.

"*Grab her!*" one of the men yelled. Jade felt a large hand wrap around her arm with bruising force. She kicked, scratched, and screamed, but the man's grip only tightened as he dragged her towards the other men.

"*No!*" Abby screamed, launching herself at the man who held Jade. He cried out and staggered back as she clawed at his face, blood flowing down three long scratches now. Jade twisted free as her mother attacked her captor, but their victory was short-lived. Jade could only watch as the man clenched an angry fist, which he brought down with brutal force on her mother's face. Abby cried out in pain as she fell to the ground; another cry left her as a kick landed on her unprotected stomach.

Whatever restraint Jade had left was torn away by the sound of her mother's pain. Her wolf surged forward as Jade was overwhelmed by the animalistic need for blood. Before any

of the men could stop her, Jade was in wolf form. There was no uncertainty in her as she leaped at her mother's attacker.

Blood. The salty taste of it filled her mouth as her teeth sunk into the man's throat, a perfect bite. She didn't let go when she felt his terror fill her through the packlink. She didn't let go when she heard his gurgling breath as he choked on his own blood. She kept her jaws locked as she felt his heart slow until it stopped pumping his life force into her mouth. Only when she felt his body fall limply against her, and only when she watched as his eyes grew wide and lifeless, did she release her hold and let his dead body slump to the floor. His blood continued to pool around him.

Jade slipped back into her human skin as she stared blankly at the body in front of her, the body of her packmate, the body of the man she had just killed. She waited for the guilt to come, waited for it to rush in and overpower her, but it never came. Instead, she felt numb, almost empty. Killing someone wasn't supposed to feel this way, was it?

"Jade! Run, baby, run!" Jade's mother's voice broke through the mental fog that surrounded her. The other men were yelling at each other and pointing angrily at her.

"It killed him! Someone grab it before it gets away!"

It.

They would no longer call her a girl; now, she was just It, the monster.

"Run!" Jade turned to see her mother lunge for her. Scooping her up in her arms, she sprinted into the bedroom, locking the door behind her. Quickly, she ran to the open window. "Go, baby girl," she urged as she pushed Jade up on the edge. Jade could barely reach it even with her mother holding her up.

"But Mom..."

"No buts!" Abby set Jade on the ground, shaking her shoulders slightly to get her attention. "I want you to leave; don't look back no matter what happens. Don't come back here, understand me? Never stop running, not until you're far away from here. I'll find you when I can. Now go!" Abby ordered. Giving her daughter one last kiss, she pushed her up to the window, Jade's knees scraping against the rough wooden frame.

Like a silver bullet, she was off the moment her feet touched the slick grass even though every instinct screamed at her to turn around and go back. Her mother's words steered her feet onward, silencing any cruel ideas the beast inside her head whispered. But all of it, her mother's strength, the burning in her lungs, or even the blood drying under her fingernails, all of it meant nothing the moment she felt a hand latch onto her arm. Nails dug into her skin as she kicked and screamed, but the man never loosened his grip as he dragged her back towards the yells and the pillar of smoke-

Jade startled back to the real world, air flowing into her burning lungs. She wasn't dead, not yet, at least. Rearing back, Ash released his hold on her, blood and saliva spraying from his mouth as a gargled cry escaped him, giving Jade just enough time to scramble away. Black spots still covered her vision as she sucked in gulps of air, readying herself for his next attack as best she could, but it never came. Still thrashing about, Ash clawed at his head and eyes as he let out an agonized howl, oblivious to his surroundings.

She didn't know what had happened while she had blacked out, but one thing she was certain of, whether she had meant to or not, she was the cause of whatever had possessed the ghostly wolf.

Chapter 37

Ash

It was impossible to slow his racing heart as images of the frightened girl played on a loop. It shouldn't be possible; it had been years since the visions had plagued him. He had them under control! At least he had until the moment Jade's blood had touched his tongue.

Desperately, he fought to rein in his emotions and the images that bombarded his mind, but it had been years since he had experienced a vision so powerful. He watched as Jade rose shakily to her feet, ready to fight once again. He'd only meant to make her lose consciousness so he could finish everything for them both since she wasn't strong enough to do it herself yet. Now she was in the way again, forcing him to change his plans once again.

He needed to find Alpha Power and his mutt son and end them both.

Shallow breaths as she listened from behind the door to the hatred on the other side.

He could still finish his plan; he could still bring the packs to justice. He just needed a little more time.

The taste of blood after her first kill.

It would not end this way; he was stronger than the visions. He hadn't come as far as he had to be bested by them again!

Lungs burned as she ran through the forest on legs of jelly, the yell of angry wolves pressing her forward.

There was too much. The weight of Jade's memories and emotions intertwined with his own, making it nearly impossible to tell them apart. He clawed frantically at his eyes, trying to banish the images from them, but he knew it was too late. He could feel the vision already branding itself into his memory, forever becoming a part of him. Forever connecting him to the dark, demon-eyed wolf in front of him.

A phantom pain throbbed in his ribs; his throat felt bruised and swollen. But he had no blood pouring from his side, and he bore no markings on his throat that would ache in such a way. He could only stare in shock as blood streamed down Jade's dark coat as she gulped down air in greedy gasps.

It was all too much; he couldn't concentrate enough to separate the cries from the present from the echoes of the past. He could hardly tell Jade's confusion from his own. Their panic equally quickened his heart and breath. He had to get away from it, or he was going to go mad! Without thinking, he let out a call for retreat and ran. Ran from the girl whose pain was slowly becoming his own, ran from all of the horrors she held within.

Shame threatened to overpower him as his wolves, shifters and non-shifters alike followed his call. Even without a packlink, he could feel their confusion like knives in his back. Perhaps that was a good thing, though, it kept them from feeling his disgust at his own weakness. Years of fighting, planning, and mental training were wasted in one day, all because of the one wolf he truly wanted-no needed to understand. It didn't matter, though, none of it did. His plan would still work. He could still carry it out at another time, in another place.

All he needed was more time. Time to rein the visions back under his control, time to sway the breathtakingly dark wolf

towards him. Then he could finish his mission, and he could end the Alphas once and for all.

Chapter 38

Darren

It was strange, Darren thought, how a single color could inspire so many emotions inside of someone. Orange, the playdough that stuck to your fingers as a child. Blue, sticky popsicles on the front porch in the summertime. Pink, the last light of every sunset that spread across the mountain sky. Or red, the maple leaves before they fell from the trees, or fresh raspberries straight from the bush.

But it was also the color of death.

Everywhere Darren looked, there was red blood dripping, flowing, gushing, slowly draining the life from its owners. It seeped from the angry slashes across a packmate's chest. It stained a she-wolf's hands as she held her dead mates close, their pup weeping in confusion beside them. Darren's stomach roiled as he looked down to see the blood that pooled around his own feet, making the grass slippery. How could there be so much blood in one place?

There were no cheers of victory as their attackers retreated, only a hollow silence that settled over those that remained, broken only by the heart-wrenching sobs. As he made his way through the courtyard, he found himself praying to whatever Goddess was listening that he wouldn't recognize any of the blank, unseeing eyes.

The pain was nearly unbearable, not only his own but the pain of the entire pack. It overwhelmed the packlink, shadows of every member's sorrow and fear seeping into Darren until it

was difficult to tell which emotions were truly his own. Another pain tore at his heart in an entirely different way. It slashed through him from the inside out, leaving his heart feeling hollow and raw. Despite its unfamiliarity, Darren knew exactly who that pain stemmed from.

Jade

It didn't take him long to find her. His eyes were drawn to her as if she were a lighthouse in the middle of a raging storm. Back in her own skin, the mere sight of her had a weight lifting off of Darren's shoulders that he hadn't realized he had been holding. In the middle of all of the heartache, bloodshed, and tears was his own personal light leading him out of the darkness that surrounded him, but his relief was short-lived as he took in the state she was in.

She knelt in the grass, holding herself up with shaky hands, her eyes shut tight as if she were trying to escape her horrific surroundings. Her pain crashed over him in waves that nearly knocked him off his feet. It took nearly all of his strength just to keep his feet moving forward. Slowly, he sank to his knees beside her and tried to pull her into his arms, but he let his arms fall limply to his side when she flinched away. Darren tried not to let the small rejection sting; she had been through hell in the last twenty-four hours. It made sense that she would need some distance; he just wished that it wasn't distance from him.

As she sat in front of him, her body shaking in tearless tremors, all Darren could do was soak in every detail about her, and the longer he looked, the angrier he grew. Blue bruises were slowly revealing themselves on her throat's irritated skin, and blood was drying on her cheek from a new scratch. Ash had hurt her. Darren's mate had been hurt, and he hadn't been able to do a single thing to stop it.

With so many emotions fighting for his attention, Darren found it increasingly difficult to hold any of them at bay, especially the guilt that would have been debilitating if it wasn't fuel for his wolf's anger. The sight of Jade's injuries gave his wolf newfound energy as he fought to rise to the surface, forcing a growl to rumble in Darren's chest.

"Jade! Dang-it, Jade, answer me!"

Darren looked up through the enraged haze to see a male wolf running towards Jade in his human form. A snarl ripped through him as the other wolf reached for her. Instinctively Darren's arms snaked around her, pulling her to his chest.

"Darren, it's me, Desert. I'm Jade's friend. Please let me take her; we need to find her some help," the other wolf said, his wide eyes panicked as he took in Darren's yellow eyes. But Darren's wolf had taken too much control, and he wasn't about to let Jade out of their sight. "Please, Darren, if she loses too much blood, she'll die!" Desert yelled, desperately trying to get closer. His words were enough to shake Darren's wolf to step back and allow Darren behind the wheel again. Sure enough, when he looked down, he felt his heart drop into his stomach. Jade's small frame was now limp against his own, his hands wet with new blood, blood that oozed steadily from her side.

He didn't protest when he felt Desert lift her from his trembling arms and hurry off. Shakily, he rose to his feet and followed Desert through the crowd towards the pack's hospital, already overflowing with his injured packmates.

"We need a doctor over here, quick!" Desert called out, frantically searching the faces for assistance, but all he found was still hands and downcast eyes as the Northwind wolves did all they could to avoid meeting his gaze.

"Did you not hear him? We need a doctor now!" Darren yelled, finally finding his voice.

"But sir, we have enough of our own that are injured. Do you really think your father would want us using resources on...them?" a middle-aged she-wolf in a nurse's uniform asked, hesitating as she eyed Desert's pale packmark.

"I think my father would be more upset to find out that you refused care to wolves that just fought alongside us," Darren snapped, but it came out closer to a snarl, the poor she-wolf's eyes widening in fear.

"Uh-I...you can follow me," she stuttered as she turned to rush down the hall, Desert close on her heels. Darren followed them, but not before turning around to see every eye in the room on him, most of them shocked and not all friendly. He had no words to defend himself from their silent accusations, no justification they would understand if they didn't see it for themselves already.

Everything continued to blur together as Darren ducked into the small hospital room, buzzing with a frenzied energy. The blood wouldn't stop coming. It stained the sheets of the bed she was laid on, a doctor and on side giving orders to the same frightened nurse. Darren watched in silent horror as the nurse held bandages to stay the flow, the doctor trying to stitch what parts of the wound that he could, but the blood was making it difficult.

It should have stopped by now. Even if she had been any other she-wolf, her healing should have at least slowed it, but with a wolf awake within her, it should have sped up that process. Was it because she was a Blood Wolf? Or because she was a female shifter? Darren's mind raced with each new fear as it arose, shadowing everything else around him besides Jade. He

could hear the others speaking, knew that he should be listening, but it was hard enough to process their words with the fog hanging over him.

"Just stay with us a little longer Jade, you promised you'd take everyone home. Don't break your promise now," Desert tried to reason with her still body, her sun-kissed skin ghostly pale under the fluorescent lights.

"The bleeding is slowing. Finish that up quickly," the doctor said, tying off the last of his stitches. "Let's get her hooked up. We need to try to get more blood into her now."

"She's going to be alright, isn't she?" Desert asked.

"Right away, sir," the nurse said, rushing past Darren to get the requested supplies.

"Is she going to be okay?" Desert yelled again. Darren wished they would answer him, then maybe his mind would stop screaming the same question.

Then something changed.

Darren felt the shift of energies before he understood what it meant. The nurse tried to jab a needle into Jade's exposed arm when the she-wolf let out a surprised squeal and scrambled back from the bed. A string of curses escaped the doctor as well, and Darren pushed past him to the bedside. Jade's eyes had snapped open wide and alert as if she had startled awake from a nightmare. Darren assumed the screaming resulted from the eyes staring back at them, not the stormy grey he had come to look forward to each day, but the red eyes, those of her wolf. Pushing away Darren and Desert's hands, Jade struggled into an unsteady sitting position, her breathing unnaturally even for someone with extensive injuries.

"It's okay. You're safe now. Just lie back down and let the doctor do his job," Darren said in an attempt to soothe her, unable to hide his relief at the sight of her looking alive.

Alive may not have been the right way to describe her in that moment. Her ashy skin was still covered in blood, only some of it her own. A necklace of dark blue bruises covered her throat, and with her devilish eyes, she looked like something out of a story meant to scare naughty pups. Frightening or not, Darren couldn't deny the pounding of his heart had little to do with her appearance and more to do with being in such close proximity to his mate.

She brushed his hands off again as he tried to ease her down, scooting herself to the edge of the bed.

"I have to go," she said. Her voice was quiet and robotic as if she wasn't truly awake. She pushed herself into an unstable standing position, Desert's hands shooting out to catch her, but she didn't fall. "I'm fine. I have to go," she repeated, her voice a little louder.

"No, Jade, you were hurt. You need to lay back down and let your wolf do its job," Desert said gently, as he tried to block her path as she moved towards the door. It had to be the shock. That had to be it, the shock of everything was going to her head, and she wasn't thinking clearly. At least, that was what Darren kept telling himself as she pushed past Desert. She didn't bother to answer any of his many questions as the confused doctor and the rest of the group followed her down the hallway. Her steps were unsteady, but she still refused the hands of support that were offered, opting instead to lean against the wall as needed. She seemed to know where she was going, which left Darren wandering behind her and wondering how worried he should be.

After they passed a few occupied rooms and some seemingly random turns, Jade finally stopped in front of an open door. Darren couldn't see much from where he stood, but he could tell there was a single hospital bed in the middle of the room, one of the newest rooms they had set aside for the ill she-wolves. Slowly, Jade stepped through the doorway, the rest of them following her hesitantly.

"Jade, come, let's go back to your room. You're going to wear yourself out," Desert said in a hushed tone as he saw who Jade had been searching for. In the bed lay a sleeping young woman, her washed out skin making her once rich brown hair stand out against the white pillow. Darren's heart sank at the sight as he nearly choked on the lump that formed in this throat.

Valery

Monitors beeped and blinked all around the bed, letting him know she was still alive, although her ashy skin said differently. Darren had seen many deaths in his short life, but he'd never seen anything like this. He'd never seen someone so dear to him slowly eaten away from the inside out by an invisible enemy.

"I'm sorry, but you're not allowed to be in here," the doctor said, but no one bothered to reply. Jade stood at the edge of Valery's bed, silently watching her. "All of you need to leave, now." Darren heard them moving towards Jade. Without thinking, his arm shot out, blocking the doctor and nurse's path. He wasn't sure what Jade was up to, but something inside whispered that he needed to see what was about to happen.

Gently, almost as if she were afraid she would break her, Jade brushed Valery's hair away from her face and leaned in close and what she did next sent chills to Darren's bones. But nothing was louder than the nurse's bloodcurdling scream.

Chapter 39

Jade

Jade didn't have time to think as she felt her canines slip into place, aiming for the perfect spot on Valery's neck. She didn't know how she knew it, but then again, she didn't need to. She wasn't the one in control.

For the second time that day, the taste of warm blood coated Jade's tongue as her teeth found their mark. It filled her senses with nothing but the girl in front of her. She could feel all of it, every shaky breath that filled her lungs, the heat of the fever that raged inside, the achy limbs that were crushed under an invisible weight. She could nearly taste the sickness as it festered and rotted away whatever goodness came across its path. Yet, underneath all of the suffering and the sourness of death's looming hand, Jade could feel what she had been searching for.

It might as well have been hidden behind a wall of glass, clearly seen but untouchable. Jade's wolf gently coaxed the sleeping creature, but it seemed to be just out of reach. When it didn't stir, she pushed harder, wincing when a sharp pain exploded in her head as the wall pushed back. As she pressed harder, the pain only grew, beating down on what little strength she held onto, the battle from earlier leaving her with little to work with. Could she really do this?

She didn't have a choice, not if she wanted her friend to live. With new resolve, Jade pushed back against the wall, the pain turning into a shrill, unending whine that made her ears want to bleed.

You have to wake up, she called out, her voice muted.

She was so close, yet she could feel her hold slipping, the distant screams tugging at her consciousness, begging her to let go. But she couldn't, not yet.

Wake up! She commanded, nearly collapsing when the barrier shattered into a million pieces. Someone ripped her away from Valery's writhing body, pulling Jade from the internal war she had just won.

"What did you do to her?" the doctor yelled as he rushed to Valery's side. Jade collapsed against Darren's chest as his arms wrapped around her protectively, but she didn't need anyone's protection in that moment. A new strength flowed through her as she pushed off of Darren, her feet steadying beneath her.

"I saved her." She heard herself answer, her wolf choosing to speak for the both of them. No one replied to her, their mouths open as they stared at her in horror. With her wolf so close to the surface, Jade was sure that her eyes were still a haunting shade of red, and her canines had yet to retreat back into her skull. Even without the blood that she could feel running down her chin Jade was sure that she looked like something from their darkest nightmares.

The snapping of bones made them all turn back to the unconscious girl. They watched in horror and amazement as one by one, each bone snapped and changed.

"What's going on?" the nurse screamed at Jade, but she couldn't bring her attention away from the change that was happening in front of them. All at once, grey fur sprouted over the girl's skin, her arms turned into another set of legs as her face lengthened.

"She...she-!" the nurse stammered.

"She shifted," Desert said in amazement as they all stared wide-eyed at the very awake and very terrified wolf that stood in front of them.

"How did this happen? Someone better have an explanation, now!" Luke Power yelled. Although he didn't need to, he already had the attention of every doctor and nurse in the room. Even from where Jade stood just outside of the doorway, she could hear every hushed word that was uttered as the confusion spread throughout the room. Faces flinched, and eyes stared at the floor or walls, anywhere but the man standing in front of them, demanding answers they didn't have. It was almost enough to make Jade feel sorry for them; after all, it wasn't them that Alpha Power was really angry with. It was her.

Valery was finally resting after having help shifting back into her human form, which was no easy task with an anxious wolf making its appearance for the first time. But with some gentle coaxing from Darren, he was able to convince the frightened wolf to allow Valery to take control once again, the girl just as scared as the beast had been.

"We are unsure of how it happened yet, sir. But we believe that the young woman may have been going through a difficult or forced change," one unlucky doctor summarized, doing everything in his power to avoid eye contact with Luke's glare.

"Is that all you *believe*?" Luke asked, narrowing his eyes as he watched the doctor shuffle his feet uncomfortably.

"We have an untested theory that the other ill she-wolves may be going through something similar if not the same thing."

"Females haven't shifted in centuries. Why would they start now? What do you mean by forced?" Luke all but snarled at the unfortunate spokesmen.

"We're not certain how it is happening yet, but it doesn't seem as if the change is happening naturally. Something is forcing their wolves to come forward, but because it isn't happening naturally, they are unable to complete the change. Much like complicated shifts with male wolves. Valery seems to have been able to successfully complete her shift the same way that we help males that are trapped in between the shift." Luke raised a brow, his eyes darting to where Jade stood for only the slightest second.

"And how exactly do we do that?" he asked, clearly understanding the process the doctor spoke of. It was a silent dare, a dare to say what he knew everyone was thinking.

"Um, well, with the bite of an Alpha wolf. An Alpha is the only one able to make a direct connection to the wolf. Allowing it to fully come forward and complete the shift with the human part," the doctor practically mumbled, his words trailing off hesitantly. Jade wasn't surprised when Luke's gaze shot directly to her own, his eyes flashing with anger.

"That's a good theory, but I have one question. How is that possible when the bite Valery received wasn't from an Alpha?" he asked, never breaking eye contact with Jade.

"Well, as far as our evidence suggests, contrary to our history, this rogue female has most of the traits that we would find in a true Alph-"

"She is not an Alpha!" Luke Power's anger boomed through the room, a terrified silence hovering over the group. Jade's own anger bubbled up inside of her, threatening to spill over the shattered wall within her to the wolf she had in check. It was her

friends that had saved his entire pack from Ash, and now she had discovered a way to save the very she-wolves that he had blamed her for infecting, but none of it was enough. Luke Power would never see anything more than a worthless, dangerous outcast when he looked at her, no matter who she saved.

They needed to get out of there before he decided to act on the fury that would keep growing.

"I'll be right back," Jade whispered to Desert, pushing off of the doorframe. She felt another pair of eyes on her but chose to ignore them for now. Darren would have to wait. Desert moved to follow her, but she held up a hand. "No, stay here and see what else Luke has to say. I just need some fresh air." Without another look at Luke or his blue-eyed son, she limped her way outside.

Wrapping her arms around herself to fight off the chill of the night, she couldn't help the ache that bloomed in her chest as she breathed in the crisp air, so much like the late fall nights in her own mountain home. In just a few days, she could be in that home again, and this time with her own pack, but she suspected that the heartache was far from over.

Connecting with Valery's wolf had helped Jade's own wolf kick start the healing process, but there was a lot of damage to heal. Thankfully, most of her friends had fared better than she had. Besides a few stitches, most of the group had made it out with nothing more than shallow cuts and bruises, and they were as anxious to leave as Jade was. She'd had Chris and the others take the pack to the warehouse to rest for the night. They would head out in the morning, hopefully, while Luke was still distracted by the she-wolves debacle.

As excited as she was at the prospect of being home soon, she couldn't avoid the way the mate bond throbbed every time

she thought of leaving the Northwind Pack's home. Darren's home. Despite the pain, she had little doubt that leaving Darren was what he needed. As long as she was around, he would never be able to live peacefully with his family, and that was the one thing that she would never think of asking him to give up.

Letting out a sigh, she let her arms loose, allowing them to swing back and forth as she sucked in one last breath to clear her head before returning inside the hospital, back to the disarray that seemed to be her life, but something made her pause. It was faint, almost impossible to sense, but she was certain something was wrong.

Someone is here.

That was all the warning she had. Whirling around, she heard a small pop just before she dropped to the ground with a scream as the silver bullet pierced her shoulder. A snarl ripped through her clenched teeth as her eyes skipped frantically over the trees and shadows, searching for her attacker. There was only one enemy of wolves that chose silver as their weapon.

Hunter

Acknowledgements

In the years it has taken to create this book and its characters I have learned just how essential it is to have a team of amazing people surrounding you. I have been incredibly lucky that many of my close family and friends make up the bulk of that team for me. Sometimes it feels as if the list of people to thank is endless, but I will do my best to fit everyone in.

It wouldn't be right to start with anyone other than my wonderful parents, Tanya, and Kenny Simler. Ever since I told you I was writing a book you have been nothing but supportive. Over the years you each have not only given time and financial support, but you never once doubted that my words would reach others and that people would actually have a desire to read the works that my messy mind creates.

Next would be my siblings and cooky sister-in-law for reading and rereading this book countless times. Thank you for being my willing test subjects and biggest cheerleaders.

And I could never forget my husband, Ian Graham. Not only have you listened to me obsess over these characters and their stories, but you read this book multiple times and created the breathtaking cover and interior artwork. And my wonderful mother-in-law, Ann Graham, thank you for being the first one to edit this book for me. Your enthusiasm with it was a great motivator to help me push through the editing process.

Last but certainly not least is all of the people who read this book in its earliest stages on Wattpad. It was each of you that made me realize that writing wasn't just something that was a fun hobby but something that would be a defining part of me forever. Thank you, to each and every one of you.

The Author

K. R. Simler always had an appreciation for the written word and the world of storytelling that was fueled by her parents who both regularly read to their children. Stories from C. S. Lewis, David Eddings, and J. K. Rowling often filled the house and provided the inspiration for many imaginary games that were filled with their own quests, magic, and dragon slaying.

But Simler's complete adoration (and borderline obsession) with books didn't start until she was a preteen. Armed with a library card and an empty backpack she was well known at her local library for the stacks of books that would come and go in her arms on a weekly basis. During this time, she explored all different genres such as fantasy, horror, mystery, and many others that she came to love. Although adulthood may have slowed the rate at which she consumes books Simler still isn't picky about the genre, but when she is offered the chance, you can most often find her diving into the pages of fantasy and paranormal novels filled with witches, vampires, and werewolves. Oh my!

K. R. Simler resides in Colorado with her husband and their cat and two dogs, and their ever-growing backyard garden. When she isn't writing her next novel or curled up with a good book, she can be found in the kitchen whipping up culinary experiments or finding new hobbies like gardening, beekeeping, and wherever else her heart takes her!

For updates on book two of The Blood Wolf Trilogy and other projects follow her on and Instagram @k.r.simler.